The Latchkey Children

André Launay, born in London of French parents, is the father of three children. The author of several works of non-fiction and two other novels – *The Girl with a Peppermint Taste* and *The Innocence Has Gone* … – he spent some time in America before settl… Southern Spain, where he now lives.

André Launay

The Latchkey Children

Pan Original
Pan Books London and Sydney

First published in Great Britain 1985 by Pan Books Ltd,
Cavaye Place, London SW10 9PG
9 8 7 6 5 4 3 2

ISBN 0 330 28686 2

Photoset by Parker Typesetting Service, Leicester
Printed and bound in Great Britain by
Hazell Watson & Viney Limited,
Member of the BPCC Group,
Aylesbury, Bucks

They went missing.

One after another.

Three children.

Without trace.

First it was a twelve-year-old girl whose mother worked nights and was unaware that she had not been home for two days till a neighbour asked after her.

Then it was a boy, eight years old, who never got back from a fishing expedition. His mother felt no concern over his absence for more than twelve hours.

Another girl was believed to be staying with a friend till the friend rang up asking why she had not turned up.

Three days passed before the police became involved, four days before a newspaper published the strange facts, and a whole week before the local television station thought the story worth a mention.

Interest in possible tragedy, fascination in the anxiety suffered by the parents, only then gripped the lives of everyone in the small town of Avalon.

chapter one

'Day 8,' wrote Zuke Donoghue in her private journal. 'They're dragging Westcoat Pond where Judd was last seen and flashed Joleen's and Bonnie's pictures on TV again. No one has asked me anything.'

She studied her handwriting.

It was neat. She had pressed too hard with the ballpoint and it would show through to the next page, but it was neat.

She snapped the journal shut, got down on her knees and eased up the floorboard she had loosened specially under the bed, and tucked the book quickly in its hiding place.

No one knew about it, not even Dillon.

If she died suddenly the secret hiding place would die with her and the contents of her journal would never be revealed.

So there would be a few more sleepless parents in Avalon tonight and more pointless searching in the streets and woods, but that's what they deserved.

She opened the bedroom door and shouted.

'Dillon!'

He was watching television again.

Sighing at the thought of all the responsibility her mother had saddled her with, she went down the stairs and into the living room.

He was there, deep in the armchair in front of the screen chewing more candy. Her kid brother who wouldn't eat his supper.

Why did it bug her?

Why didn't she let him fill himself up with that garbage till he was sick, and why did she get angry at him watching that crap?

Because he had a brain.

No one else appreciated it, but she did.

Dillon had a brain, and he wasn't using it, and nobody cared except her.

'OK, asshole, you either give me the chocolate or I switch off.'

He was quick.

Off the chair and down on the floor covering the switch with his hand and stuffing the rest of the bar into his mouth.

Stomach and brain gunge was more important to him than wholesome foods and knowledge. He'd grow up a real dummy.

'I'm not cooking you anything. It would be a real waste.'

'I don't care.'

'You will when you see me eating what I got us. A new recipe pizza, mushroom and pepperoni and a new jar of Thousand Island.'

That got him.

He opened his mouth wide and let the gob of chewed chocolate drop into his upturned palm.

Sometimes he was disgusting.

'You can come and help me cook.'

She went into the kitchen, opened up the freezer and brought out the pizza pack and read the instructions.

Twenty minutes! She wouldn't have time for that. No oven for her. The grill with extra cheese and butter.

'When's Mom coming home!'

'Why ask?'

'I want to know.'

Now he was sitting at the table reading his comic, waiting to be served. The domestic scene, often enough experienced when Dad had been around, the harassed wife slaving over the cooker for her husband, only it was sister and brother, and still a game, with everything in the kitchen a toy.

On Sundays, maybe, her mother thought it was her kingdom, but it wasn't. She'd made sure of that. She was the only one who knew where things were. She was in charge.

'Where did you put the ketchup, honey? Have you seen

the egg slicer, the cheese grater, the potato peeler? Why put it there? I always hang it up by the sink.'

The simple, straightforward explanation calculated to make her mother feel guilty.

All the utensils she needed had come down from the top shelves and were now at eye level. Her eye level. Reachable. Her mother had to stoop.

That first battle had been won, and then the whole war.

After the first two weeks, the kitchen had been hers to claim as her own.

And more.

'Honey, would you like to do the shopping, as you've more time than I have? On your way back from school?'

The complete and unconditional surrender, her mother handing over money and she spending it, occasionally putting some in her own pocket.

Independence had dawned on the day a letter had arrived from San Diego.

Independence for her.

Reality of middle age for her mother, Angela Donoghue, who wasn't quite pretty any more, but kind of stocky. There was weight there. It didn't show as fat, but in the solid bone structure and the way she walked.

She was dark with very brown eyes and a sallow complexion, and there were tiny creases nearly everywhere on her face when you looked at it close to, which is why she took such pains to make up in the morning if she knew she was going to meet a male of importance.

Her expression was one of general surprise. She was perplexed by life. She was particularly perplexed by Zuke, whom she had one day decided was more intelligent than herself. As was young Dillon, who astounded her with his knowledge.

It was all inherited from their father, which was probably why she had become estranged from her own children. They were not hers, they were his. They always would be, despite the fact that he had deserted them all.

On coming back from shopping one day she had found his car gone and a note on the table.

There had been pretended surprise, shock, but Zuke knew it might well have been the other way round, Mom writing the goodbye note and saddling him with all the responsibilities.

Zuke knew that if her mother felt any bitterness or regrets it was because she had been too slow off the mark.

Father had left the mess first.

Zuke had understood all that on eavesdropping a phone conversation between mother and friend.

The one remark still burnt.

'The bastard beat me to it.'

It had never been discussed, had never been mentioned. Whether both parents wanted to be rid of each other or of their own children would never be known. Angela Donoghue had dutifully soldiered on and met her responsibilities until Zuke, slowly but surely, had taken over, because it was easier and made more sense.

Mother, eventually free of guilt, free of the chores, had come to terms with the new situation and had thrown herself into a job.

'Dad's not coming back, honey, so from now on I'll have to go out to work.'

'What work?'

'Kind of secretary, I guess.'

Kind of.

Part-time receptionist in one of the three local hotels. The seediest, the one with the worst reputation. The Greenhook Chalet Motel.

She had to be there early in the morning to serve breakfasts, and late at night to work behind the bar.

Some nights she never came back at all.

She'd never tried too hard to make a real home, either for herself or for her kids.

Dad had done all that.

When Grandma died, leaving them the two-storey

clapboard house, he'd worked out the alterations so that she and Dillon could each have their own rooms. They'd chosen the colours, had helped him paint.

That had been a good time.

Then he'd found himself another lady in San Diego, and had abandoned them.

It was two years now since she'd seen him. Two whole years. And she had to look at his photograph and stare at it to remind herself what he looked like.

What hurt most was that this woman had two kids of her own. She'd heard that one of them was probably his, and that was why he had run away.

So maybe she had another brother, or sister.

Who cared?

He had gone and mother had been relieved.

That first Christmas, before the divorce had been talked about, when her mother still thought he'd come back, she'd made the effort to keep them happy by buying some nice presents and wrapping them up and posting them as though they had come from him.

The postmark was Avalon, and neither she nor Dillon had said anything, but had gone through the expected 'oohs' and 'wows'. Inside there had been a Christmas card signed 'Dad' in her handwriting, and she had forgotten to take the price tags off and the price tags had Warshall's name on them, Warshalls of Main Street, Avalon.

She had no idea how to gauge their awareness. Most adults didn't. Some couldn't tell the difference between a twelve-year-old, a ten-year-old or a six-year-old. To them they were all children until girls developed breasts and boys started driving cars.

When the divorce had come through her mother had thought herself rich. The house was hers, she was the owner, which sounded great, but it turned out to be a disaster. The upkeep, the repairs, the insurance. Fine to have a house to do with what you wanted, but it was expensive to maintain.

She'd tried to sell it, found it was in need of so many things doing that it wasn't worth what she'd expected, so she'd stayed on at the motel. Three days a week to begin with, then four, then weekends as well, and then, 'Seeing as you can manage so well, honey, I've decided to give you the latchkey.'

It had been the gift of freedom, adulthood hung round her neck on a silver chain.

'Wear it always, never take it off.'

The chain had broken the following day, after which she'd used a leather shoelace, which stained and cut into her, so she'd changed it for an old piece of string, and her mother hadn't noticed for a week.

'You'll be responsible for Dillon too, you know.' She hadn't minded.

Four years younger and impossible, but with brains.

Dillon could do anything with numbers, a genius at mathematics. She'd given him a calculator when it had slipped into her pocket while she was looking around the hi-fi store, and she'd told him not to take it to school or show it around but only to use it at home.

He'd understood why.

He was bright that way.

So her days had shaped up into a routine, a necessary discipline. She got up first and made coffee for her mother who hurried off to the motel in the old station wagon. Then she got Dillon up, and made him breakfast, and they went off to school together.

When they got back it was to unmade beds and washing up in the sink which she coped with systematically. She shouldered the burden of carrying on without Dad and had watched Mom go through a drink problem, a drugs problem and a sex problem, and had survived.

It had been a real education, the behaviour of adults in a crisis. They lied so much.

They lied to each other and to themselves.

She'd explained it all to Dillon who'd understood, and

had explained it to Joleen and Bonnie and Judd who'd also understood because they were going through similar experiences.

The Latchkids, others called them and, because they had to fend for themselves and came up against the same problems and needed each other's advice, Zuke had started the Latchkey Club.

She grilled the pizza after adding slices of cheese, pickle, thousand island dressing, ketchup and apricot jam, and when it was sizzling and about to burn she set it on a plate before Dillon and sliced it up.

He didn't pause reading his comic book but grabbed a piece and munched into it.

She ate hers more delicately, watching him.

When he'd finished she took a chocolate ice cream out of the freezer and gave it to him, washed up the one plate and wiped the knife clean. She'd got feeding Dillon down to a fine art, no forks, no knives or plates. Convenience foods, convenience eating, and a tin of Coke with a straw if he asked.

'I'm going out now,' she said, brushing the pizza crumbs off the table on to the floor.

'Fort Knox?'

'I'm going for a walk first.'

'They OK?'

'Who?'

'Joleen, Bonnie and Judd.'

'How would I know?'

'You know.'

'Well if you know I know, remember not to tell anyone.'

Dillon looked up and studied her for a moment. 'Can I join them?'

'Maybe, but not yet.'

'OK.'

He never argued, always accepted her decision, and quite happily went off to watch television again.

As she was about to leave he shouted.

'Zuke! Here! They're on!'

'Who's on?'

She didn't rush, though he made it sound vital.

'Bonnie's parents, look!'

It was an in-depth interview with an in-depth interviewer swivelling in a chair about to question Marina and Bob Sharp. The station had pulled out all the stops and had a blow up photo of Bonnie flashed on a screen and the interviewer was giving his audience a character summary of the missing child.

Bonnie, according to him, was a strange little red-headed girl, often nicknamed Orphan Annie, who loved dogs and horses, and already showed talents as a painter. Zuke knew Bonnie was indifferent to dogs, had never ridden a horse and couldn't draw to save her life, what she was good at, however, was gauging adults to perfection, she could play to them, pretend to them and twisted her parents round her little finger.

Marina came into close up now, a large, plump woman, wearing dark glasses, with platinum hair, a deep voice, arms as thick as other people's legs. Bob, her husband, as was so often the case, completely the opposite.

Zuke decided Marina's hair was a wig, or very heavily lacquered. She was a hairdresser, owned the hairdressing salon on Main Street. She smoked, obviously drank too and ruled the roost.

She was answering some dumb question asked her by the interviewer.

'I guess I've just been too busy to notice what was happening,' she admitted. 'My Bonnie's always been able to look after herself and I've never really worried about her.'

At which point she decided to burst into tears, which clearly pleased the show's producer because they went into a big close up of the mascara running down the fat cheeks.

'I mean . . . I can't stay at home all day just waiting for her to come back from school, or come back from wherever she goes during the vacation. She's old enough to look after herself surely?'

It was the husband's turn. Concerned only about himself he claimed he was a sick man and whatever the question was about Bonnie he managed to blame the problem on his own health.

It was because he had had a hernia operation, because he had mouth ulcers, because he had lost weeks of work while in hospital and had had to go out on the road when he had recovered, that Bonnie had disappeared. He had wanted his wife to stay at home, but they needed the money and, if truth be known, she was more successful than him.

Yes, they had a large house, with a pool, but it was run down, they had seen better days. For Chrissake there was a recession on and no one could afford house help anymore.

The camera panned left and Nancy Delora came into shot, Joleen's mother, New York hooker and Avalon's own best little whorehouse, as Zuke had heard her described.

Joleen's blow up came on, the blonde pigtails in ribbons, the upturned nose, the bright blue innocent eyes. They didn't show her legs. Joleen had long legs that made men turn round in the streets when she wore white socks.

Nancy stared steadily at the camera. She was in leather boots and tight leather skirt, her long nails flashed silver in the studio lights, her eyelids pale blue, her lashes longer than ever. She was introduced as a model hailing from the East Coast.

She first of all stated categorically that she didn't think her daughter was dead. She believed the girl was in the hands of some pervert who had a sex problem, who would suffer the consequences because Joleen, she was sure, could look after herself.

'But she's only eleven,' the interviewer protested.

'I've been on the streets all my life,' Nancy Delora suddenly spat out. 'And I can tell you that some of you men need women like me around. It's because we're illegal and you have to go underground for your kicks that you take up on little girls.'

Zuke clapped her hands.

Nancy Delora was using the programme as a free commercial and the interviewer was really riled.

Pointing out that not all men were sex-starved, that some actually worked hard at running good homes and were happy with their wives, he admonished her for judging others by her own, not particularly high standards of morality.

But she just laughed.

'It's the husbands I get, sonny. And I'll tell you something,' she touched her temple with a long index finger, 'I have here in my head the names of all my clients, and if certain guys in key positions who are just sitting around on their butts don't do something about these missing kids quickly, I'm going to start talking. I give them twenty-four hours.'

The interviewer made no comments but quickly turned to the next parents, first Judd's father, Mike Reidy, who had been specially flown in from Dakota by the station.

A heavy man, burly, he had absolutely nothing to say for himself and hardly seemed to know why he was there. He drove long distance trucks, he explained, was home a couple of days every three weeks, earned a great deal of money and would willingly pay a big reward to whoever found his son. When asked Judd's age, he was out by two years, but didn't seem to mind the correction. He was a kid himself, wide-eyed at everything that had happened, still hadn't got over the fact that he had been in a plane and had been flown home because his boy was missing.

His wife Selina, who worked as a packer at the Avalon Fruit Canneries, sat quite still, knees together, hands clasped on her lap, dreading her turn, but when it came she answered clearly, with a smile. She didn't believe Judd was in real trouble. A feeling. If he had been murdered or been in an accident, she would know, she would have felt it, would have had a sign, a warning. She was a Libra and Judd was a Pisces, and there had been nothing in either of their stars hinting at disaster. She was sure all three kids had decided to go off somewhere together and would probably be found in the next day or two, maybe in Disneyland. They had just run away from home because home had nothing exciting to offer. They were bored, it was vacation time. Nothing more.

And Zuke considered her the most sensible and most dangerous of all the parents, because she was so near the truth. Fortunately the interviewer, winding up the programme put everyone back on nervous alert with sincere overkill.

Seven days was a long time for children to go missing. Everyone was concerned, should be concerned, and everyone in Avalon had a citizen's duty to help look for them.

Zuke left the house.

It was a warm evening, hot even, the smell of fruit in the air from the surrounding orchards, from the Canneries, the glow of the pinkish sun making her happy, but the excitement of how well things were working out cramping her stomach.

It was some distance to Westcoat Pond but the whole of Avalon would be there and she wasn't going to miss that for anything.

She walked quickly down Cedar Avenue, turned left along 6th Street, cut down behind the row of shops, the gas station, past the church where, already, there were signs of activity.

A squad car cruised by.

Then another.

And another.

Familiar Avalon faces were there hanging around, men studying maps spread out on the hoods of their cars, dissecting the area.

As she waited on the sidewalk to cross, she watched another squad car coming slowly towards her.

It stopped and one of the officers beckoned to her.

'Where are you going?'

'Why?'

'Know Joleen Delora or Bonnie Sharp?'

'Sure. Found them yet?'

'No. We're still looking. But we're not too happy about kids like you being out alone.'

'Guess I'm not too happy about it myself, but I've got to go shopping. Mom's working and Dad's in San Diego and my little brother needs feeding.'

'When does your mother get home?'

'Eight, nine, ten? Who knows?'

'She give you the key to the house?'

Zuke showed him the latchkey round her neck.

'What's your name?'

'Zuke Donoghue.'

'OK, Zuke. Just take care, and don't speak to strangers. And if you see either Joleen or Bonnie, let someone know immediately.'

So new cops had been brought in from somewhere to cope with the emergency. She knew the locals by sight, Sergeant Oates and Sergeant Finch personally.

She walked across the road, waited for the patrol car to disappear, then climbed over the white church fence into the graveyard, round the back to the path that led up the slope towards Westcoat Pond.

The long dry grass whipped against her jeans as she started running, burrs collecting on the canvas of her trainers. In the distance she could hear the whines of the police sirens. The whole of Avalon was out for the great evening search.

When she got to the top of the hill she was amazed to see the organized army of parents, police and helpers moving in a line across the flats south of the pond. A fire engine had half-drained the pond and men were wading about in the water prodding the mud with sticks.

As she got nearer Liz Kleiner spotted her and called out.

'Come to watch, Zuke, or help?'

Liz Kleiner was a pain. Her new home room teacher, she always went on at her for being late at school though she knew she had to get Dillon up and do all the housework.

'Help,' she shouted back. 'What are you looking for?'

'You know what we're looking for. Anything that might belong to Judd, Bonnie or Joleen. Judd was last seen here two nights ago with a man carrying a fishing rod. What each of us is doing is searching an area of six feet to the right and six feet to the left as we move along. You can work with me.'

'Who saw Judd with a man?' she asked.

'I don't know, but that's the information we're working on.'

'And you believe it?'

'Why not?'

'I wasn't believed when I was abducted three years ago. Maybe it's the same man?'

'I didn't know you'd been abducted, Zuke.'

Liz Kleiner was from the East coast, and Zuke guessed she got pretty lonely during the vacations. She was always organizing bazaars and picnics and this whole business was completely ruining the pageant she was producing.

'Tell me about your abduction, Zuke,' she said.

They moved forward side by side, Liz Kleiner beating the long grass down with a walking stick, looking for things all the time, sometimes stopping to pick up a bottle top, or an old can, a screwed up candy wrapper. Occasionally someone shouted out, a button had been found, a piece of cloth. Everything mattered and the officer in charge rushed over to check.

'When was it and what happened?'

'Oh,' Zuke said, 'I've told the story so many times I'm kind of bored with it, and no one's ever believed me. People think I invented the whole thing because Ma was pregnant. As it happened Ma wasn't pregnant and it truly happened. But what the hell?'

‘I’ve never heard the story. Tell me,’ Liz Kleiner insisted.

She was lying. She had heard it. The shrink’s report was in her Grammar School file which had followed her to the Junior High with such remarks as ‘Imaginative and Over Inventive’, suggesting she was a liar.

‘I was nine, wearing a new yellow dress for the August Regatta. I was watching some kids on the lake in the boats and this man came up to me and offered to buy me a ride. Pretty stock stuff like you see in the movies. Which is why no one believed me. People want thrills and new ideas all the time. The truth is very repetitive and dull, you know.’

‘I know,’ Liz Kleiner said kindly. She was like that, leaning over backwards to help.

‘Anyway, I said I didn’t like boats so he asked me if I’d like a ride in his car.’

‘What sort of car?’

‘It was green, and the inside was kind of homely, padded with sheepskin, you know, white and woolly and he had a stereo system with really loud music. I mean, it was very exciting, and the windshield was green too, not all over but from the top down. He drove fast and didn’t turn left when I asked him to, which was when I started getting frightened.’

‘Where did he take you to?’

Zuke was about to answer when whistles started blowing, a call to stop. At the far end of the line someone had found something. A body? An amputated arm? A severed head? The anticipation of horror was expressed on everyone’s faces.

It was a small pair of swimming trunks, wine coloured with no name tag, found hanging on the lower branches of a thorn bush.

Liz Kleiner sat down, pulled at a blade of grass and started sucking it.

She didn’t ask Zuke about the abduction again. It obviously hadn’t interested her that much in the first place and had been forgotten.

Typical.

Zuke had noted that of adults. They asked you a question then didn't care a damn about the answer.

'I think I ought to be getting home now. Dillon's alone,' she said.

'All alone?'

'Sure. Mom's working. I don't like him being by himself in the house when it gets dark.'

Liz Kleiner smiled kindly at this, recognition that this young girl was very aware of her responsibilities however imaginative and over inventive she might be.

Zuke walked down the slope towards the pond, passing Judd's parents who were hurrying up to identify the swimming trunks.

They were Judd's.

Zuke knew.

She knew because she'd hung them on the low branches of the thorn bush early that morning.

Zuke went home.

Dillon was back in front of the television but not watching it. He was reading.

She made a few futile noises around him to make her presence known, then went into the kitchen and filled an empty garbage bag with a pack of twelve quarter pound hamburgers, twelve rolls, a jar of mayonnaise and a bottle of ketchup. She threw in a few apples, oranges, bananas, and a quantity of candy bars, all bought that morning.

She swung the bag over her shoulder and left by the front door.

She crossed the Prestianni lawn, joined the sidewalk outside Grandma Olsen's house, then turned right into Dry Creek Lane.

She bobbed up and down as she walked, amused by the sound of her hair smacking lightly against the plastic bag across the back of her neck. She'd kept her hair short ever since Rick Prestianni had told her she looked like Joan of

Arc. She'd liked being compared to the Saint, though she didn't see herself in religious terms at all. It was the girl in armour she'd identified with, going off to war.

She checked to see if anyone was around, then darted up the drive of the derelict old house known to the locals as Mayor's Folly because one of Avalon's first Mayors had ruined himself building it, but known to the Latchkeys as Fort Knox, because that is what the house had become to them.

Built of grey brick and flintstone, it had four storeys, a verandah round three sides on the ground floor, wooden balconies jutting out on the first floor and three gables decorated with elaborately carved eaves. It stood in two acres of abandoned land, most of which was used for dumping old kitchen sinks, baths, bicycle frames, and anything else which had proved too much for the local consumer society.

She strode purposefully to the back of the house and dropped her garbage bag by the stone steps leading up to the double doors which had opened out on to the once well laid out garden, then sauntered on round to the east side and along the path and back to Dry Creek Lane through the overgrown laurel bushes.

The kids would have seen her, they would have been watching out for her and for anyone else hanging around. If anything was wrong they would have left a piece of pink tissue out as a warning, and she would have carried on, even gone back to the house with the supplies.

But clearly all was well and tonight Bonnie, Joleen and Judd would be joined by Steve.

Zuke felt her heart miss a beat at that thought.

Things were really beginning to hot up.

The success of 'Mission Steve' depended on the boy's father, Dan Mollman, behaving as he always did on Wednesday nights, that is returning from his day's surveillance of the Chittuck Solar Energy Laboratory, where he worked as security officer, at nine o'clock and immediately settling down to watch the Vietnam veterans' soap before putting Steve to bed.

It was likely that because of the crisis he might not come home as usual, but join the others in the search for Judd, a now obvious possibility which she should have foreseen. But the programme was important to Dan, and so was the welfare of his little boy.

Of the four Latchkids Steve was the only one who did not know what was going to happen, because Zuke thought him too restless and she could not trust him to keep his mouth shut for too long. What he could be trusted to do was enjoy an adventure. Anything to get away from his father who, through a determination to bring his son up as a happy and normal all American boy, over compensated for the loss of Steve's mother who had died two years back after a long illness.

Steve was hardly ever allowed to do anything once his father was home. It was total freedom all day and prison time at night and Zuke knew that all she had to do was tap Steve on the shoulder, ask him to come along with her, and he would.

Steve's abduction was the most important in her plan to terrorize Avalon. Because his father was a respected citizen who led an exemplary life. She wanted the disappearance to be sudden and inexplicable. She wanted Steve to be in the house one minute and gone the next. She had therefore questioned Steve about his daily routine when his father was home and learned about the nightly feeding of his rabbits which were kept in a regularly cleaned hutch at the bottom of the tidy garden.

Every night at five minutes to ten, Steve, accompanied by his Dad, went to feed the rabbits before going to bed, except on Wednesdays when he went alone because Dan Mollman watched his favourite programme.

So now, on her way back from Fort Knox, at half past nine, she went over to the Mollman house, unobserved, hid by the large rabbit hutch at the bottom of the neat garden and waited very patiently for Steve to appear, because patience was what it was all about.

It had got dark, the lights were on in the house, but the curtains not drawn. She had seen the grey-haired Mollman sitting in front of the TV, so everything was going according to plan.

Patience was one of her gifts which she was aware few people possessed, and she was capable of sitting for hours, sometimes without moving a muscle, if there was good reason to do so.

Now there was good reason.

She checked her watch.

Five minutes to go.

The moment Steve went missing the balloon would go up, the sparks would fly and his father would make sure the police hotted up their inquiries.

The kitchen door opened and Steve appeared holding a large plastic bowl.

She didn't move but remained quite still in the shadows.

He came along the path, then suddenly stopped to empty the contents of the bowl on a compost heap hidden in among the bushes half-way down the garden. Then he turned and went back into the house.

A change in routine? What about the rabbits?

She waited, tried to guess what was happening.

Steve would be going to the living room, sitting down next to his father to watch TV, the programme would end and he'd be sent to bed.

The plan was going to fail.

But Steve came out again carrying another bowl.

He came down the path, straight to the hutches.

She'd have to let him feed the rabbits, she'd have to do that, then she'd have three minutes to run with him to her house and hide him there.

Steve started talking to the animals.

'There you are Lincoln, Jefferson, Washington . . .'

Dan Mollman must have chosen the names. Educational, patriotic and dumb. The man was a real pain.

As Steve stepped back, away from the hutches, Zuke reached out and grabbed his arm, clapping the palm of her hand over his mouth.

'OK, Steve, this is it. Follow me. Just take the bowl and follow me.'

Improvisation.

The bowl would be an unexpected bonus.

She'd drop it somewhere to cause confusion, just as she had Judd's swimming trunks.

Everything was falling into place.

'Where are we going?'

'Just follow me, keep down low and don't make a sound.'

She'd plotted the route. Along the back path under cover of a hedge, along a ditch behind Grandma Olsen's and the Prestiannis', then in by her own back garden to the side door.

They did it in half the time she had allowed, went straight upstairs and into Dillon's room.

'Hi, Steve. Glad you could make it.'

'What's happening?'

'We're going to the moon,' Dillon said, making the kind of face that suggested a lunatic plan.

'In a rocket?'

'Bicycle,' Dillon corrected.

'Mom not back?' Zuke checked.

'She rang. She'll be late.'

'Great! Just stay here you two, for a few minutes, OK? I've a few things to do.'

She went downstairs to check that everything was as it should be, all the lights off except the one in the hallway to help Mom see up the stairs when she got in.

She checked the time, then went to look out of the front window. If Mollman acted quickly all hell would break out in the area any minute. So there was no time to lose.

She went back upstairs.

'Right. You, Steve, get to the Knox without being seen. The others are there waiting for you. You, Dillon, follow a bit behind to make sure he's not seen. If anyone asks you where you're going, or where you've been on your way back, act dumb, you're just out for a walk.'

'OK.'

'If this succeeds I'll get both of you new GI Joes.'

'I don't take bribes,' Dillon said. 'But the spaceman would be appreciated.'

Dillon grabbed Steve's hand and started pulling him down the stairs.

'I've got the spaceman, I want the marine,' Steve said.

'Just move it.'

They were gone, out of the kitchen door. Zuke crossed her fingers. Steve would be OK, though he lived in his own fantasy world. He had strange eyes, something unsettling about them. Calculating. Inherited from his mother, because he didn't look a bit like his father, and the mop of blonde hair was odd too. Silver it was, sometimes.

Zuke went to the bathroom and looked out of the window, watched Steve and Dillon dart along the hedge. She went back to Dillon's room, picked up the rabbit bowl and switched off the light.

She was tense, aware that the consequences of something going wrong now would be terrible, but then she smiled at the thought of success.

It would shake the adult community when they found out what they had allowed to happen under their very noses, what dangers adolescents could be in.

They never listened.

They never wanted to believe.

'You'll be OK, Zuke. Dillon'll be OK . . .'

They had no idea of the fears kids suffered when left alone, fears of unexpected adult behaviour, the psychopath's violence, the madman breaking in.

The three children missing had already unsettled some.

Now the whole town would get worried.

The phone rang.

She took her time going down the stairs and into the living room.

'Hallo?'

'Is that you, Zuleika?'

In all the world only one person called her by her full name, Dan Mollman himself.

'Is Steve with you?'

'Nope.' She managed to sound surprised by the question.

'Is Dillon?'

'Sure.'

'Is Steve with him?'

'Dill!' She shouted up the stairs, then into the phone she said, 'Hang on. I'll go check.'

She put the receiver down and went up the stairs, looked into Dillon's room and the bathroom. She must not lie. She must not say that Dillon was there in case he was seen. She bit her lower lip and went back down the stairs.

'Nope. Neither Dillon nor Steve.'

'Do you know where Dillon might be?'

'Gene's maybe? Gene Prestianni?'

'Thanks.'

The way he hung up quickly was proof it had worked. He'd ring the Prestiannis', or go round, and God knows what he'd do after that.

She switched off the hallway light and went out on to the porch, sat down on the steps and waited for developments.

A few minutes went by before she heard an engine start up in the distance, saw the headlamps light up the under foliage of the trees lining the road, then the grey car pass.

Dan Mollman in a hurry, maybe going to the police.

She felt a cramp in her stomach.

Then there was a noise behind her.

'Zuke?'

It was Dillon, back much sooner than expected.

She stopped him coming out, led him into the living room.

'How did it go?'

'They were waiting for him, the panel opened up and they pulled him in, head first. Never seen anyone go through so quickly.'

'Anyone see you?'

'No.'

So it had worked.

It had all worked.

The four Latchkids were now safely hidden away.

'Can I go read my book?'

'Sure.'

'What are you going to do?'

She picked up the plastic bowl from beside the phone, and put it on her head.

'I'm going for a walk.'

chapter two

Eugene Prestianni stared at his birthday cake and counted the twelve candles.

They were all blue, stuck in pink roses, in a circle on thick white icing.

HAPPY BIRTHDAY GENE was written in blue, and under that was a simple blue sailing boat on a wavy sea.

Grandma Olsen next door had made it, had brought it round, lit it and set it before him.

Not his father, not his mother, but Grandma Olsen, no relation, just a neighbour who seemed to know that his parents had forgotten what day it was.

'I know your boat hasn't got a sail,' she said, 'but the thought of you enjoying yourself on the lake is what I wanted to picture.'

'That's a really nice present, Gene. You must say a big thank you,' his mother urged him. 'That's a really nice surprise.'

It had embarrassed her, of course.

'I just brought this over for Gene's birthday,' the old lady had said.

'Birthday?' His mother had become confused, then turning to him had reproachfully asked, 'Why didn't you tell me? I can't remember everything.'

'Once a year is difficult to remember,' Grandma Olsen had agreed, and there had been a hateful exchange of looks.

Now the old lady was outside again and coming back with a cardboard box tied with a blue ribbon. She handed it to Gene.

He took it from her, felt something moving about inside, pulled off the ribbon and eased the lid off.

Inside the box was a tiny black and white rabbit breathing rapidly on a bed of grass.

'He's for me?'

'He's for you. He was born three days ago, at Dan Mollman's, and his name is Ulysses, after Ulysses S. Grant.'

'Where am I going to keep him?'

At that moment Rick Prestianni joined them, hands deep in his jean pockets, unshaven, red-eyed, and smelling as always of drink.

'What've you got there?'

'A rabbit, Mr Prestianni,' Grandma Olsen said. 'A birthday present for Gene if you'll let him keep it.'

'Why shouldn't I, if it's his birthday present?'

And to Gene's amazement his father picked up the tiny animal, put it in the palm of his large hand and stroked it gently with two fingers. 'I used to have one like this. Same colours. A doe it was. This one's a buck,' he said turning it over and examining it. 'He'll need a hutch and regular feeding, Gene. Animals like this need care.'

Suzy Prestianni snorted.

'Don't say it, Suzy,' his father warned. 'Just don't say it!'

'Don't say what?'

'That you don't want the rabbit in the house. The boy knows you don't want it in the house, and I know you don't want it in the house, but I'm going to build it a hutch and it can stay outside.'

'*You're* going to build it a hutch?' Her voice pitched high with the mockery.

'And Gene's going to paint it.'

With Grandma Olsen standing behind them like a referee the hostilities did not develop.

'I'll get you your present tomorrow, Gene,' his mother said. 'That's a promise.'

He shrugged his shoulders, embarrassed for her.

She'd forget again. She always did.

'Let's go see what we've got in the way of wood,' Rick said handing him back the rabbit. And Gene, with the animal cupped in his hands, followed his father down to the bottom of the garden.

Rick Prestianni started taking everything out of the shed, old flower pots, the perished rubber dinghy that should have been on board the cabin cruiser on the lake called *Water Fox* that they never went out in anymore, the filter machine that had been bought for the swimming pool which had never been dug, the lawn mower for the grass that had never been sown. The garden was not a garden at all, but a yard.

His father rummaged further in the dusty darkness and brought out an old dish rack that had once stood beside the kitchen sink.

'We can use these bars for the front, and an old box as the back, then he'll have a real airy home.'

The building of the hutch depended entirely on Rick Prestianni finding everything he needed immediately. If there was one short delay, one hiccup in the endeavour, he would never do it.

Gene knew this, so went back into the house, put Ulysses in his cardboard box and ran to the garage to get the essential tools.

When he got back, Rick had already slowed down, had lit a cigarette and was staring at the dish rack and a wooden box.

'The front's too small. It'll leave a gap,' he said.

'We can put two pieces of wood on either side, or one on one side,' Gene suggested.

'You got the wood. You know how to do it?'

The aggression was building up.

'Maybe . . .' Gene said, shrugging his shoulders.

'Then I'll leave you to it!' And Rick walked back to the house.

The effort was over.

If the hutch was to be built, Gene would have to do it alone, and if he succeeded it would be held against him as an affront.

He thought of leaving everything, it was getting dark, but then he decided the rabbit was the most important thing in his life, so he started measuring the rack and the box, and started sawing and nailing and by the time night had fallen he had built a good enough hutch for the tiny animal to sleep in, with a strip of wood running along the bottom to stop it getting through the bars.

It was while he was tearing at some long tufts of grass in the garden of Mayor's Folly that he caught sight of two small figures making their way hurriedly towards the back of the old house. He ducked down the moment he saw them and watched till they had disappeared.

Latchkids.

They were always running around there, playing their silly games.

He didn't care.

He took the grass back to Ulysses, bid the rabbit good-night, then made his way to bed.

The next morning, watching the breakfast show on TV, he looked up from his cornflakes when there was a newsflash. A fourth Avalon child had gone missing.

At about the same time that he had seen the two furtive figures round Mayor's Folly, Steve Mollman had apparently disappeared from his home.

The Sheriff himself came on the programme asking everyone to give a hand in the search for the missing children. An orange plastic bowl used by Steve Mollman for keeping his rabbit feed had been found on the side of the East Avalon Highway near a farm, and the area was going to be combed.

'I thought I saw Steve Mollman last night,' Gene said. 'Down by the old house.'

'Yeah? Well it couldn't have been him could it? Not if they're hunting around the East Avalon Highway. Want to join me in the search?'

His father was being real nice.

The summer vacation mornings could sometimes be difficult, specially if the old man was hungover. Mom usually left for work in a hurry leaving a disaster trail behind her, and it was up to father and son to tidy up. Sometimes his father didn't feel like it.

But today seemed OK.

Gene washed up the breakfast things while Rick showered and shaved and dressed, then they locked up the house and got in the old green Lincoln.

Gene sat in the front as they drove to Cold Spring Farm, the meeting point of all volunteers. As they got near he noticed Zuke Donoghue walking alongside the road, a piece of grass in her mouth, looking cool and casual as she always did.

He thought of asking his father to stop to give her a lift, but knew some remark would be made about Zuke and Dillon and the way they were being brought up. There was a gulf between the two families, had been ever since Mr Donoghue, Zuke's father, had moved away.

He and Gene's father had been the best of buddies, both crack salesmen for the Avalon Fruit Canneries; but after Zuke's father had left to seek his fortune elsewhere, Rick had started drinking and had eventually lost his job.

Everyone from Avalon seemed to converge on Cold Spring Farm, and a field was designated as a starting point. Dan Mollman was at the gate with the Sheriff giving instructions to the volunteer helpers as they drove in. Each was given a photocopied map of the area with roads traced over in different colours.

'You take the amber road, Rick, if you don't mind. Just cruise along it slowly, looking to left and right. Gene can be a great help too. Anything suspicious, stop and search and report to us. Good luck! And thanks!'

They moved off, Rick studying the map as he drove.

Gene felt good. It was like the old days when they went for long drives and picnics and Dad was always cheerful and cracked jokes.

There were no jokes today because it was a kind of solemn occasion, but he felt good, and last night's bad vibes over the rabbit hutch had been forgotten.

'I don't want you wandering around on your own anymore, Gene, not until one of those kids has been found and we know what's happening. There could be some homicidal maniac around with an axe or something crazy. You've got to be careful. This is where we start the search.'

He turned off the highway and started driving very slowly down a shadowy lane lined with thick trees. He'd never been down here before.

'You look out to the right, I'll handle the left. Stop me if you see anything.'

They cruised for a hundred yards or so, then Rick stopped the car and got out. In a ditch he'd spotted something metallic, but it only turned out to be an old length of drainpipe.

They moved on.

Gene saw a few pieces of paper, a can or two, but didn't say anything. Then they came to the end of the lane and a junction where a squad car was parked and a few people were hanging around not sure what to do next.

He recognized a face or two, old buddies of his father's, Vietnam veterans grown fat, rednecks soured by failure who would ignore him or not even notice him, so he stayed in the car and wished he'd brought Ulysses, who could have hopped about on the back seat. But then maybe he'd go down the hole in the upholstery where the springs had come through.

One of the men was passing round a bottle, everyone having a swig, including the cop. They didn't care a damn about Steve and the others, this was just an excuse to get out of the house and meet up.

He thought of Zuke on the fence.

What was she doing there anyway?

It would be nice to be with her.

She'd know what was happening.

'Are you dating Zuke Donoghue, young man?' Old Grandma Olsen had teased him once. 'She's a fine intelligent young lady, bright as a button and pretty too.'

He'd blushed.

He'd carried her books back from school just the once but had got laughed at too much by the adults to do it again.

'It's the freckles that get them, Zuke, eh?' Joleen's mother had said one day when they were all down by the lake. Joleen, Bonnie, Zuke and another girl from Cedar Avenue. He'd favoured Zuke and had been the only boy there. 'I sometimes paint freckles round my nose,' he'd heard her go on in a whisper to his own mother, 'and business usually picks up.'

The adults had laughed, but he hadn't understood.

The remark had puzzled him for days till he had asked Zuke, who'd explained it as though the whole world but him knew what it meant.

'She does men favours.'

It hadn't helped him a bit.

The group decided to split up and they all returned to their cars, Rick laughing at some off the cuff remark, chuckling to himself as he got in behind the steering wheel.

'What are we going to do now?' Gene asked.

'I don't know what you're going to do, but I'm driving over to Westcoat to have a beer. Want to join the men or go home to your bunny?'

'I'll go home,' he said.

His father wasn't generous, but dropped him off at Cold Spring Farm where he reported his negative findings.

'You can walk from here, can't you? Across the fields and round by your school. You know the way.'

Hadn't he been asked not to go anywhere alone barely an hour ago? He didn't say anything but just got out of the car and started the long walk.

Maybe he'd meet Zuke on the way.

But he didn't.

When he got back to his house he was surprised to find the front door open and his mother in the living room talking with two friends over coffee. He stood in the doorway and listened to them bitching about Latchkid parents for not keeping more of an eye on their children.

'Jack McQuare's closed part of the factory and offices for the day, Gene, so's everyone can help in the search,' Suzy Prestianni said, looking up.

Jack McQuare, her boss, was always giving her days off.

'I'll go feed Ulysses,' he said.

'Ulysses is his new pet rabbit,' he heard his mother explain. Then over her shoulder to him, 'Call me if you need me,' just to show the others what a good mother she was.

She'd forgotten his birthday present of course, as expected. Who cared?

'Gene!'

He'd just got to the kitchen.

'There's something for you upstairs on your bed.'

She hadn't forgotten!

He rushed up.

It was something small wrapped in red paper. He tore off the paper to find a white plastic box that promised something valuable. Inside was a digital quartz watch, all black and silver, the smaller figures on the right of the dial changing every second, the date above, a button for a light, another for a stop timer. It wasn't an alarm, but who needed an alarm?

He strapped it on his wrist, it was a bit loose, but looked really great. Then he rushed down the stairs.

'Thanks, Mom. Thanks a lot.'

She allowed him to hug her, and gave him an affectionate kiss, looked at the watch, made sure the other mothers admired it.

'I'll get you your lunch, then you can go out and play.'

He ate alone while his mother went back to entertaining her friends. He was used to it. His father hardly ever ate lunch and Mom had hers at the factory canteen along with all the other secretaries. Maybe she'd had hers. It was pretty late.

When he'd finished, downing a glass of water because he didn't like the taste of her beetroot salad too much, he went to see Ulysses tucked under the grass in his hutch, fast asleep. He pulled him out and watched him breathing in the palm of his hand. It was nice having him but there wasn't much you could do with little rabbits except look at them. Ulysses wasn't exactly interested in his new watch.

Then he decided to paint the hutch and found a can of blue paint in the garage, but when he eased off the lid the contents were all solid and shrunk, and anyway he didn't have a brush. So instead he started tidying the shed, putting the perished dinghy back, the filter machine, the flower pots.

Something attracted his attention beyond the shed and he looked up.

Dillon, in white T-shirt and jeans, carrying a heavy brown paper bag, was hurrying towards Mayor's Folly.

He put Ulysses back quickly in the hutch, then rushed to climb over the wire fence, ran down the path behind the hedge and caught sight of him again.

Then Dillon disappeared.

Over by the old house he suddenly disappeared.

Puzzled, Gene ran on forward to the thick line of laurel bushes and got down on his haunches.

No sign of anyone.

It was as though the boy had gone through the wall of the house like a ghost.

Gene looked at his watch. 16.05 and 22 seconds.

Two of them last night.

Now Dillon.

Supposing the Latchkids were all hiding in there for some reason. Supposing they'd all got into some kind of trouble but nobody knew and they were hiding?

He got up cautiously and looked through the dusty dark green leaves at the old house some fifty yards away. He'd never really studied it.

The casings round the windows, the verandahs and the doors had all once been pink, but the paint had dried and peeled off and only the grey cracked wood underneath, matching the grey black stone, gave the place a deserted haunted look, that and the boarded-up windows and boarded-up doors. It would make an ideal hiding place, once you got in.

He moved along and through the laurels, then decided to make a run for the large square water tank that had been dumped half-way between himself and the back verandah. From there he'd be able to observe anything that was going on inside, if anything was.

He got down to a sprint start position, then made the dash, his jeans catching on to something sharp, tearing the material.

He hurled himself to the ground. The tank gave perfect cover. He'd stay there for a while before moving even closer.

16.07 and 43 seconds.

He couldn't wait.

He looked round the side of the tank, decided on a hollow

in the ground some ten yards on and started the long crawl.

He moved slowly, like a marine, on his stomach, pressing one knee down and thrusting forward, the other knee down, forward, like a chameleon, as camouflaged as a chameleon too, for his faded blue check shirt and jeans blended in with the dusty grass, only his white sneakers might show up against the background. Not that there wasn't plenty of colour about, old cans, waste paper.

He reached the hollow and let himself roll down into the dip, ended up on his stomach again, taking his weight on his elbows, stretching out his legs.

He eased himself up so that he could see the house, checked the time once more and decided to stay there till five o'clock.

Three quarters of an hour.

If he saw nothing by then, he'd go back and give Ulysses his supper.

Gene waited for the figures to change on his watch. A few more seconds and they would all go at once, more quickly than the eye could see, and without a sound, even if you put it to your ear.

The zeros came up.

Time: 17.00.00.

He looked towards the house again.

Nothing.

No one.

He heard a noise to his right, a rustling. In there among the tangle of grasses, hardly bigger than his thumb, was a field mouse. It was sniffing, its tiny pink nostrils lifting up in the air and sniffing, its black beady eyes darting all around, its pink paws, sharp, skinny, scratching at the dust beneath.

He didn't move, held his breath. If a mouse hadn't sensed his presence, then no one else would either.

He checked the time again and let out a long sigh, forgetting about the mouse, and when he looked for it again it had gone.

He moved the long grass around but it was nowhere to be seen. Like Dillon, it had vanished. Though he was sure Dillon was in the house, he just couldn't work out how he'd got in.

Now he was beginning to feel thirsty.

He reached out and pulled at a bright green blade of grass, stuck the end in his mouth and started chewing. He should have brought some gum.

The white of a T-shirt showed up suddenly, just a flash, but enough to make him sit up. It was Dillon crawling out of a hole right there in front of him, twenty yards or so, a gap below the steps that led up to the porch. He was crouching, looking around.

The boy stood up, then strolled off casually round the side of the house, through the laurel bushes and out along Dry Creek Lane.

Gene waited. When he was sure no one else was coming out, he got to his feet and started slowly towards the steps till he reached the shadow of the porch.

He dropped down on his knees wondering where Dillon could possibly have come out.

Then he saw it.

You had to know, it was so clever. Just the one board under the steps which looked as solidly in place as all the others. He moved over, studied the board, saw the way it was fitted. Any kid could get his finger through the small hole and pull.

Which he did.

Now he slid down through the narrow gap which no adult would dream of trying. It hardly looked wide enough for his own head.

He lay flat on his stomach and eased his feet in, his legs, squeezed his hips through, his chest. He was caught now, like a rolled up newspaper in a mail box, and his feet didn't touch anything on the other side.

How much of a drop was there?

He threaded himself in some more, had to turn his head

to one side to get it through the gap, then he touched bottom with his toes.

He was through.

Darkness, dry earth. He could just reach for the board and pull it back into position.

What a hiding place!

He waited for his eyes to get accustomed to the darkness, then things took shape. It was just a space under the porch steps, nothing more, but there was a wooden crate against the cement foundations and when he stood on it he saw the way into the house, a short man-made tunnel.

He pulled himself up and in and along, and again he was through, this time on to a dusty wooden floor, a back room of the house with enough light coming from the boarded up windows for him to see exactly where he was.

It had been a sitting room maybe, a dining room?

He tiptoed through into one of the living rooms, stepped on a loose board which squeaked.

He stopped dead in his tracks, then moved on.

He checked the front hall, the other front room which led into yet another. It was a big house, a mansion of a place. Round the back of the staircase, the old kitchen, dark, dank, a spider's web in the corner of the doorway, an old sink, an old stove. Another spider's web in the pantry. It made his flesh creep. He hated them.

He came back the same way. No evidence of the kids here. He started carefully up the stairs.

Wood, old, creaky.

First landing. He stood still. The house had another two floors, maybe an attic. He went round the rooms quickly, checked them all out. The bathroom smelled foul, no water, nothing there, but it smelled foul.

He went on up, the stairs narrower, the ceilings lower, then he smelled it, very faint, but different to the dust, a scent, a perfume. Orange. The smell of oranges. He was getting near. He was getting very near.

In the front room on the second floor there was a ladder going straight up into the attic. That's where the scent was coming from, and every rung of the ladder was clean, no dust, used daily.

He climbed up, popped his head above the attic floor and wanted to shout for joy.

It was all there.

Unbelievable, as large as the whole house, with a carpet, cushions, and furnished. Wow! Was it furnished!

'Anyone here?' he said, his voice timid, tight.

No answer. Stillness itself.

But he had found it. He had found the Latchkids' room, their hideout. He pulled himself right up and stared and stared at everything around him.

He could see Zuke's touch. The movie posters, the travel posters, the large Supergirl doll, even a fruit machine! There was a battery operated record player, LPs, comic books, a case of Coca Cola, cigarette cartons, and rolls and rolls of different coloured toilet tissues.

Where had she got it all?

On one wall, surrounded by pictures of JR and Superman and Luke Skywalker was stuck a large sheet of white card with all their names – Joleen Delora and Bonnie Sharp, Steve Mollman and Judd Reidy, Dillon Donoghue – topped by Zuleika Donoghue herself.

'We've got a camera too, if you want to photograph it all,' a voice said.

He froze.

Slowly he turned, looked round. No one in the room, no one in the hatchway, no one in any of the corners.

'You're an asshole, Gene,' the voice said.

It was Zuke and it came from directly above him.

He looked up.

She was sitting on the huge crossbeam, her legs swinging, a menacing look of contempt in her eyes.

'How did you find your way in?'

'I . . . I . . .'

'You watched Dillon.'

'Yes.'

'Get out of the way, I'm going to jump.'

She jumped.

'Know what we do to kids like you?' she said, stepping forward and standing real close to him.

'No . . .' He caught his breath, tried hard not to show he'd been frightened.

'We do what we did to Rufus.'

'I don't know who Rufus is.'

'Rufus was Bonnie's dog.' She stared at him, narrowing her eyes, pursing her lips, daring him to look straight back at her. 'Rufus *was* Bonnie's dog,' she repeated. 'He died. He died because we killed him.'

Gene didn't move a muscle.

'Know why we killed him?'

'No . . .'

'We killed him because he found this place. We couldn't have him sniffing around looking for Bonnie, following her in. He's buried out there in the garden, in the very dip where you were lying all this afternoon spying on us.'

So she'd seen him.

'How did you kill him?' he asked.

'Electrocution. It was kind of horrible. We tied wires to his front legs and his tail and all his hair stood up on end. It was nearly funny, Gene. Nearly. Took ten minutes.' She reached out and lifted a strand of his hair, then let it drop. 'I guess you'll look pretty funny too.'

'You can't electrocute me,' he protested.

'Why not?'

'It would be murder.'

'Who'd get to know? I wouldn't tell anybody, Bonnie wouldn't tell anybody, nor Joleen, Judd or Steve or Dillon. And you wouldn't tell anybody 'cause you wouldn't be around to do so.'

She put her right hand around his throat and squeezed it a little. 'Maybe we'll garotte you.'

He didn't know what that was.

'That would be more suitable for you, being Mexican. That's what they do in Mexico. Garotte you.'

'I'm Italian,' he said.

'Oh yeah? I always thought you were from Mexico. How do they execute criminals in Italy then?'

'They shoot them,' he said. 'I think.'

'Can't shoot you. Haven't got a gun.'

'What's garotting then?' he asked.

'They tie you to a post, real tight, slip a metal ring or wire round your throat then tighten it, real slowly, by means of a screw, till you're strangled to death. Sometimes,' she added for effect, 'they twist the screw through into the back of your neck till your spine splinters.'

She smiled now, and he smiled back.

She'd gone too far and knew it. The threats had run into fantasy and it had become funny.

She still stared at him but the look in her eyes was different. It was interested. He knew she liked him, really. He'd felt it when she'd put her hand round his neck, when she'd first reached out to feel his hair.

'Want a Coke?' she asked suddenly. 'Cigarette?'

She turned on her heels and went to one of the cardboard boxes in the corner, brought out two cans of Coca Cola and a carton of Marlboro.

'Got this stack two weeks ago, round at Warshall's in Main Street. It was reported in the paper. Didn't you read about it? We got a video too and two thousand cigarettes, enough chewing gum for a year and this watch.' She held up her wrist and proudly showed him the large quartz watch. She pressed a couple of buttons and an electronic noise played 'Ol' Man River'. It was better than his.

'I can only wear it up here or they'd get to know,' she said through a sigh. Then, 'Sit down.'

He sat down on one of the huge bean bags and pulled back the metal tag on the Coke can she gave him.

'We've got stealing down to a fine art. Ever read *Oliver*

Twist by Charles Dickens? Fagin, that's me. I plan, the others collect.'

'You shouldn't be telling me all this,' he said, 'I might report you.'

'To who? Your Pappy? I'm not frightened of you, Gene. I'm not frightened of anybody. Know who's married to my Aunt in Washington DC?'

'No.'

'Senator Carl Hapsburg. I'm a Senator's niece. Just remember that.'

'You're full of shit, Zuke,' Gene said, surprised at his own bravery. 'I don't believe anything you say. I don't believe you ever killed that dog the way you said.'

She put down her tin of Coke, crossed her arms and studied him.

'And I don't believe there's a Senator Carl Hapsburg,' he added.

She studied him some more.

'OK. So I never killed the dog because Bonnie never had a dog anyway, but how did I get all this? Look at that tape-deck behind you, all those tapes. We've got the whole Golden Metropolitan Opera collection, the whole Golden Metropolitan Ballet Music collection, and the History of Jazz volumes one to twenty-five.'

'You like all that stuff?'

'No, but it's educational. If there's a nuclear war we've got enough cans of beans to last us three months, and enough to drink, and we got two boxes of spray-on furniture polish.'

She reached out and took a further sip at her Coke.

'Games. We've got all kinds of games. And Joleen, Bonnie and I have enough cosmetics to last us till we die.'

He was impressed. He had to be.

'How do you think all these things got up here, magic? You think I'm some kind of magician?'

'Witch, more like,' he said.

She liked that and laughed, then stopped and stared at him again.

'Why did you come up here?'

'Curiosity.'

'It killed the cat.'

'I'm not a cat or a dog. And you won't kill me.'

Sitting back as he was, his legs stretched out, ankles crossed, he felt confident, manly. He was in command of himself. And Zuke was only a girl, a bit older but his size.

'I'm going to give you a hard time,' she said, standing up. The hard look was back in her eyes, she could switch it on and off and really unsettle him when she pleased.

He pulled back his legs instinctively and sat up to be more alert.

'You're scared of me, Gene. You're scared of me because you don't know how much power I really have and I'm never going to let you know. But just remember this, always, I know how to twist adults round this little finger. Whatever I want them to do, they do. Whatever I want them to believe, they believe. And you're no different.' And she stuck the middle finger of her left hand rudely up in the air and circled it with the index finger of her other hand.

'I've got two books up on the shelf behind me, Gene, which have more information about adults than the whole school library. One's about child psychology which tells you just how wrong adults are about us, the other's on body language. Know what body language is?'

He sat up a bit more and tried to cover his ignorance by shrugging his shoulders.

'Body language is the total give-away. Like you, now, trying to pretend you know what I'm talking about. I can read people. Specially adults. They're dim. They lie, they cheat, they deceive each other and all you have to do to know this is study them. Right now you're as nervous as you were when you first came up. Look at your fists, they're as tight as your toes which are curled up inside your sneakers. Your feet are together, your knees. I've manipulated the whole interview, Gene, played with you like a fisherman plays with a catch. Five minutes ago you really thought you had the better of me because I patted you on the head. You're pretty sexy Gene, I'll say that much for you, but I'm not into that yet, and neither are you.'

She opened her eyes wide, not having thought about it before.

'Are you sexy, Gene?'

'I don't know. I don't think so.'

'You don't *think* so? You want to kiss me?'

It came up, as it did often enough, from somewhere along his jaw line, the flush, the heat, and the moment he realized he was blushing it pulsated all the way up to his eyebrows.

'Wowy! Little ole Gene's got sexy feelings! I bet you haven't even got pubic hair.'

He hated that. He really hated it and wanted to get out. He didn't want to have anything more to do with her, wished he'd never come up.

And she started laughing. She laughed at him and stared at him and all he could do was look down at the carpet, unable to face her.

When she stopped laughing, he looked up.

'You know, some grown up men, I mean real grown up men follow me sometimes,' she said. 'They follow kids like you as well. Pretty kids with nice faces. Girls' looks. That's what I think happened to Steve and Judd, Joleen and Bonnie.'

She was being serious.

'You thought they were hiding up here, didn't you?'

'Yes.'

'I think I know where they are, but if I tell anyone they won't believe me.'

'Why not?'

'No one believes me, Gene, you know that. I was abducted two years ago, the guy did awful things to me and no one, not even my own mother, believed a word of it. So no one listens to me. But I'm pretty sure I know where they are.'

So he'd been wrong all the time.

'Where?' he asked.

'What'll you do if I tell you? I mean, just what will you do, exactly?'

The straight look again. The steel-grey eyes.

'I'd try to rescue them,' he said honestly.

'How?'

'I suppose,' he said slowly, half-expecting to be damned for ever, 'I'd go to the police.'

She didn't explode.

She didn't spit or hiss or laugh.

She just said very quietly, 'I don't think the police would listen to you. They don't take us adolescents seriously. What you'll have to do is tell your father and get *him* to go to the police.'

She was going to confide in him? Recruit him to do something for the Latchkids?

'Come over to the house first thing tomorrow morning. By then I'll have all the information.'

chapter three

Zuke watched him through the peephole in the boarded up window on the ground floor.

You could see the whole of the back garden, the path behind the laurel bushes leading to her house, to Gene's. With binoculars you could see right into Grandma Olsen's kitchen and watch anyone in Dan Mollman's garden.

From the front rooms it was even better.

Through gaps in the shutters you could see down the whole of Sherbrooke Drive. Observation post Numero Uno. No one could come to the house without being spotted a mile down the road. Not that anyone came to the house, it had been empty ever since the last owners had died and most of the kids at Avalon Junior High thought it was haunted.

But Gene hadn't thought it was.

She saw him now, cautiously emerging from the secret exit, keeping low on the ground, looking around to see if anyone had spotted him.

He'd been easy enough to convince, had fallen into every trap she'd set him. The perfect dupe. If he carried out her instructions this time she'd use him again, but she'd have to find out how close he was to his parents.

Living daily with parents was unhealthy. They asked too many questions, were too curious for comfort. Without his father at home all day he'd be good material. But he couldn't qualify as a Latchkey. Not unless his old man went out to work. Or divorced his mother.

Or died.

She watched him crawl under the wire fence, straighten up and walk down the lane, hands in pockets, whistling maybe. Then she checked her watch.

Seventeen forty-five.

Stage two of the great SF Operation would soon have to get under way.

She sucked her breath in through clenched teeth.

The adrenalin was flowing.

She felt her heartbeat quicken, felt the flush coming to her cheeks, felt the urgency now to activate further what she had set in motion.

The whole town and nearly half the State had been on the move for the last five days because of her.

Now a culprit would be fingered.

And he'd defend himself.

And the law would accuse.

And she'd work all the puppets from behind the screen she had so carefully put up.

She went along the dark passage to the kitchen and opened the door that looked like a cupboard. Steep cement steps led down to a cellar.

'You can come up now, you guys. Our guest has gone.'

They came up one at a time, Joleen, Bonnie, Judd and Steve.

'How are you, Steve?'

'OK.' It didn't sound too happy.

'You want out, Steve? We can abandon the whole mission now if you want out.'

'No, I don't want out!'

'Worried about hurting your Dad's feelings?'

The look he gave her instead of an answer was proof enough. He didn't like his father any more than any of them liked their parents. They had all talked about it enough times, the need to teach the adults a good lesson, the longing to remind them that though mothers and fathers had to go out to work, though the whole damn family had to be fed, though they were all old enough to look after themselves, they needed some kind of recognition, some occasional show of affection.

'You guys going to be OK? Tonight's the Big Night!'

They all nodded.

She could do anything with them if she wanted to, they respected her so much. She was their mother, the only person they could turn to in time of trouble. And they'd been in plenty trouble. She'd seen to that.

'Up you go then and get some rest. You'll be hearing from me as soon as it's safe. And keep the voices down.'

She made her way to the low opening in the back room, slipped herself through the short tunnel to the space under the verandah steps, then eased the board carefully away to see if the coast was clear.

By this time tomorrow, it could all be over.

She was watching TV with Dillon when the phone rang.

Zuke picked up the receiver and signalled her brother to turn down the sound. He immediately crawled across the floor on his stomach like a snake because they were watching a snake movie.

'Hello?'

It was her mother ringing from the Greenhook Chalet Motel. From the way she started with a pleading 'Honey . . .' Zuke knew it would be good news. Either she wasn't coming home, or she was coming home really late.

'Honey, we've got a party of tourists from Texas here tonight and Mr Greenhook wants me to stay on, so I guess I might be a bit late.'

'Don't worry, Mom. Everything's OK here.'

'Got enough to eat and drink?'

'Sure.'

'Ring up Suzy Prestianni if you get worried about anything. She'll come over.'

Sometimes her mother sounded as though she actually cared. But then she used the same excuse so often. Tourists from Texas, visitors from the East Coast, Mr Greenhook's birthday. He'd had three birthdays this year already. She just had to ring up her little daughter to clear her conscience. Soon, maybe, she'd crack, like the Sharps. She'd heard Marina Sharp was quite hysterical about Bonnie's disappearance and was thinking of closing the hairdressing salon. But she'd only got as far as thinking.

So it was now a question of waiting and of being patient. She'd cook Dillon his favourite hamburger dish with cheese slices, and onion slices and pineapple slices, top the vanilla ice cream with chocolate sauce and a cherry, then tell him that it was Zero Hour for Operation SF.

She played around in the kitchen emptying a large bag of peanuts into a jar, turning the water on really strongly to foam up the detergent bubbles, trying to float the plates and spoons on them.

The doorbell rang which made her jump, and she realized she was nervous. She'd have to calm down, keep really cool.

Dillon went to open the door.

'Zuke!' he shouted, going back to his viewing. 'It's the police.'

But it was only Sergeant Finch.

'Hi, Zuke. Know your mother's out, so I thought I'd drop in and see how you were. Not heard anything from Steve or Judd have you?'

'No, Sergeant.'

'Got any plans for tonight? Going out anywhere?'

It had to be a routine check.

'Nope. Just sitting here and watching TV and feeding Dillon.'

'Good, good. You know the number to ring me if you need any help?'

'Why? Do you think some psychopath's doing the rounds?'

Sergeant Finch looked at her with a mixture of irritation and wonderment.

'Where did you get hold of that word? Television again? Just don't let anyone into the house you don't know. OK?'

She shut the door and locked it loudly to give him a sense of their security.

The hamburgers were nearly burnt, but Dillon liked the charred taste, and she served them to him in front of the TV and watched his stupid programme as well, a family quiz during which he answered nine out of ten questions while the contestant only managed three. She had to admit she could only answer three herself.

When the show ended she got up and switched off to protests from Dillon who didn't want to go to bed.

'Nobody said anything about going to bed, stupe. Tonight is Operation SF. Like now!'

'Now? With the blacking?'

'With the blacking, and everything else we prepared.'

It was like giving him a Christmas present, like Halloween, like a Trick or Treat expedition.

'We may not be back till half midnight. Think you can keep awake till then?'

'You bet! But what about Mom?'

'She won't be back till much later. That's the only risk we

have to take, so put your pillow down in the bed in case she comes back before we do.'

They went upstairs to her bedroom where she had everything ready in a canvas bag tucked away in a corner of the cupboard. Navy blue polo neck sweaters, acquired from Warshall's, their darkest jeans, black socks, also acquired from the store, Dillon's blue sneakers with the red toe-caps painted over black, her own dark brown shoes, two pencil torches.

She handed him a dark woolly hat and the boot polish to black his face, and stuck a black beret well down on her own head.

They'd done a sortie like this before when she'd first formed the club, Joleen, Bonnie, Judd and Steve. Dillon had been too young. They'd raided the Greenhook Chalet Motel, her mother's very own place of work just for the hell of it, and because her mother always left the reception keys lying on the kitchen table begging for something to be done with them.

They'd all cycled across town in the dark to the motel and broken into the kitchens while the residents were snoring. They'd taken a whole lot of spoons, glasses, batches of raisins and cookies. It hadn't been reported in the paper like the later Warshall raid, but then Warshall's had been truly dangerous. They'd set off the alarm and had only got away because no one imagined it was kids and no one had noticed the loose air vent low in the wall by the car park gates.

She went to the bathroom with Dillon, washed her hands and made him wash his really clean, dried hers, made him dry his, then after giving him his pair of expensive leather gloves, she threaded on her own and made sure no traces of black boot polish remained anywhere.

Next she went to her room and stuffed a rolled up blanket and some clothes down into her bed while Dillon did the same with his. She then got down on her knees and eased up the secret floor board under her bed and felt around for the all important key and Bonnie's even more important medallion. She tucked both in her back pocket and stood up just as Dillon came in looking like one of the chimney sweep boys from an old English movie.

The medallion was a Roman coin on a silver chain which Bonnie had worn around her neck since an Aunt had given it to her on her sixth birthday. Everyone at school knew the medallion. It was Bonnie's trade mark and an ideal clue for someone to find.

'The whole operation may take us a couple of hours, so have a pee, a drink of water, eat a few cookies and take some chewing gum.'

She made sure all the lights were off except in the hallway, led Dillon out to the back door and gave him instructions to make his own way, as quickly as he could, to the Knox where the others would be waiting for him.

She stealthily made her own way down the garden and out along the hedge to Dry Creek Lane then, leaving Fort Knox to her right, cut through the private gardens backing on to the lane and made it to Polk Street without incident. She paused for breath behind the music store, then ran down a passage leading to Main Street.

Speed was less important than making absolutely sure that nobody was seen. She had instructed them to go in pairs. Joleen with Steve, Bonnie with Judd. Dillon was to follow behind simply to make sure that no one had spotted them.

It was nearly midnight. The only likely people around would be the squad car cops, or someone taking a dog for a walk. She flattened herself against the wall and peeped round.

Death City. Not even a cat in sight. The Ipaca Knitwear Store brightly lit as always, Silvo's Hardware sign sizzling and flickering on and off, most of the light up the other end.

She darted across and took refuge in the entrance of the office block. Armaflex Security Services, First & Second Floors. Dan Mollman's employers.

She ran on round the corner, down Chittuck Road to Sam

Finer's yard on the corner of First Street where they would all meet.

She crouched down by the gate and listened to all the sounds around her. She then pulled the key out of her pocket.

SAM FINER'S GARDEN CENTER

Two summers back, during the vacation, she had been walking by on her way to the Old Town Store on First Street and had noticed that the yard, always closed and barricaded, was open. Intrigued, she had walked in and looked around and Sam Finer, a man in his sixties, sporting a stetson stuck well down on long white straggly hair, had loomed up behind her.

'Can I help you, Miss?'

'What's happening?' she'd asked.

'I'm opening a garden centre. Want a job?'

It had never occurred to her to have a job, but all he needed was someone to help him take the potted plants out of a log cabin he had built in the yard, arrange them along the wall for display and water them every morning. He'd pay her a dollar for the couple of hours it would take.

She'd started immediately and had become a regular employee.

Sam Finer had farmed oranges down in San Isidro Valley most of his life, land inherited from his grandfather who had been one of the Gold Rush pioneers. When his wife had died he hadn't wanted to lead the lonely life anymore, so had bought up the Old Bank building on First Street, now such a backwater since they'd built the new town centre that it was sometimes called Old Western Street. The atmosphere of the Old Bank and the Saloon Bar opposite, and the tiny drugstore further down with the two clapboard houses in between, made it likely that the Magnificent Seven might stroll down it at high noon.

She'd helped Sam Finer move in during those summer weeks and had spent a good deal of time down in the vaults under the Old Bank where she'd been fascinated by the ancient safe, a massive iron-lined room, big enough to walk into and hold a party in and where Sam Finer said he'd probably grow mushrooms, because there wasn't much else you could do in there.

He'd turned the front of the bank into a pet shop, selling puppies, kittens, birds and goldfish, the exotic fish proving the most popular so that he now had more than twenty tanks bubbling away. It was a good business, with one assistant, and Sam lived upstairs by himself in a couple of rooms which looked like the inside of a gypsy caravan.

He was regular in his habits, obviously missed his old country life, though he swore he much preferred the town. He'd moved there, he said, to be opposite Joe's Saloon, where he met up with Rick Prestianni, another regular.

He'd never had children of his own, for one reason or another, and whenever kids came to the shop he always stood around making sure they didn't damage anything. Two boys had broken some terracotta pots during his first week, since which time anyone under the age of eighteen had become suspect.

Zuke had noticed, after a few days, that he got irritated with her. Nothing specific, nothing she could put her finger on, but it was clear he hated kids coming into the store and staring at the fish, tapping the glass, leaving sticky finger marks on the tanks. Understandable in a way, but running a pet shop was rather asking for their attention.

She'd been dismissed, of course, and replaced by an adult. She'd expected a bonus, a little something more than the money she'd agreed to work for, but he'd paid her the exact amount, calculated to the hour, making her work that last hour to the full filling flower pots with a smelly compost.

No gift rabbit or free goldfish which she would have liked. Maybe he wasn't mean but just didn't understand children.

Not many people did.

She'd picked Sam Finer as her victim, not because of his attitudes but because he happened to have that safe in the basement of the Old Bank and she knew the layout of his house and she had the key to the gate of the yard.

One day Sam Finer had asked her to get another key cut for the Garden Center gate. Instead of getting just one copy, she'd got two, pocketing the spare for no other reason than that she liked the idea of having access to the place without his knowledge.

Now she was taking full advantage of her talents to improvise, making use of what she had, what she knew. All she had to do was find a way in and out of the Old Bank and she didn't think that would be a great problem because Sam always left the window at the back open for air, and regularly went to visit his sister in Masanoby every Thursday night, staying over Friday to return late with new stock.

Making sure that no one was around, Zuke stood up and inserted the key in the lock. It turned with a squeak and a clank, she waited, listening for other noises, opened the gate and slipped in, leaving the gate ajar and the key in the lock.

She crossed the yard and quickly hid behind the log cabin.

She did not pause, but took a ladder down from its hooks on the wall of the hut and set it up against the back wall. Slowly, cautiously, she climbed up and looked over.

There was a danger that someone living in the flats above the terrace of shops on First Street might be awake and looking out, but it was dark and as she was level with the tops of the potted cypresses and the branches of various fruit trees, she would just be another shadow.

Once on top of the wall, she dropped down on the other side into Sam Finer's private yard behind the Old Bank.

The all important bathroom window was open.

While weeding the garden one day she'd noticed that the glass had been put in the wrong way. It was one of those mottled wavy kind of windows through which you could see out but definitely not in, and he was unaware that the way it had been fitted you could see in.

She had watched the big man pull down his trousers and expose a huge arse and she'd been fascinated to see a large purple birth mark on his left buttock.

When he stood in front of the pan to pee he was always too far back for anything else to be studied, though it had intrigued her enough to get closer on two or three occasions.

She was safe now, well hidden from view by the house itself, by the garden walls. She pushed the window up, climbed in, and made her way to the kitchen and the back door, which she unlocked. She pulled open the cupboard under the sink to make sure a bucket was still kept there. Then she heard a car out front. Quickly she tiptoed to ease open the door to the shop.

Moving headlights panned through the windows from the street and she ducked down behind one of the fish tanks to watch through the glass and the bubbling water. The vehicle was cruising slowly down the road. It had to be a squad car.

She waited till it had gone, then dug down into her other pocket for Bonnie's medallion and placed it on the floor under the fish tanks.

Sam Finer or his assistant might find it when sweeping out. If not, she'd make sure Gene did.

She quickly retraced her steps in the darkness to the door, pulled it shut behind her and unclipped the pencil torch from her belt.

Switching it on she let the sharp circle of light dance down the steps leading to the basement. Boxes of bird seed and fish food were stacked at the bottom, so she tiptoed down to check that the safe itself was empty.

There were a few bird cages in there, empty cartons, a broken fish tank. It would be OK.

She rushed up again, pulled the back door wide open and made her way stealthily down the garden, crouched in against the wall, and waited.

Her eyes were used to the dark and she could see that there was no one at all up at the windows.

So far, so good.

She heard the gate creak, whispers, someone climbing the ladder.

The first of the mohicans.

It was Steve with a heavy torch, followed by Joleen with the first canvas bag. She waved them over to the open door. She could hardly recognize them, they were so blacked up.

Bonnie with the second canvas bag came over, followed by Judd, two dark towels tightly rolled up and strung to his back.

She led the way in, switched on her torch and took them straight down to the cellar. On the plan she had drawn for them for the briefing she had omitted nothing but the bird seed boxes.

Once at the bottom she switched on the big torch and they all moved into the large safe. Zuke now went back up to the kitchen, grabbed the bucket from under the sink, filled it with water and carried it down the cement steps making sure she did not spill a drop.

By torchlight, Steve, Joleen, Bonnie and Judd had already unpacked their essential rations of potato chips, cookies, chocolate bars and dried fruit and had taken off their gloves, dark caps and sweaters, and put these in the now empty canvas bags. They took it in turn to wash their blackened faces.

Under her jeans and sweater, Bonnie was wearing a pink frock, she took off her sandals and put on a pair of patent leather shoes. She had supposedly disappeared on her way to a friend's party.

Joleen was in a T-shirt and skirt, Steve and Judd in jeans.

When Zuke was satisfied they were cleaned up, she went upstairs to change the water in the bucket and came down again. The clean water was for drinking.

She stuffed the dirty towels into the bags with the discarded clothes, took the big torch and checked one last time that nothing was left in there that their supposed abductor would not have provided himself.

'Remember,' she said to them when everything was ready. 'Twelve hours, don't start worrying for twelve hours. If by two o'clock this afternoon nothing has happened, then start screaming.'

She stepped out of the safe, waved them goodbye, swung the heavy door shut and shot the two massive steel bolts across.

It occurred to her, right then, that they were all remarkably trusting, because, if she chose, she could leave them to rot there, except that they might be found before they expired and tell the world everything that had happened, in which case she would be accused of attempted murder.

Well, she had thought often enough of killing one or two particular people, but none of her kids. They were too much fun, and too vulnerable.

She made her way up the steps, tucked the heavy torch in one of the bags, opened the door of the shop to check that all was well out front.

There were no sounds, and no sign of headlights shining in the street.

She closed the shop door, retraced her steps to the kitchen. Closed the back door and locked it, then slipped out of the window, bringing it down to its original position before padding down the garden to the wall.

She slung the canvas bags up and over, stretched and pulled herself up, climbed down the ladder to the yard on the other side and crouched down to listen for any unwelcome sounds.

Silence. Total silence.

She moved the ladder and hung it up on its hooks, picked up the bags and made her way to the gate.

In the silence of the night she decided to wait for five minutes, just to go over in her mind what they had done, what they might not have done, and also to listen, just in case one of the kids got frightened, though each of them had spent time locked up in a dark cupboard at the Knox by way of training.

That had been Judd's idea, Judd believing himself to be a future astronaut. He'd stayed in there the longest, a whole day from nine in the morning till seven at night, without food or water. The others had managed half that time, which was enough. Now it would be longer, but they would not be alone.

Even during the training none of them had known what it was all for. A no-question operation, she'd told them, and the club rules said that a no-question operation was just that. Trust each other, trust her, don't trust adults ever.

She'd made up most of the rules, had had them agreed by vote. There had never been any objections to what she proposed. She always managed to make them believe she knew best. She had the brains. It wasn't a question of age, it was a question of know-how, of experience. They believed she had both.

She'd started the club with Joleen when they had found their way into Mayor's Folly one day. They'd discovered the attic and had realized it was perfect for secret meetings and somewhere to while away cold afternoons.

It had been about eight months back when Joleen's mother had needed to use her apartment to entertain men guests during the day and she had kicked her daughter out, told her to go stay with friends, anything, but not come home till nightfall when she went out to work the clubs.

They hadn't known how to furnish the attic until Bonnie had come up with the brightest idea of all. Richer than either of their families, hating her parents who were mean and could have afforded a home-help to look after her when she came back from school, she'd dreamed up the robbery.

They'd ransacked Bonnie's house.

Everything that could be concealed in brown paper bags

had been taken casually to the old house attic over a period of hours and the big stuff, the living room carpet, the bean cushions, the hi-fi and portable TV set had been hidden in the garden till night-time when they were sure no one was looking.

Immediate searches of the surroundings by the police had been delayed by the violence Zuke and Joleen had worked on poor Bonnie. They'd trussed her up like a chicken, had gagged her and dumped her in the empty bath, after smashing up Mrs Sharp's expensive vanity suite, with its pink mirror and pink light bulbs, and pouring tomato ketchup down the white satin bedroom curtains to suggest a bloody struggle.

They'd used gloves of course, and had been careful about foot marks, and Bonnie had made the adults feel so guilty that they had never questioned her story of the two men with stockings over their faces who had attacked her. Besides, one of them had left prints in the dust where the living room carpet had been. Just the left foot. An old boot Zuke had found in the Mayor's Folly garden.

They'd been daring then, but not as daring as now.

Satisfied that all was well, Zuke slipped through the gate, locked it, put the key in her pocket and started her shadowy journey back to the house.

The light was still on in the hallway, which meant her mother wasn't back.

She went up the stairs quickly and pushed open her brother's bedroom door.

'Dill?'

'Yep?' He stirred in his bed.

'How did it go?'

'No sweat. No one was around.'

'How long have you been back?'

'Couple of minutes.' He pulled back the bedclothes. He was still dressed. 'Thought you might be Mom. How did it go with you?'

'AOK.'

'Can I have something to eat?'

'Like what?'

'Like a hamburger with Thousand Island and some french fries.'

'Jesus, Dill. I'm tired and it's one o'clock?'

'But aren't you hungry?'

'Sure I'm hungry.'

'So let's have a midnight snack.'

'What if the neighbours see?'

'We can cook in the dark.'

And they did.

It was a continuation of the fun time they had had, moving silently around the kitchen in the red glow of the cooker ring, Dillon going as far as switching off the ice box so that the inside light wouldn't go on when they opened the door.

They ate two quarter pounders each with potato crisps, pouring on the sauce, and followed that up with ice cream and a can of Coke. They washed up and put everything away, and then Zuke caught sight of herself in the hallway mirror.

'Shit, Dill, I'm still all blacked up!'

'Yep.'

'Why didn't you tell me?'

'Didn't notice the difference.'

'What if Mom had come back?'

'You'd have thought up something clever.'

She went to the sink, squeezed the washing up liquid into her hands and started the big scrub.

'Where did you clean yourself?'

'The bathroom.'

She'd have to check up. Knowing Dillon there'd be black boot polish all over the soap, all round the washbasin and impregnated into the towel.

As it happened she found the bathroom spotless, the towel unmarked and no evidence of Dillon ever having been in there. Switching on the light, however, drew the attention of someone outside, for the front door bell rang almost immediately.

She experienced what other children alone in a house

might have experienced, doubt and fear that it might be the psychopath.

But it couldn't be.

Of all the people in Avalon, she could be certain of that.

She quickly changed into her pyjamas, made sure little brother was tucked up, and went downstairs.

'Who is it?' she shouted.

It was Sergeant Finch again. She opened the door.

'Your Mom back yet?'

'No.'

'Everything OK? I saw a light on, and movement.'

'Bathroom.'

'Dillon OK?'

'Fast asleep. You're certainly checking around tonight, Sergeant, are things that nervous?'

'No sign of any of the other Latchkids, Zuke. Bonnie's mom's been taken sick and is in hospital. Things are shaping up badly. Been more than five days now.'

She was about to correct him, but stopped herself.

'Well, we're OK, Sergeant sir.'

'All the same, be careful.'

He touched his cap in way of salute and walked back down the porch steps.

She closed the door and raised her eyebrows at the behaviour of everybody. Her little Operation was having a good deal more effect than she had expected, though it had taken time to gain attention.

She went upstairs.

As she slipped into bed, content at what had been achieved, she deliberately made herself think of Joleen, Bonnie, Judd and Steve.

Would a fear have set in that they might be trapped in there for ever? Or were they playing word games as she had advised them to?

Joleen would be OK. Steve would enjoy it all providing he was entertained. But the other two might crack. Providing they didn't crack completely it would be fine. In fact a little crying, red eyes, genuine fear, would do the Operation no harm.

She might leave them in there an extra hour to achieve the right effect.

They would be loyal.

They owed it to her.

Without her what would their life be like?

She remembered well enough the day when Joleen and Bonnie suggested they should look after Judd and they'd brought the boy over to her house. She'd felt like a head mistress interviewing the two mothers of the same child.

That was the trouble with both those girls, they were timid compared to her. They needed to be led, to be told what to do. They only had themselves to think about whereas she'd always been responsible for Dillon. One reason why she didn't have that many friends. She'd sussed Judd out the moment he'd stepped in through the front door. He was terror stricken.

Since he was six, for two whole years, he'd been left alone by his parents and lived in fear of being attacked by humans, by monsters, by ghosts. He'd been bitten by his own dog once and could have died of rabies without anyone knowing. The rules imposed on him by his parents only made matters worse. When he came back from school he rang up his mother who worked at the factory, nine times out of ten she couldn't come to the phone herself. His father was always a thousand miles away, trucking. He'd said he was so frightened of noises he couldn't do anything but lock himself up in the bathroom for hours, the only safe place in the house. And he wasn't allowed to have more than one light on at the time because his mother wanted to save on power bills.

She'd made him a member, a genuine case. It had made her feel good, Joan of Arc, the Saviour of Lost Souls. Then Judd had brought along Steve who had similar problems. Rules imposed by a strict father that made the days longer and impossible. No TV, no cooking, no leaving the house. Electricity of any kind was dangerous, and the house couldn't be left unguarded. He hadn't taken much notice, but one day had burnt his arm flash frying some steak he'd stolen from the supermarket. She and Bonnie had treated the burns and had given him an alibi. Zuke herself had rung up Steve's father asking if his son could come round for the afternoon, then they had brought him home later bandaged up with the story that he'd put out a small fire and had been real brave.

Joleen and Bonnie would keep the boys happy, their motherly instincts would come into play if any of them started having problems.

She hadn't begged them to do this for her, they had volunteered.

She'd just been pretty convincing. 'Time we terrorized the town, made people realize what crappy kind of parents we've got . . .'

She really wanted to cause anxiety, she really wanted to put Marina Sharp, Nancy Delora, Dan Mollman, Selina Reidy and her own mother through the kind of anxieties Latchkids went through.

They didn't care enough!

And the anger made her sit up.

Jesus! Even now the adults were still playing games, turning the searches into jamborees.

They had never believed her rape story.

She'd make them believe this one.

The front door opened and she heard voices.

So Mom had chosen to come back with someone, this night of all nights. Unless it was Sergeant Finch inviting himself in for a coffee. But it wasn't. They'd have gone straight to the kitchen. Instead Mom was leading whoever it was into the living room. Another lover. Oh Mom! Would it be like last time? The guilt making her so ratty and so unpredictable the following day?

Sometimes she wished her mother was like Joleen's. At least Nancy Delora kept her men under control and got paid for it.

She heard the glasses and bottles being moved. A drink as

a preliminary. No way was dear Mom going to come up and see if her honey children were alive. They might be sawn up in little pieces for all she'd care. She'd probably forgotten she had any children.

Last time a male had been brought home, Dillon had walked straight into the bedroom the next morning and had walked straight out again.

'Mom's got another man in her bed,' he'd reported.

Simple statement of fact. It didn't affect him, it didn't annoy him. He had no feelings about his mother at all.

'What's he look like?' she'd asked.

'Got a beard and hair on his shoulders.'

'She likes hairy men,' she'd said, and Dillon had thought that very funny. She was always surprised at what made Dillon laugh. That's what she liked so much about him, he was easy to amuse.

She'd gone down to the kitchen and had made her mother and new partner coffee, toasted some bread and in the end had prepared a whole breakfast tray, decorating it with a plastic flower taken from the kitchen drawer where she kept all things plastic.

'Where's the corkscrew?' her mother had asked on another occasion when entertaining another man.

'The metal corkscrew's in the metal drawer, the wooden corkscrew's in the wood drawer.'

'Zukie's a Virgo, you know,' she'd heard her mother explain. 'Tidy as tidy can be. Neat. She's got everything in separate drawers, the plastic together, the metal, the silver. It drives me crazy.'

She'd stuck the plastic daffodil in a little jar, taken the tray up to the loving couple.

'Oh, Zukie, you shouldn't have. That's very sweet of you.'

'Who's this?' the bearded man had said. Then, to Zuke's astonishment, he had turned and stared at her mother and genuinely asked her, 'Who are you?'

How could that happen?

Just how could that happen?

Going to bed with people was supposed to be intimate and loving. But then she'd seen a similar scene on TV, some drunk at a party going to bed with a woman he'd never met before and waking up not knowing who she was, not even sure who he was. Maybe men did that all the time. Dillon had thought that funny too. But then he was a man. Kind of.

Despite wanting to hear everything that was going on downstairs, despite her burning desire to follow every one of her mother's movements, she felt herself dozing off, sleep overwhelming her. So she let go.

It had been a long exhausting day.

In the morning she woke up early, crept across the landing to her mother's room, and peeped in.

No man. Mother fast asleep, alone in her bed.

Zuke went downstairs to the living room. A bottle of vodka, two glasses, cigarette ends in the ashtray evidence that it was not a dream, but the man hadn't made it upstairs and somehow she was disappointed.

She went to the kitchen and started making breakfast, then heard the row break out next door.

It began, as it always did, with that raucous scream from Gene's father, 'You fuckin' bitch!' followed by a string of other compliments.

Suzy Prestianni usually gave as good as she got. Tall, thin, dark, she was as nervous as a racehorse and her youth had passed her by because she worried so much about everything. She could not accept that life was full of trials and tribulations and wanted every day's problems to be resolved the same night so she could think clearly about the next morning's. It had driven her husband to drink, or so he claimed in the high-pitched shouting matches. She fussed continually about his addiction, was heavily into tranquillizers to help her cope, but all the same went to work in the belief that he could look after Gene. She had got herself a great job as Jack McQuare's secretary, the wealthy president of Avalon Fruit Canneries, the local Mr Big.

This morning she had no doubt again suggested he should get out of bed to help her do something. So they rowed endlessly, which was why Zuke sometimes found herself feeling sorry for Gene, though he didn't always make it easy.

It was that doleful look, that 'pity me' look.

OK, so he had parents that rowed. Better to have parents that rowed than no parents at all. Not that she was an orphan, but then she might just as well be.

Certainly she had no loving parents, no parents that appreciated what she could do, what Dillon could do.

'Why don't you ask Gene to come over and play?' her mother had suggested once in the early days following Dads exit.

'Because I don't like him.'

'I think he's a very nice, quiet boy.'

'He's a mess.'

'It would help me, Zuke. If you were friends with Gene you could go stay there some nights with Dillon so's I wouldn't worry about where you were. The Prestiannis would love to have you.'

She couldn't think of anything the Prestiannis would love less.

And since when had she started worrying about the whereabouts of her children?

Now, Rick was really letting it flow.

It went on and on and on, and if she bothered to go upstairs and look out of her bedroom window she'd see little ole Gene kicking his heels at the bottom of the garden, waiting for the row to be over.

'I know why you don't like Gene,' her mother had also said. 'You don't like him because he's still got his father. You're jealous.'

She hadn't answered. She'd looked at Dillon who had looked back at her weighing up the comment. He'd clearly thought it quite truthful.

Maybe she did resent Gene still having his father around. After all both men had been great friends.

'Better to have a drunk dad than no dad at all,' she had finally countered, and had looked to Dillon again for support.

Her mother had looked at Dillon for support, too. Little Dillon, eight, genius of the family, was a kind of silent arbitrator. A look of approval or disapproval from him could win an argument.

'I don't think that's true, Zuke,' she'd said. 'Men who drink can really give you a hard time. We don't see much of each other, we're not much of a family, but we don't have that bad a time. You don't get slapped around like Gene does, and you don't get me screaming at you, do you?'

That was the trouble with her mother, she could be really down to earth on occasions, calm, intelligent and even kind. Usually after her periods. Three or four days before, her moods could be gauged like a barometer reading. Randy time followed by dust, sweep and clean time, followed by the migraines and tantrums, followed by a loving depression.

Maybe she'd be like that. Moody, bitchy, unreliable one day, the opposite the next. A fate to come. Dillon wouldn't have that problem. Nor would Gene. Maybe that's why she didn't like him. She was jealous of men!

She went upstairs to her bedroom and looked out of the window. Predictably he was down there by the shed with his new rabbit waiting for the conflict to end.

What next?

A screaming fit from Suzy Prestianni, the slamming of a door followed by frenzied abuse from Rick and the throwing of a bottle. One had gone straight through the window once.

After the rows Gene usually caught the backlash, which was why he was making himself scarce.

She'd helped him out, had waved him from the verandah on one bad occasion and asked him in to the safety of her own house, a friendly gesture, made out of pity for the circumstances, which had backfired.

'Thought you'd like to get away before he hit you again.'

'He never hits me.'

Poor Gene couldn't admit it, couldn't admit that his father was a drunken ogre. And that was what had jarred the most.

The love, despite.

Because she still loved her father.

Despite.

They had been real buddies and he had been fun, but had deserted her, and deserted her for another woman. Which was why she forgave her mother everything, deep down. Forgave her for looking so desperately for another man. She'd hoped for a replacement, but as time passed she'd learned the unpleasant truth that fathers could not be replaced, surrogates just got in the way, came between mother and daughter demanding attention and always getting it.

Activity next door now. Suzy Prestianni rushing out, tears streaming down her face, running to Gene, down on her knees holding him, hugging him, talking rapidly. Gene, typically, sticking his thumb in his mouth till his mother slapped it away. He was nodding his head, understanding what was going to happen, what his mother had decided was best.

Suzy off to work, or off with some excuse leaving Gene to face the ogre by himself, as she always did.

And out came the ogre himself. Not big, not brawny, an absolutely average man, average height, going bald, but with those crazy eyes and broad grinning, winning smile. He could clown, Rick Prestianni, specially when he'd just had a drink. He'd raise his eyebrows, wrinkle his nose, purse his full lips in a grimace that always made her laugh.

'Hi, Zuke. You're going to be very pretty one day!'

It was because of Rick Prestianni that she had cut her hair short. 'Know what's wrong with you, Zuke? You've got a boy's face and you're trying to look like a girl. You should try thinking you're a boy then you'll look like a girl. You've got a nice neck. Men like necks, Zuke.'

She had thought him quite mad at the time, but all the same had studied herself in the mirror. She'd taken her long hair and put it up, and for the first time had noticed her neck. It was quite long. She'd moved her head about, looked left and right staring at her reflection from the corner of her eyes. She'd got hold of some scissors and had slowly started cutting, snip, snip, the mouse-coloured hair dropping to the floor. 'Comb your hair for goodness sake,' Liz Kleiner had said. 'Why don't you wash your hair?' her mother had said. Nobody had suggested cutting it. She had gone on snipping until it was as short as Dillon's.

She had combed it through and had liked the feeling. She'd brushed it through and it had been so simple. She'd washed it, which was easy, it hardly needed drying and she'd felt light-headed all that day, truly different.

Every time she caught sight of herself in a mirror or a shop window it had been magical. The new Zuke. It had made her eyes bigger somehow, and Dillon had looked at her amazed.

'You look like a boy,' he'd said. 'Not a real boy, but a page-boy, or like the Prince in Cinderella.'

'Yeah?'

And he'd shown her the illustration in her own book of fairy tales, and she'd been quite pleased.

She'd deliberately gone out front when Rick Prestianni was getting in his car, had pretended not to notice him, and he had leaned out of the window and nodded his head in approval. 'Nice . . . nice. Know what, Zuke? If you'd cut your hair sooner, maybe your dad wouldn't have been so keen to leave.'

It had upset her so much that she had wanted to ask Dillon if it were true, then had decided that it was one of those screwball things Rick said that had no meaning. Her father had not left because of anything she had done or not done, he had left because of another woman.

Her mother had come home, tired, peeved, exhausted from a long day at the motel, had slumped down on the sofa as she always did, had kicked off her shoes, opened up her blouse and fanned herself with a new magazine she'd bought. But she hadn't noticed.

Her own mother had not noticed her hair.

Not until Zuke had gone out to the kitchen to get her a drink and come back into the room, had she asked Dillon, in a half-whisper 'When did Zuke cut her hair?'

'This morning.'

Only then, when she was sure that it hadn't been like that the day before, the week before, maybe the month before, she made the reproach. 'I don't like it like that, Zuke.' As though she could go upstairs and pick out the pieces from the waste basket and stick them all on again.

'Why not?' she'd asked.

And through a long desperate sigh her mother had admitted, 'I don't like it because it reminds me of your father's girl friend. That's how she had her hair cut.'

Gene was still out there alone, standing stock still stroking his rabbit's ears with two fingers. Now would be the time to hook him, when he most needed a friend.

She tapped on the window, he looked up, and she beckoned.

chapter four

Gene ran out of Zuke's house and headed straight for Sam Finer's Pet Shop and Garden Center.

His heart was beating very fast. Pounding. That was it. Pounding.

He couldn't believe his luck.

She'd waved him over from the window, had met him on her own doorstep and had asked him in.

'OK, Gene. You want to join us?'

'The Latchkids?'

'The Latchkey Club,' she'd corrected.

'Yes. Yes of course.'

'You'll have to do a few things before I can propose you to the others to prove to me that you can be loyal and can keep a secret. Secrets are everything.'

'Try me,' he'd begged. 'Try me.'

She'd studied him with those searching grey eyes, had weighed him up. It had really seemed that way, looking at every one of his limbs as though figuring out how much they weighed.

'When you came to the old house yesterday you thought Steve and the others were there, didn't you?'

'Maybe.'

'Why?'

'Thought I'd seen him the night before, kind of close by . . .'

'You thought wrong. I've had a lead today which might help find Steve and the others,' she'd said. 'You know Sam Finer's place on First Street? I was in there this morning and saw something suspicious.'

He'd waited for her to go on.

'Did you ever notice that Bonnie wore a medallion round her neck?'

He couldn't be sure. Girls wore all sorts of things round their necks.

'Along with the Latchkey?' he'd asked.

'Right. It's a Roman coin. Well I saw it under a fish tank in the middle of Sam Finer's shop. I'd like you to go check if it's still there.'

'Why don't you?' he'd asked, not rudely, but curious to know why she should ask him.

'Rule One. Don't ask questions when given an order. There's always a good reason.'

'Sorry, Zuke . . .'

'The reason I don't want to go back myself is that I think Sam might know where the kids are and has something to do with their disappearance. If I go there twice in one day he or his assistant might get suspicious themselves.'

'What do I do if the medallion is there?'

'Pick it up and take it to the police, but without being seen. If you have the chance look in the basement too, stairs lead to a cellar under the shop. I'd like to know what goes on down there.'

He'd been about to ask why but remembered Rule One.

'Whatever you do, Gene, never be afraid to tell me anything. If you goof on a mission, just admit it. We all make mistakes. We all get frightened. The most important thing is always, always, to tell me about it, or then things go wrong. Adults, you see, lie to each other continually. We Latchkeys never lie. *Never*. Not to each other and not to ourselves. That's why we're so strong. We know exactly what is happening all around and we know we can trust each other.'

He slowed down at the corner of Chittuck Road and walked the rest of the way as casually as he could.

First Street was pretty quiet, Joe Tatillo sweeping outside his saloon bar, a few people shopping, a few cars cruising.

He walked straight into Sam Finer's shop. A woman was sitting on a high stool behind the counter filing her nails. She was wearing a pink nylon overall and looked unfriendly with her pointed black glasses.

'Can I look around?' he asked.

'If you don't touch anything.'

He mooched, making his way to the middle section of the fish tanks. He saw the medallion straight away where Zuke had said it would be, but he didn't try to pick it up because the woman was watching him. Instead he studied the various labels on the tanks.

He was close to the door at the back of the shop, so he went through, along the short passage to the top of the cellar steps. He felt pretty nervous.

'Where do you think you're going?'

'I . . . I thought there were more fish downstairs . . .'

It was Sam Finer himself, coming down from the first floor.

'All the fish are in the shop.'

'Isn't there anything downstairs?'

'Nothing that's got anything to do with you.'

Gene back tracked and pretended to take an interest in more of the fish, only the tank he chose to look at was empty.

'How's Rick, your father?' Sam Finer asked with a softer tone in his voice.

'He's fine.'

'Tell him to come over and have a drink some time.'

'Yes, sir. I will.'

And he was out in the street, his heart pounding more than ever.

Then he realized he'd forgotten to pick up the medallion. He hesitated for a moment on the sidewalk, then moved on quickly round the corner, back down Chittuck Road.

He'd have to tell Zuke.

Oh Gee! She'd think him really dumb, but she had said never to be afraid of telling the truth, it's what kept them so successfully together.

He started running, more to get rid of the feeling that he'd been real stupid than to get back to Zuke quickly.

He could kick himself!

He found Zuke in her kitchen, and started to blurt everything out.

She stopped him. Put one hand on his shoulder and her fingers gently on his lips, and stopped him.

Patiently, calmly, she told him to sit down, have a drink of Coke, and tell her everything that had happened, slowly, and in detail.

So he did, from the pink nylon overall the woman was wearing to Sam Finer's plaid slippers.

She seemed surprised at that, the slippers and the fact that he was there at all. 'Do you think he'd just come down after waking up?' she asked.

Gene shrugged his shoulders.

She wasn't a bit concerned about his not having picked up the medallion. 'I'd like you to go to your father now and tell him you went to Sam Finer's and saw Bonnie's medallion,' she said. 'But don't mention me.'

Gene hesitated.

'Something bugging you?'

'Dad will kill me if I tell him I've been there.'

'Why?'

'He and Sam had a quarrel way back. I'm not supposed to go there.'

'You didn't tell me that when I asked you to go there.'

'Would it have made any difference?'

'No,' Zuke smiled.

'I'm not frightened of my dad. I just like to keep out of trouble.'

He felt he'd gained a point, that Zuke appreciated the fact that he hadn't chickened out of going where he wasn't supposed to.

'O. . .K. . .' Zuke drawled, thinking something out. 'Now if you'd been with us longer I would have known that your father and Sam didn't get on, and maybe I'd have taken a different course of action . . . but everything can be turned to advantage . . .'

He watched her thinking, feeling he was unable to help out himself.

'Why would you go to Sam Finer's against your dad's wishes?' she asked.

'To buy something for my rabbit?'

'Such as?'

'Dunno? Rabbit medicine?'

'Is he ill, your rabbit?'

'No.'

Zuke bit her nails, looked at her feet.

'I could think he was though.'

'But you didn't buy any medicine, or even ask about rabbits. You asked to see the fish.'

'Right,' he said.

'Not bad thinking though, Gene, you're on the right lines. When's your dad's birthday?'

'October.'

'Your mom's?'

'February. Why?'

'Flowers. You could have gone to ask the price of potted plants or something.'

'Yes!' he said with enthusiasm. 'I went to ask the price of a coffee plant. Dad smashed the one on the porch the other night. He was drunk again. I could say I went for that, then sort of forgot.'

'Bright Gene. Bright. Tell him you went for the coffee plant, looked at the fish, saw the medallion and Sam Finer who acted kind of funny.'

Someone tapped at the window.

It was his father, anger clouding his face. What the hell had he done wrong now?

Zuke opened the door.

'I've been looking for you everywhere, Gene! I even nearly rang the police!'

'I went down to Sam Finer's.'

'To *where*?'

He'd said it, had come straight out with it regardless of the consequences. He had to prove to Zuke he wasn't frightened.

Rick Prestianni was so shattered by his son's admission that he just looked wide-eyed at both of them.

'I went down to see if I could replace the coffee plant that got bust.'

'The *what*?'

'The one that got knocked over the other night.'

Rick's eyes widened even more, then narrowed. Gene was daring to mention the unmentionable.

'There's something else,' Gene said quickly, but his father grabbed hold of his arm and pulled him out of the door.

'Then come and tell me at home. I don't suppose Zuke wants to hear your whole life story.'

He was led out, and as Gene glanced over his shoulder he got his reward of the year.

A wink from Zuke.

On the way back to the house, his father put his hand heavily on his head. 'Sonny boy, let me tell you something about which you don't seem to be aware. Every day this week a little boy or a little girl has gone missing. Now you may not think, by my behaviour, that I care a shit about you, but in fact I care a lot. Also Mom would not like the neighbours to think we didn't care about you because what the neighbours think seems to be very important to your beloved mother. So, when we're in the middle of a scare like we are now and the police are banging on people's doors at all hours of the day and night and Dan Mollman is doing his nut because he thinks his dear little son's been decapitated, don't, do not, leave this house without telling me where you are going. I'll tell you how important this is. It is so important that your mother just rang me from her office to tell me that she and her friends and Miss Kleiner your teacher, have decided to cancel this year's pageant. Can you imagine? So what were you going to tell me?'

'I think I may have a lead on the Latchkids,' Gene said simply.

The ride was good, his father suddenly cheerful, no longer threatening, taking the medallion find seriously. They turned into First Street and parked outside the pet shop.

Sam Finer was in the doorway, smoking a pipe and contemplating the world. He looked big in his loud lumberjack's check shirt, his old jeans, the thick black belt, the long white hair curling at the nape under the oil-stained stetson he always wore. He was a cowboy from the old days, right down to his boots which were cracked dry and dusty.

He didn't move at all but watched as they both got out and sauntered over to him.

'Second visit in one day! You got something in mind you want?' He ruffled Gene's hair, then held out his large coarse hand for Rick to shake. 'Do I owe this honour to your son?'

'Maybe, maybe,' Rick said. 'We'd like to look at some fish.'

'What kind of fish did you have in mind?' Sam asked leading the way in. 'We've got all sorts.'

'What would you suggest for a beginner?'

'It doesn't have much to do with beginners, it's all a question of water volume. How big a tank do you have, or want, or need? How many fish?'

'We hadn't thought about that. Guess we'll have a look around and see which pretty fish takes his fancy.'

Rick turned to Gene and raised his eyebrows. Where had he seen the medallion? Gene led him to the center tanks as casually as he could, and looked down. It had gone. He moved along the line. Nothing. It was nowhere to be seen.

'It's gone,' he whispered.

'Which one's gone?' Sam Finer asked, picking up the exchange. 'I haven't sold a fish in two days, Gene, so if you saw one you liked this morning, it must still be here.'

'He wasn't talking about a fish,' Rick said.

Gene felt himself go cold.

'He was talking about a medallion he spotted on the floor.'

'A medallion? Gold was it?'

'What kind of medallion, Gene?'

'Roman. A Roman coin. Maybe gold.'

'Valuable was it?' Sam Finer asked, more condescending than curious.

'He says it belonged to Bonnie Sharp.'

'One of the missing kids?'

'That's why he was interested.'

'And you saw it in here, Gene, this morning?'

Sam dug deep into his jeans pocket and brought out the medallion, held it up between forefinger and thumb.

'This it?'

'Yes, that's it.'

'And you think it's Bonnie's?' his father asked.

'I know it's Bonnie's. See, there's a hole there. She had a chain running through it and always had it hanging round her neck along with her latchkey.'

'Well I guess the right thing to do is for you to take it round to Bonnie's parents and see what they want to do with it,' Sam said. Then, giving the medallion to Gene, turned to Rick and slapped him hard on the back. 'How about a drink, for old time's sake?'

And the two men, arms round each other's shoulders, started out of the shop and across the road.

'I'll wait for you at Joe's, Gene.'

The paternal concern had lasted less than an hour. Faced with evidence that one of the missing children might have been in the shop in the last day, all the two men could do was go and have a drink.

He walked along the hot summer pavement looking for something to kick. There were weeds growing between some of the paving stones, First Street hadn't been looked after by the City Council for years. All their funds went to the upkeep of the newer part of town where the police building was, and that's where he was going.

He cut up Wood Drive under the thick line of trees. The houses were new here, smaller, but somehow fancier than those in Cedar Avenue and most had swimming pools round the back. They were executives' homes, managers at the Avalon Fruit Canneries or Armaflex Security Services, or the Solar people down in the valley.

He saw Dave and Ben on their bicycles, freewheeling down the short drive and up again. He didn't even have a bicycle now, not since he'd outgrown his first Schwinn and Dad had lost his job.

'Hi there, Gene!' Ben shouted.

'Hi, Ben . . .' He didn't stop. They were silly kids, had too much of everything to be interesting.

He turned up Main Street, passed the Supermarket, Silvo's Hardware with all those super penknives, passed the drugstore. He turned left again into Third Street and the police headquarters, the flat cement driveway and garage area where all the shiny squad cars were normally parked, but today were all out, searching.

He felt important as he walked up the seven long flat steps to the glass swing doors, and wished a few of his friends could see him. Inside he made his way across the air-conditioned reception area to the desk.

The cop behind it looked up from some paper work.

'I want to report a finding. It's to do with the missing kids,' Gene said.

The cop chewed on the inside of his mouth for a moment, picked up the phone and pressed a couple of numbers. 'What's your name?'

'Gene Prestianni.'

Into the phone the cop said, 'George, I've a kid here, name of Gene Prestianni, says he has some information.'

He put the phone down and stood up. 'Follow me.'

Up some stairs along a sunlit corridor, a row of offices on the left, into one of them where another officer was sitting behind a desk looking through some files.

It was Sergeant Finch. Gene knew him well enough.

'Hi, Gene. Sit down. Want a Coke?'

The full treatment. Gene guessed that the search had gone on long enough with no results and the police were only too pleased to have any lead, specially one from another of the children.

'You found something then?'

Gene took the medallion out of his pocket and placed it on the desk and told the Sergeant the whole story, and

Sergeant Finch buzzed the Sheriff who came in and listened to the story again while Sergeant Finch took down the statement.

'I think we should go see the Sharps. Would you mind taking a ride in one of our squad cars?'

They knew how to get people on their side, the police.

As he left the main entrance, between the Sheriff and the Sergeant, both putting on their caps, tightening their holster belts, he wished to God someone he knew would see him.

And someone did.

From the corner of his eye he spotted Dillon, kicking his heels at the turning of Wood Drive.

So Zuke Donoghue was having him watched.

Well, this would please her.

Sheriff Oates was chatty, sitting in front with Sergeant Finch who drove, Gene on the edge of the back seat leaning forward between them.

The Sheriff asked him a few questions about school, about his mom and dad, nothing tricky, just to put him at ease. They were heading west along Fifth Street. Sheriff Oates was nice.

They turned into Westcoat Road and stopped outside Number Fourteen, a white house with a green-tiled roof and green shutters. Bonnie Sharp's home.

'Stay in the car with the Sergeant, Gene, I'm just going to check that they recognize the medallion.'

Gene watched the Sheriff amble up the garden path, up the steps, slam the black iron knocker.

The door opened and he disappeared into the darkness beyond.

Gene threw himself back in the seat and spread his arms out, his hands, his fingers. It was hot.

Sergeant Finch lit a cigarette but kept it well down out of sight.

'Your mom still working over at the Canneries?' he asked.

'Yep.'

'Jack McQuare's secretary, isn't she?'

'Yep.'

The door of Number Fourteen opened and the Sheriff stepped out, adjusting his cap on his head, bidding whoever was inside goodbye. 'OK,' he said, getting back into the car, 'let's go see Sam Finer.'

The drive was silent, a left and right turn, down Main Street, then up Chittuck Road to the corner.

First Street was as deserted as it had been earlier. The Sergeant parked the car and both he and the Sheriff eased themselves off the hot leather seats. Gene followed, feeling nervous.

Sam Finer came across the road from Joe's.

'How's business Sam?' the Sheriff asked.

'What business?'

'This was found in your shop this morning,' the Sheriff said, showing him Bonnie's medallion.

Sam Finer nodded.

'Mind if I take a look around?'

'Be my guest.'

Gene automatically followed Sam, the Sheriff and Sergeant Finch into the shop, and they looked at all the fishes in the tanks.

'You found this on the floor?' the Sheriff asked.

'Right here, centre stack,' Sam said.

They went through the door at the back.

'What happens upstairs?'

'My flat,' Sam said.

'And below?'

'Store room. Mainly seeds and other stock.'

He found the light switch and led the way down the cement steps to the basement, a small room, whitewashed, with bags of corn stacked against one wall, birdcages, empty fish tanks, empty cartons.

There was a massive safe door which was bolted.

'I never closed that!' Sam said, puzzled, more to himself than anyone else.

'Listen!' the Sheriff said, putting a finger to his lips.

Everyone listened.

There was the faintest sound of scratching. Very faint.

'Oh my God! That'll be Kitty, got herself locked in.'

Sam immediately started pulling back the bolt and tugging at the heavy metal door. Sergeant Finch helped him.

It swung open.

First a sickly odour made them all step back, then they saw four children sitting on the floor hugging their knees, numb, dumb, pale, shielding their eyes from the light, shielding each other from expected terror.

'How in the hell did you get in there?'

The Sheriff stopped a suddenly incensed Sam Finer from reaching out to grab them. 'How did you get in here?' he asked, more calmly.

One of the girls got awkwardly to her feet, stood there in her party frock, trembling with fright.

It was Bonnie Sharp.

'We don't know. Each of us was blindfolded and pushed in here. And one of us has been sick.'

chapter five

Zuke was nervous.

She had put the successful outcome of the whole Sam Finer Operation in the hands of a boy she hardly knew. On a whim, a hunch, she had improvised the discovery of the Latchkeys. It could go very wrong.

Gene had left with his father, grinning from ear to ear with the pride and joy of being allowed to do something for her. She hated him for that, hated anyone to be so servile, but realized that this annoyance was because she really wanted to like him. He had it in him to be devious, and they were fellow travellers in a world of slow-witted adults. He was weighed down by the guilt and neuroses piled on him by his terrible parents. She'd sort him out, if her trust in him paid off.

She decided to make herself another strawberry milkshake when the kitchen door burst open.

It was Dillon.

'They've arrested Sam Finer!'

She hadn't expected it to happen that quickly.

Dillon was soaking wet, his brow streaming with sweat, he was panting, flushed, hardly able to stand up with the exhaustion and excitement.

'Sit down and tell me about it.'

She'd give him a glass of water when he had cooled off.

'Gene left the police station with Sheriff Oates and Sergeant Finch in a patrol car, direction of Westcoat, the Sharps' place, I expect. They were about twenty minutes then turned up at Sam Finer's.'

'Did anybody see you?'

'Gene, early on. No one else. The whole of Avalon's out in First Street. People are going mad!' Dillon could exaggerate. 'They found the kids.'

'Are they OK?'

'Fine! Piled into two squad cars. Why don't you come over and see for yourself?'

There was no reason for her not to go, not to become one of the curious. In fact if she didn't go it would look suspicious.

'OK,' she said.

She followed Dillon out of the front door, left past the Prestiannis'. Grandma Olsen was out in the street looking anxious, having heard a rumour.

'Is it true they've been found?'

Kathie Stone who lived up the other end of Cedar Avenue came by on her bicycle. 'They're at police headquarters, that's where everyone is going!'

Dillon ran, Zuke ran.

They weren't the only ones.

Excitement, elation was in the air and when they eventually got to Third Street she was astonished at the number of people milling around. She hadn't expected this to happen at all. Not at all. She had figured that it would be a quiet little reunion of parents at the pet shop, Joleen, Bonnie, Steve and Judd, looking a bit weak, a bit bedraggled, but she hadn't expected such a crowd emerging from every corner.

Zuke mingled and listened to what was being said.

'Heard it on the radio . . .'

'They found them in Sam Finer's store, locked up in an old safe.'

'Did he do it?'

'Who knows? No one knows.'

'How are they?'

'In a terrible state. The little boy was nearly dead. No air in there. Five days without air.'

Had they acted, or had there been no air?

'They smelt terrible,' someone said. 'No bathroom.'

She'd thought of that. Hadn't said anything to any of them, but she had thought of it. How else could it look real? Clean well-scrubbed kids would hardly have been believed.

'Gene Prestianni found them.'

That was the first relief.

'Found a watch belonging to one of them in the shop. Spotted it on the floor. That's what led to them.'

She had anticipated the misinformation, but not what suddenly turned the corner.

'Look!' Dillon shouted. 'The TV truck!'

If they were going to be interviewing in the front line there was only one sensible thing to do and that was go home and watch the match at close quarters through the camera.

'I'm going home,' Zuke said. 'We'll see it better live on screen.'

Two dumb adults close by nodded their heads in agreement. The kid was bright. It was true, and they started leaving.

Zuke ran, Dillon followed.

They got home, switched on. It was already on the screen, the confusion, the reporters, an officer holding up his hands for quiet, Sergeant Finch smiling in the background.

The officer managed to get some calm, he cleared his throat, turned towards the handheld microphones.

'The Sheriff will make an announcement later, but the four Latchkids have been found, they are safe and well, are undergoing minor medical check-ups and will be going home very soon.'

The camera zoomed in and out of the crowd and around, then suddenly spotted Marina and Bob Sharp, the first parents on the scene.

Instantly they were surrounded, bustled, hustled.

'We understand . . .'

'Please, I want to see my daughter . . .'

Marina Sharp of Marina's Hairdressing Salon and the pink Cadillac who a week ago hadn't been aware she had a daughter. Dark glasses, plantinum blonde hair, wearing a near see-through blouse which was hardly right for the occasion. Zuke sensed that she was already recovering from the traumas and even maybe beginning to see a profit in the ensuing publicity.

Bob Sharp was a few steps behind her, more humble, more concerned maybe, but concerned about what? He was checking his watch. Was he missing a ball game or something more important than a reunion with his long lost Bonnie?

Close up suddenly of Marina again whipping off her dark glasses to reveal her sad puffy eyes, weeping with joy, she was explaining, after weeping so much with grief.

Wasn't it just incredible? They hadn't cared a damn. Now it was tears all the way.

A voice over told the viewers that they were going to First Street outside Sam Finer's Pet Shop and Garden Center where the children had been found. And there they were in the middle of the road between the shop and Joe's saloon and Rick Prestianni, eyes glistening with booze, holding on to Gene's hand.

'This is Gene Prestianni,' the voice-over told the viewers as Gene made Avalon TV history. 'The boy who found the kids in Sam Finer's safe. What led you to them, Gene? A great bit of detection work.'

'I . . .' Gene started, but the adult interviewer wasn't going to let any kid upstage him, no way. 'I have to tell you folks that Gene Prestianni is going to be the Hero of Avalon, singlehanded he did what the police have been trying to do and failed, working on his own, on a hunch, while we were all hunting for the kids outside the town, he figured, didn't you, Gene, that they might be in the very centre and, hunting every shop, going over every street he found the one clue that led to them, Bonnie's watch.' And unbelievably the interviewer now came into shot pulling a girl's watch out of his pocket and holding it up for all the world to see.

Gene stood there looking at it, amazed, as he well might, and Zuke allowed herself a big grin.

'Of course we now know . . .' Mr Intelligent went on, 'that there was no cause for alarm at any time, each Latch-key managed to survive for six days without air or food or water in the vaults originally built by Wells Fargo back in the Avalon of the goldrush days . . .'

The adults were going to play the game for her, muddle it up, screw it all up, all she had to do, all any of them had to do was keep silent for as long as possible, the heinous stories would be invented for them by the media, they had already started. Not a medallion but a watch, not four days in the safe but six, not a few biscuits and water but starved, it was all going to be fearful and Sam Finer, poor old Sam Finer, who had probably never hurt a fly in his life, was going to carry the can and his misery would go on for ever.

She would just keep right out of it, which wouldn't be too difficult, because the last thing the press would want now was another damn kid getting in on their act.

Adults were God's gift to the Devil.

Now the commercials interrupted the news bulletin, and Dillon turned to look at her.

'Guess this is going to make the headlines, put Avalon on the map.'

'Guess so, Dillon.'

'Poor kids though,' he said. 'Fancy going through all that pain and that fear.'

'It could have been one of us,' Zuke said, shaking her head.

And Dillon shook his head with her in sympathy.

There was a noise in the front hall. Both got up to see who it was and found their mother at the door, home early, for the first time in months.

'Have you heard?' she said with great emotion.' 'They've found Bonnie and Joleen and Steve and Judd. Isn't that wonderful?'

She actually had tears in her eyes.

'I bought this for Gene, do you think he'll like it?'

It was a Lego set, the like of which she had never bought either of them. She had never had enough money, or enough time. Now she was going to give one to Gene.

'What for?' Zuke asked, puzzled.

'Zuke. He's our neighbour, and if it hadn't been for him . . .'

Oh boy!

'Don't you think it's a nice thought? Other mothers are buying him presents.'

'I think it's very generous,' Zuke said.

She had made Gene a hero. Without meaning to, certainly without planning it, she had made Gene a hero, which would at least guarantee his silence.

The commercials ended and it was back to the Big News.

Nancy Delora now in the middle of the screen, not too made up, not dressed to kill, not putting on airs.

She didn't seem to care too much for the cameras and even less for the reporter who blocked her way up the steps.

'How do you feel now you know Joleen is safe?' he asked her.

'How do you think I feel, asshole?' she replied. And he wasn't given a chance to stop the sudden flow of anger.

'You slave and you work for your kids, you know, you suffer for them, hate leaving them by themselves all day, then comfortably off guys like you who can afford to have housewives at home looking after them, who can hire nursemaids, have the nerve to make more money out of our anxieties. I'll tell you this much, I'll never give you another interview, or agree to help your lousy programme, nor your sponsors, and I'll add this much for free, that new range of shampoo you've been promoting . . . a load of shit, man.'

It made an impact.

The reporter turned it to his advantage, let her go and informed the viewers that they had just seen the best example of what tension could do to a parent who had nearly lost her only child.

Zuke wanted to weep, till she looked at her own mother who was genuinely on the point of tears again.

Sirens took over and a long shot of Third Street showed two police cars turning into the headquarters yard.

Zoom.

Close up of the first car. A cop getting out, Sam Finer, another cop holding Sam's stetson.

Hustle. Bustle.

'Have they arrested Sam Finer?' Zuke's mother asked, incredulous at the possibility.

Zuke said nothing but shrugged her shoulders.

The camera moved in on one of the arresting officers, a microphone was thrust at him.

'Is that man being detained?'

'Not for me to say,'

'The kids were found in his vault!' An angry voice shouted from the crowd. 'He abducted them!'

Then chaos.

Everyone at once, accusing, defending, shouting abuse.

'Sam Finer wouldn't do a thing like that!'

'One of the kids fingered him!'

'Bullshit! They just got themselves locked up in there.'

The camera pulled back and up over the heads of the crowd. It was surprising how many people were there and it made Zuke realize just how big Avalon was and how involved every one of its citizens had become in the childrens' disappearance. It made her feel unsettled. There were certain faces in that crowd that frightened her. The intelligent faces, the ones with discerning expressions, the adults who might guess at what had really happened, understand why.

She had originally conceived the whole operation as a practical joke, but by the time she had talked it over with Joleen and Bonnie, it had become a lot more serious, as a way they, the forgotten children, the ignored children, could satisfy their resentment against their parents.

'Let's really disappear,' Bonnie had insisted. 'Let's disappear for several days, let's vanish one by one till maybe they call in the police to search for us. Then we'll find out how much they care.'

She had allowed it to escalate out of proportion.

Certainly out of her control.

The conspiracy had worked because all of them had kept quiet, because she had not got involved with the parents, with the search itself.

She had not read the papers either, and had hardly watched the early news reports. Maybe she should have. Maybe it had all been taken far more seriously than she had realized.

They were showing Sam Finer's shop now and interviewing Grace in her pink overall and spiky glasses. She was talking about Gene and the medallion, putting that part of the story straight at least.

Then the camera went in among the fish tanks and down the narrow steps and showed the viewer the inside of the safe.

'They were locked up in there for a week?'

It was her mother, sitting on the very edge of the sofa, appalled, unable to believe what she was being told.

Zuke got up and announced she was going to make milkshakes for everyone. She needed to be alone, needed to think, to prepare herself for real trouble.

Joleen might hold out, Bonnie definitely, but she couldn't be sure of Judd, and even less of Steve. If Dan Mollman started suspecting it had all been a game, he'd cross question his boy till he broke.

She poured the milk into the mixer, added the strawberry flavour powder, switched on and watched the white liquid turn a pale shade of pink.

Shit! All it needed was for one of them to mention her name and the law would be round in a flash.

So she'd tell them why she'd got it together. She'd put up a defence, play the abandoned child. It might make headlines and remind her dad she was still alive. She'd get the shrinks to believe that that had been her motive anyway.

She switched off, poured the strawberry foam into three glasses and stuck straws in each, placed them on a tray and took them to the living room.

On television a whizz-kid in collar and tie behind a polished desk surrounded by big books, was fingering a brass paperweight. He was either some dumb politician or a lawyer.

'Who's that?' she asked, handing Dillon his milkshake.

'The Assistant District Attorney.'

The hollowness came back to her stomach.

She wasn't too sure what a District Attorney did, but it sounded unpleasantly official.

'What does he do?' she asked her mother.

Angela Donoghue hid the embarrassment of her own

ignorance by taking an extra long sip at the milkshake and making sounds of delight at its taste.

'He prosecutes,' Dillon said. 'That's what he's on about now.'

The whizz-kid was answering an interviewer's questions.

'There are situations when prosecution may be dropped. Yes. When public opinion does not demand punishment for example, or where prosecution will not serve any legitimate purpose. When criminal conviction will ruin a person of hitherto good character and injure his family. Where court proceedings might have a harmful effect on the witnesses, which could be the case here, requiring children to recall details of an upsetting nature.'

'But it is a child, or at least the parent of a child, who is demanding justice,' the interviewer commented.

'I was stating examples of when prosecutions might be dropped on the supposition that someone has been found guilty, but the District Attorney must first study the evidence put before him at a private hearing.'

'Is one child's condemnation sufficient for prosecution?'

'There are three other children involved. It may depend on whether their evidence is conflicting or not.'

And the screen was wiped by an exploding star followed by the commercials.

'What particular child is he talking about?' Zuke asked.

'Steve Mollman,' Dillon said, making a rude noise through the straw at the bottom of his glass. 'Steve's dad is out for blood.'

chapter six

Zuke had wanted to make the people of Avalon aware that within the community there were some pretty unhappy youngsters, kids from so-called respectable homes who had been virtually abandoned by their parents because money and standards of living and possessions had become more important than caring and loving your own children. And, according to the press and TV she had succeeded.

But things were beginning to get hairy.

Sam Finer had been brought before Judge William Craft during a private hearing. His defence lawyer had spent a long time praising his irreproachable character, reading out countless references from friends and acquaintances who had rushed to his support, and this had resulted in the local newspaper headline THEY DON'T MAKE THEM ANY FINER.

The prosecution's four young witnesses, however, had produced sinister evidence. Though none of the juveniles had been found marked by physical violence, the solidarity of each child's story was damning. They individually claimed that they had been enticed to the pet shop supposedly to look at a newly acquired piranha in the basement and, once down there, had been gagged and pushed into the safe and locked up in complete darkness.

At various intervals the door had been opened and food hurled in. With no light they had had to crawl around on their hands and knees searching for the chocolate bars, the potato chips, the cookies, drinking water from a bucket which they had then used as a toilet pan.

Joleen Delora had apparently voiced the opinion, and the others agreed, that Sam Finer was a nut, a psychopath, who for some reason saw children as animals and had locked them up and fed them as he locked up and fed the pets he sold.

Maybe in his demented mind he'd wanted to sell them off too.

The children affirmed that the abduction had taken place in the early evening, around seven when the shop was closed and Finer had no alibis to counter those accusations, nor could his defence lawyer come up with a reason why the children should want to accuse him. They had no motive and without a motive that line of thought was illogical.

The question therefore was whether Sam Finer was mentally unstable. The defence was asking for more time and for the police to investigate each child's character and background, which might prove dangerous. What the prosecution needed, Zuke realized, was something to top its case, a surprise witness, a damning slur against the accused.

She would have to think up something clever very soon for if either of the girls, Judd or Steve felt they were losing ground, they might panic and crack.

For the last two days each child had been kept in protective custody by the Juvenile Department, well guarded from the press and in isolation from each other and from any friends who might act as go betweens. A precaution insisted on by Finer's lawyer and agreed by the Attorney.

'The eyes of the world are on Avalon,' were the words with which the twice daily television report started. The eyes of the world were not, but certainly a large number of people in the State were taking a keen interest in the case.

A helicopter's view of Avalon with Lake Avalon in the foreground opened the programme, followed by an old photo of the Wells-Fargo bank, followed by a new photo of Sam Finer's Pet Shop and Garden Center, finishing with an exterior view of the Avalon Court House.

The town had filled up with media men and women from all over the country, the Greenhook Chalet Motel was full, takings in the bars were breaking records, everyone was in a great state of excitement, so, if nothing else, Zuke had at least generated a boom for which the population should be grateful.

One person who was not grateful, however, was her own mother who came back earlier than usual one evening, seething with anger, an unexpected attitude that inspired Zuke to throw herself in at the deep end.

Rumour apparently had it that Nancy Delora had sold Joleen's story to the *National Enquirer* for a lot of money, that Judd was going to be featured in *Time* magazine, Steve in *Newsweek* and that the Marina Hairdressing Salon had become such a center of gossip that the Sharps were buying out their rivals simply to accommodate the increasing number of customers they had queueing up for appointments.

To top all that Warshall's were presenting Gene Prestianni with a brand new ET bicycle and giving his mother five hundred dollars credit to buy anything she wished in the store, all this in recognition for what the family had done for the community. She wished to God Zuke or Dillon had been abducted as well, that way they might have benefited from the bonanza. The next thing would be Sam Finer getting off and expanding his emporium on the strength of all the publicity! To which Zuke remarked, 'Why shouldn't he get off? He did before. Why not this time?'

'What do you mean he got off before? When? Got off what?'

'Well we don't want to go into that again, Mother.'

'I don't understand you sometimes, Zuke. You talk in riddles.'

'Sam Finer,' Zuke sighed. 'I recognized him on the television.'

'What do you mean, you recognized him? You've seen him before. You know him!'

'Two years ago, Mom?'

'What happened two years ago?'

'I nearly got raped, remember? Only you wouldn't believe me, like nobody wants to believe Steve or Bonnie or Joleen or Judd now. Nobody wants to believe children. It was Sam Finer then, it's Sam Finer now. I didn't realize it until I saw him walking out of the back of the Court House on TV today. Something about his broad back and small head without the stetson.'

It clicked.

Like computer lines on a screen joining up to make a picture, she could see the information being processed behind her mother's knitted brow, the widening eyes and the smile as it dawned on her what it could mean.

'It was Sam Finer?'

'Yes.'

'Would you go to the Judge and swear it was?'

'What for, he wouldn't believe me.'

'Yes he would.'

'Why? You never did.'

'There was insufficient evidence.'

'What evidence is there now?'

'We'd be saying he's tried it before. Those children were found in his shop.'

'He's saying that they locked themselves in there.'

'But if *you* accused Sam Finer . . .'

For five hundred dollars credit at Warshall's she would sell her daughter's reputation. Marvels never ceased.

'I've got no more evidence now than I had then.'

'Will you let me talk to someone about it, Zuke? This *is* important. Men like that can't be allowed to go free.'

Now she suddenly had a social conscience?

'Who would you talk to?'

'Someone I know works at the radio station.'

'Why not the police?'

'I think it would be wiser to have someone else's opinion first.'

'Why not a lawyer then?'

'They cost money.'

'TV would be better than radio if it's publicity you're really after.'

Her mother was too preoccupied to be sensitive to that remark. She just took in the suggestion, sat down, lit a cigarette and thought; knees together, elbows on the knees, hands clasped, cigarette between extended fingers. An uptight lady, sensing an opportunity, terrified of doing the wrong thing, even more terrified of missing out.

Suddenly she got up and left the room.

She was looking for the telephone directory which she couldn't find because Zuke had put it away in a cupboard.

'It's on the bottom shelf of the dresser,' she shouted.

'What is?'

'The local directory.'

'You psychic or something?'

'The number's 322 3221.'

'What number?'

'The TV station.'

'And how do you know the number?'

'They sing it and flash it on twenty times a day, Mom. That's where you phone in to place ads.'

Angela Donoghue came back in, sat down by the phone and, hunched again, thought for some time more before picking up the receiver and dialling.

As the number rang she looked up.

'Do you happen to know the name of the newsreader?'

'Ask for the newsroom.' This from Dillon who appeared unexpectedly in the doorway wearing an Indonesian funeral mask cut out of a comic.

'Could I have the newsroom,' Angela asked nervously into the phone.

The other end queried the reason for her call, which threw her. 'It's in connection with the Latchkids trial. I have some information about Mr Finer.'

She was told to whom she was going to speak, and looked at Zuke.

'Chris Feebs. Heard of him?'

'Nope.'

They all three waited patiently, Zuke glancing at her crazy brother, then at her mother wondering just what was going on in her head. Calculations of what could be reaped?

Obviously no awareness that her own little daughter might be nervous of what she was starting.

Chris Feebs came on and Angela D., ace informer and dutiful citizen, straightened up.

She explained she was a mother of two, Latchkids as it happened, whom she had been careful to keep at home during the last few harrowing weeks. Then she started on the long story about her daughter who, two years ago, when ten, had been abducted, but that no one in authority had believed her and that this same daughter watching television earlier today had recognized the man, who had worn a mask, and it was Sam Finer.

No exploratory questions from the other end, just the urgent need to know essentials: the address, the telephone number, the name again.

'Yes, she's here now . . . I'm sure she would . . . Yes she's at the same school . . . The Prestiannis are our neighbours, she's a great friend of Gene's. They play together all the time . . . No . . . no one else knows . . .'

The receiver down.

'He's coming round right away!' Victory in that smile, then concern. 'Do you think you ought to wear something different, honey?'

'My party frock?' Zuke suggested, but the joke was lost. There was no time for funny remarks now, Mom was going to be interviewed, maybe she was going to be seen on television.

She started tidying up the place straight away, pummelling the cushions, stacking the magazines, the comics, clearing the cups and glasses and plates and other debris left over from the children's day at home.

She rushed up the stairs and made the great mistake of putting on too much make-up, putting on too bright a blouse, too tight a skirt, and when the bell rang and she went to open the door Zuke calmly settled herself in the largest armchair knowing that she looked vulnerably small in it.

Dillon kneeled down on the floor and asked her what he should do. 'Just be yourself, stay around, say nothing, it's nothing to do with you,' she instructed.

Creep Feebs came in looking less young than he did on television, but also a lot less artificial. She knew his face, had seen him countless times.

He hadn't got his job for being stupid and Zuke took an instant liking to him because he pointedly ignored her mother hoping, no doubt, that it was the child who might be worthy of attention, not her.

'You, Zuke?' he asked, sitting down cross-legged on the floor next to Dillon, ignoring the fuss going on behind him, Mom offering drinks, coffee, the sofa, cigarettes. 'Short for what?'

'Zuleika.'

He deliberately positioned himself below and in front of her to make her feel more confident, but also the better to judge her, so she was careful not to let on that she had already decided she was as smart as he was.

'Your mother says that you recognized someone on the news as being the man you had trouble with a few years back. Do you mind talking about it?'

'Yes.'

'Yes, you mind talking about it, or yes, you don't mind?'

'I don't want to talk about it.'

'Zuke!' The pained reproach came from her mother, naturally, and she made a face.

'You don't want to talk about it at all?' Feebs asked.

'I don't remember much.'

'But you remember the man?'

She nodded and bit her lip. Too much. Lip biting didn't come too naturally which made her smile nervously, and that was a genuine reaction he picked up on.

'Did you know who the man was at the time?'

'He was wearing a mask, so she couldn't.'

It was surprising what mothers could remember when pushed.

'What sort of mask?' Feebs said, acknowledging that parents could be a pain by a gentle nod.

'Wool. Dark wool like the masks they wear in movies when they raid a bank.'

'Could it have been a stocking, perhaps?' Mom suggested helpfully.

Zuke shrugged her shoulders and pouted peevishly.

Feebs reacted more openly.

'How about a walk, Zuke? Got a garden? Let's go out in the backyard.'

'OK.'

Angela Donoghue, aware that some sort of relationship was developing between her daughter and the reporter, but not understanding why, made a further effort to be noticed.

'Dillon, I think you should go and play upstairs.'

'Don't worry, Dillon,' Feebs said, 'we're going out.' Then gently, squeezing Angela's arm by way of taking her into his confidence he whispered, 'Best if I have a word with Zuke alone, get the story straight from her.'

'Oh sure . . . sure. Can I get you anything?'

'A beer, when I get back.'

Out into the garden with the rusty swing put up by her Daddy and the old kennel where Fido had slept happily till he'd got run over.

Feebs sat down again, cross-legged on the patch of dry grass.

'You got a dog?'

'He died.'

She wasn't going to help him. She wasn't going to make things easy for him.

'Tell me about the trouble you had two years ago.'

'Why?'

'I'm interested.'

'Nobody else was at the time. Nobody believed me.'

'Your mother did.'

'No she didn't. She's only decided to believe me now because of all the fuss over Joleen and Bonnie.'

'You know them?'
'Sure I know them.'
'You know the boys too. Judd and Steve?'
She nodded.
'Why didn't anyone believe you at the time?'
'They didn't want to. It wasn't convenient.'
Was that being too perceptive, too smart?
'How do you mean, it wasn't convenient?'
'They were busy. And I was called imaginative.'
'Who by?'
'Everyone.'
'Who is everyone?'
'Teachers, doctors, parents.'
'You saw a doctor?'
'I saw a shrink.'
'What did he say?'
'He said I was an attention getter.'
'Shrinks do that. But are you?'

She shrugged her shoulders again. That had been a mistake, telling him she was an attention getter. It warned him that he might be dealing with just that.

She'd have to hook him again, somehow.

'I think you're wasting your time,' she said.

'Why's that?'

'Nobody's going to want to know. They called me an attention getter when there was no need for me to want attention, but now there is.'

'Why's that?'

'I'm about the only kid in the district the press haven't interviewed.'

'So we play it a certain way, if you want.'

'What way?' She was puzzled.

'We don't reveal who you are.'

'You can do that?'

'Why not? Would you talk to me and tell me everything if I swore to keep it all to myself?'

He was testing her.

'It was Mom's idea to ring you, not mine. I thought the Sheriff should be the one to go to.'

'You're right. You want to go to the Sheriff I'll take you.'

She glanced up, aware that Mom was at one of the bedroom windows looking down.

Feebs saw her and just checked his irritation. 'I think we ought to spend a little time on this. How about coming for a drive, going down to the lake maybe, having a coke or an ice cream or something?'

'I guess you'll be safe enough.'

'Shall we tell your Mom?'

'She'll probably want to come too.'

She let him chat to her mother who gave her a wink as she walked down the front path with Feebs and got into his open car. It was white with red upholstery and green tinted windshield. He opened the door for her and she sank back in the front passenger seat.

As they drove off he switched on some quiet music and she tried to look casual by putting her elbow up on the window, but it didn't feel natural, so she gave up.

She couldn't put her finger on it but there was something about Feebs she liked. So she would have to be careful. On the other hand she sensed the feeling was mutual so she could play on that.

'How old are you?' he asked.

'Twelve. Born September ninth. I'm a Virgo.'

She glanced at him sideways. He was raising his eyebrows and on the point of making a remark, but he remembered in time how old she was. Nine times out of ten the mention of her zodiac sign got a laugh, or a reaction from men. They couldn't help it.

'Were you born in Avalon?'

'Yes. In the house we're in now.'

'Father around?'

'They're divorced.'

'And your mother goes out to work?'

'Every day, most nights.'

'So you're a Latchkid as well.'

'One of the originals.'

'You have a brother. Any others?'

'No.'

'How long have your parents been divorced?'

'He left home when I was ten.' She was enjoying the drive. The open car made her feel important. 'Two years ago,' she added. 'Which is why the doctor who saw me, the shrink, thought my whole story was a fabrication. It fitted nicely into a pattern of daughter missing her dad.'

'What was your story? What did this man do?'

'He didn't rape me. I got away before he got round to that.'

'You escaped?'

'It wasn't too difficult.'

'Can you fill in a few details?'

They had arrived at the lake and he parked the car on a slope facing the water, but they went on sitting.

'I was coming back from school. It was winter. I was alone, Dillon was at home, sick. Ma was only working part time then. It was in Dry Creek Lane, pretty creepy place, there was wind and rain, a really shitty day. I saw the car parked ahead, didn't take much notice, but as I got to it, the door swung open. It was a very wide door and it blocked my way. Out stepped this figure with the mask pulled over his head. Big man. As I tried to step aside, he stepped aside too, not only blocking my way, but taking hold of me, gripping me firmly by the arms.'

'What else was he wearing?'

'Leather jacket, jeans. Boots, I think.'

'What did he say?'

'Nothing. He slapped his gloved hand over my mouth and pushed me into the car, quite violently, across the driver's seat and on to the next one. I tried to open the door but I had no idea where the catch was, and by the time I found it we were already moving.'

'Did you scream?'

'No.'

'Why not?'

She stopped to think. It had to sound real. She had to judge her instincts as to what she would have felt in the circumstances.

'This is going to sound screwy, but I didn't want to embarrass him.'

He smiled at that. Understood what she meant.

'So you weren't too frightened?'

'Fear is an odd thing isn't it? No. I wasn't frightened because I was bored at home. I mean, I didn't care about Dillon then, and I didn't get on with Mom, so if something had happened to me I wouldn't have had any regrets. If you're alone, really alone in the whole wide world and nobody cares about you . . . you've nothing to lose. I had nothing to lose. So I was kind of pretty cool, I guess.'

'Where did you go?'

'We drove out of Avalon on the Fresno road and turned left somewhere going up in the Ridgemount Hills. He switched his headlights off then. It was a bumpy track and he knew the way.'

'Did he talk at all?'

'Sort of. He mumbled, maybe had some cotton wool in his mouth to disguise his voice, I don't know. He spoke with a pretty crazy accent, put on, sort of Mexican.'

'What did he say?'

'I asked him why he was wearing the mask. 'My face is burnt,' he said, 'and if you don't do as I ask I'll show it to you. It's so damned frightening you'll die.' It intrigued me. It didn't frighten me at all. What do you want, I asked. The usual? And that made him mad.'

'What did you mean by "the usual"?'

'I didn't know. Not sure I know now. Sex, I suppose. But it made him mad. He called me a little whore and pushed me hard against the door. I thought for a moment he was going to push me out.'

'Did he hurt you?'

'Enough. I got frightened of pain, I remember that.'

'Go on . . .'

'We got to some shack, a log cabin kind of place in the hills. It could have been anywhere. He got out. By then I'd figured how to open the door, and I got out too and ran. I just ran, got to a fence, climbed over it and ran across a field, and into some woods and I stopped, hid under some bushes and waited. But he never gave chase. I waited for a long time. Then I heard his car start and saw the headlights shine down the track. He drove off, the way we had come. I waited, then went down, found the lane and walked along it till I got to a highway. I walked and walked, and whenever I heard a car coming I hid . . . till I got to the café where I thought it would be safe.'

'Where was this café?'

'Ridgemount.'

'What happened then?'

'I told the owner my story. He rang the police, they came and collected me and after that it was a matter of repeating and repeating, and signing a statement, and no one believing me.'

'If they didn't believe you, how did they explain you being in Ridgemount?'

'They figured I'd hitched a lift. I couldn't prove I hadn't done that.'

'So what makes you think it was Sam Finer?'

'His small head and wide shoulders. I always thought it was Sam Finer but had no proof. Then when I saw him on TV without his hat – he always wears a stetson – I told Mom.'

'There must be hundreds of men with small heads and wide shoulders,' Feebs said.

'Sure, but there can't be hundreds of them going round Avalon abducting little girls and boys.'

'You say the Sheriff didn't believe you?'

'He never did anything except send me to a shrink who decided from the beginning that I had imagined it all, or had made it up to get attention. Besides, nothing had happened to me. He hadn't hurt me, or knifed me, or drawn blood. No crime had been committed.'

'Did you ever go back to Ridgemount, try to find the log cabin?'

'Sure. With Sergeant Finch when he went to take the café owner's statement. We never found it.'

'Did you tell them you thought it was Sam Finer?'

'No.'

'Why not?'

' 'Cause I was never sure.'

Feebs thought things over for a moment, then started the car.

'It's getting late. I'm going to take you home, then do a bit of research on this, maybe I'll pick you up in the morning and we'll go see the District Attorney.'

He turned the car round to drive back to Avalon, stopped at the drugstore for some ice cream, then while he drove asked her typical adult questions about how she liked school, what her favourite subject was, what she watched most on TV and what she wanted to be when she grew up.

'A news researcher,' she answered to that one, but he was too preoccupied by what was going on in his head, to really react.

She was woken up the next morning by the telephone ringing, then her mother coming into her room flushed and excited.

'Chris Feebs is coming round to get you. He's taking you to see the District Attorney.'

She hadn't thought it would happen. When Feebs had dropped her off the night before she'd decided he hadn't taken the bait. But she was wrong. Not only wrong but decidedly apprehensive.

Glancing at the paper as she stuffed herself with cornflakes served, for once, by a doting mother, she saw a disturbing headline. SAM'S DEFENCE COULD NOT BE FINER. They were certainly making the most of his name. The story, as far as she could figure between gulps of milk and instructions on how to behave from her hovering mother, was that the defence lawyer and the DA were political enemies, and that the former was winning, which was bad for the latter's professional reputation. Prestige and self esteem were at stake.

Mom had insisted that she should wear a dress and socks and polished shoes so, looking like a dutiful child in some family insurance ad, Zuke waited in the front room for Chris Feebs, who collected her on the dot of nine o'clock.

They drove to the DA's office, entered the impressive building, took the elevator to the second floor and walked down a carpeted corridor to some glass swing doors. It all happened so quickly she didn't have time to think, which was just as well because the next thing she knew she was in this book-lined office staring at the DA himself behind a bright green leather-topped desk.

He was an elderly man with grey hair and a deep voice and a red nose, very clean neat finger nails, very clean neat clothes, a grey suit, a pale yellow shirt, a grey tie. He bid them both good morning as they were shown in, suggested with a nod that they should sit down, and went on studying a document.

He had both his feet up on the desk and one of his shoes had a piece of pink bubble gum stuck between the sole and the heel. It diminished his air of authority, and Zuke badly needed to feel she was in the presence of a human being.

When he'd finished reading he leaned forward to address her.

'You're Zuleika Donoghue?'

'Yes, sir.' She started getting to her feet but he waved her down.

'You think Sam Finer abducted you two years back?'

'Maybe.'

'Maybe isn't good enough.'

'OK. So it isn't good enough.'

The two men looked at each other. She guessed that she was needed, it was a question of whether they could get her to play their game in court which, if they but knew, was her game.

'We've got less than an hour, Chris, less than an hour to make her a key witness.'

'She's smart,' Chris Feebs said in her defence.

She wasn't sure why he was getting involved on the prosecuting side. To build up the story? Get more coverage, more mileage so that sponsors would buy more time?

'How well do you know Sam Finer?' the DA asked her.

She shrugged her shoulders.

'Have you been to his shop?'

'I worked for him.'

'You *worked* for him?'

Chris Feebs was surprised at that.

'When?'

'When he first moved into Avalon and started the Garden Center.'

'What sort of work did you do?'

'I put plants out for display. Potted plants.'

'So you saw him every day?'

'For an hour or so. Yes.'

'When did you last see him?'

She shrugged her shoulders again. 'Six months? I dunno.'

'How long did you work for him?'

'Couple of weeks, maybe three.'

'Then what happened?'

'He fired me. Got an older assistant.'

'It was vacation work was it, Zuke? Pocket money work?' Chris Feebs asked.

'Sure.'

'During that time did he ever treat you badly or give you cause to dislike him?'

He was bright, the DA. Could work things out, people's behaviour, motives. She liked him.

'I didn't invent the story, sir, to get my own back. Revenge didn't come into it. What came into it was me being a girl loner.'

The DA looked at Feebs who smiled rather proudly.

'How long after you left his employment did the abduction take place?'

'Six months?'

'When you were working for him, did he behave strangely towards you?'

'Maybe, but I didn't pick up on it.'

'Are you willing to swear in court that Sam Finer was the man who abducted you two years ago?'

'I'm willing to swear that I think it is.'

Looking at his watch the DA stood up.

'She'll have to do,' he said. 'I'll get John to brief her and we'll see what Judge Craft makes of it all.'

So she was passed on to John, of the Juvenile Department, who told her she would have to swear on the Bible and answer all the questions put to her truthfully, then she was given a glass of milk and a cookie by someone's secretary in an office, walked round to the Court House, which was next door, by the same woman and there she found her mother waiting for her with Dillon all neat and tidy in his new jeans and a clean shirt.

All three sat in a small anteroom outside the Judge's chambers, her mother smoking away and stubbing out cigarettes as nervous as hell. Just watching her made Zuke jumpy. What did she have to be so worried about?

When she was called her mother gave her a brief kiss and whispered, 'I hope you're not lying again, Zuke, because this time it's really serious.'

No time to question, no time to argue.

Again?

So through all this her darling mother still didn't believe her, still didn't believe the horrors of the night she had been through. She had got her into this purely for the publicity, for the kudos, but deep down she really believed her little daughter was lying.

A knot of anger inside her stomach worked loose. That's how it felt. A relief, as though a cyst full of venom had exploded, flooding her with energy. The spleen? Was that it? Something to do with the spleen? Adrenalin? She'd show them. She'd show them all.

The Judge's office itself was just like any such room with a few adults sitting at separate tables facing the wise man who was sitting on his own behind a desk.

As she walked in she immediately saw Sam Finer hunched in a chair looking weary, his white hair uncombed, his face drawn.

Next to him was his lawyer, she guessed, a mass of wavy black hair, black eyebrows, straight pointed nose, olive complexion. A real nasty.

At another table was John from Juvenile.

Judge William Craft was anybody's grandfather, behaving just like a judge should, studying her over the rims of his spectacles, glancing at documents on the high desk in front of him.

He told her to sit down on a chair near him, then asked her if she understood what was meant by telling the truth. When he was satisfied that she did, he told her that he had before him a police document relating to her abduction two years back, allegedly by a masked man, which she had signed and sworn was true.

Did she remember the incident, and if so did she have any idea who the man was and could she see him anywhere in the room?

She said she thought she could.

'Where?'

'The old man, there,' she said pointing out Sam Finer.

'What makes you so sure it is him?'

'Intuition, a gut feeling. I've always thought it was him.'

The defence lawyer raised his black eyebrows and shrugged his shoulders at the Judge. This girl was wasting everyone's time.

'Intuition and a gut feeling aren't quite enough, Zuleika. Is there anything about this man that you recognize?'

'I recognize his shape.'

'But you don't recognize his face?'

'No.'

'Because he was wearing a mask at the time?'

'Yes.'

Not a bit happy, the Judge studied the document before him again, looked at her, then at Sam Finer, and asked the defence lawyer if he had any questions to ask the witness.

Mr Suave got up and oiled his way over smiling sweetly, the epitome of the adult who is going to coat a very bitter and very unpleasant pill with so much sugar that it would only fool another adult.

'Zuleika Donoghue, you are, I believe, a friend of Joleen Delora, Bonnie Sharp, Judd Reidy and Steve Mollman?'

'Yes.'

'You are yourself what has been termed a "Latchkid" or "Latchkey Child"?'

She shrugged her shoulders.

'It would seem only right, and would make perfect sense, therefore, that you would want to prove your friends right, would want their story to be believed, would it not? But I must remind you that you are in a real court, not in a private hearing, you would have to swear on oath that you were telling the truth and one must hope that this means something to you. Would you swear on oath that this was the man who abducted you as far back as two years ago, if indeed you were ever abducted at all?'

'Yes.'

'But only on intuition, on your gut feeling?'

'No . . . more than that.'

'What more, Zuleika. What *more*?'

She pursed her lips, slipped her hands under each leg, looked down at the floor, up at the Judge across the room, at Sam Finer.

'I may be wrong, but I don't think I am . . . anyway the man who attacked me two years ago . . .' she dropped her voice to such a low whisper that the Judge had to ask her to speak up.' The man who abducted me two years ago . . .'

she paused for effect, breathed in, and stared across at Sam Finer again, sitting there, bewildered by everything that was happening to him. 'The man who attacked me tried to molest me. I never said anything about it then because I was frightened and I didn't understand. I'm older now and I do understand and the man who attacked me took down his trousers and had an enormous birthmark on his left . . . bum. Sort of purple.'

There was a roar in the Courtroom. Everyone gasped out loud, opened their mouths, widened their eyes, started talking all at once so that Judge Craft had to use his hammer and demanded silence.

Everything after that seemed to be done by signals and in whispers. A nod from the Judge, a nod from the defence lawyer, John from Juvenile asking her to follow him out, Sam Finer being led away through another door.

He was going to be examined.

And she was going to be proved right.

And he would be found guilty.

And that would be that.

chapter seven

Gene Prestianni was presented with a brand new yellow Mongoose bicycle and yellow crash helmet, yellow pads and every other conceivable accessory, by the manager of Warshall's at a morning ceremony in the restaurant to which all the press were invited.

For services to the community, for concern about his friends, for bravery, Warshall's were proud to honour one of Avalon's youngest citizens. Because his parents were responsible for the upbringing of such a fine American boy, they were given five hundred dollars worth of Warshall's vouchers and were photographed with Gene receiving the gifts.

Gene had been brave, certainly, he now realized, going into Sam Finer's shop like that, but he hadn't known that the old man might have attacked him and thrown him into the black safe with the others. Zuke might have known, but he hadn't.

He didn't say anything.

The whole affair sobered Rick Prestianni up considerably, for days afterwards he got up really early, showered and dressed before breakfast and made sure he looked respectable before going out.

He made a great effort to give up smoking, and managed not to have his first drink till midday.

In public and in private, he voiced the opinion that the Latchkids were trying to cover up the fact that they had been trespassing and had locked themselves in the safe by mistake. They were a notorious nuisance to everyone. On the other hand, kids of that age would not hold their tongues for long and the truth would come out, a viewpoint shared by the Judge who asked for each child's case history and statement to be more carefully examined and Sam Finer himself to be screened by a psychiatrist.

Generally it was hoped that Avalon would forget the whole embarrassing episode, and major attempts were made by its leading lights to dampen the media's enthusiasm for the story.

Latchkey children, it was admitted, were vulnerable to all kinds of influences and disasters, but Avalon was not alone with this problem, every township across the States had juveniles filling the courts, either as victims or petty criminals. It was up to the parents to behave more responsibly, whatever their own setbacks, and for the community as a whole to help them.

The gift and heroic image drummed up by Warshall's suddenly found Gene new interests and a good many new friends. Other boys who had Mongoose and Kyrawah bicycles invited him to join them in their activities, and he wheelied and bunny hopped and shot ramps with the best of them, mainly up on Balder Hill.

He avoided Zuke now, and made sure he never went near Mayor's Folly, not wanting to come face to face with her, or wanting to become involved again.

He couldn't work out who was telling the truth.

The kids had been found locked up in Sam Finer's safe because he had told the police about Bonnie's medallion, but he had only known about the medallion because of Zuke.

He couldn't trust her. However much he wanted to, he couldn't trust her.

Then he heard that each of the Latchkids was being sent away by order of the Judge, an imposed vacation out of Avalon with relatives, following new evidence by Sam Finer's sharp spectacled assistant that the safe had been open during all the five days prior to the Latchkids' discovery, suggesting that they had hidden themselves somewhere else in order to cause mischief.

Because they were sticking to their story and because Zuke Donoghue had come up with something casting doubt on Sam Finer's sanity, the old man was being kept in custody, but now, at least, Gene felt a little freer to cycle where he pleased, and even started riding around Mayor's Folly on his new bicycle, finding the terrain, with its dips and bumps, ideal for practising tricks.

One day, when he got home for lunch, he was surprised to see Sam Finer sitting at the table in the kitchen. The man looked a good bit older, had lost some hair, was thinner, and had come to ask Rick a favour.

The Judge had found insufficient evidence in the doctor's report to consider prosecution, and he had been released with the advice to leave town for a while till things had blown over.

He'd decided he would go lose himself in the countryside, and wanted a car ride as far up in the mountains as possible.

He'd walk for as far as he could to regain some of the happiness he had once known. Animals, at least, could be trusted not to lie.

The three ate in silence, and Rick and Sam drank a good deal, then they got into the car, with Sam's heavy backpack taking up most of the rear seat, and drove out to the foot of the Ridgemount Hills where an old goldrush trail was said to start through woods and valleys and mountain passes, leading to Fresno, then Sacramento, the original site of Sutter's Fort where the Gold Fever had started in the 1840s.

When Sam climbed over a stile, waved them goodbye, and started across the poppy field, Gene turned round and saw, on the other side of the road, a hut, a wooden hut, a stable perhaps, a farmer's cabin, and it occurred to him that maybe, maybe all along, Zuke had got her directions wrong, that her abduction might have happened here, and he just said this, casually to his father, without even thinking it important.

'Could that be the hut where Sam took Zuke?' he said.

The pain struck him so suddenly, that he did not realize what had hit him. It was so forceful, behind his right ear, so powerful, that it sent him sprawling to the ground, and when he looked up, instead of seeing a sympathetic, helpful father, he saw an incensed man who had swung out at him with clenched fist.

'Never again, Gene. Never even mention that girl's name again, or any connection with her lunatic fantasies and Sam Finer. Do you understand?'

The tears of humiliation and rage welled up and blinded him. He had begun to trust his father, but now, because of the alcohol, because he had lost an old friend, there was this vengeful, bilious man.

'Get in the car and stop moping!'

Gene cautiously got in the back, where he had spent most of his time in the past being driven to school or on crazy outings. The difference between the front seat of the car where he had of late progressed, and the back was like heaven and hell, the demarcation line an unseen chauffeur's partition keeping the two compartments worlds apart.

Silence while Rick turned the car round.

Silence while Gene nursed his head, his ear which was still stinging and ringing.

Silence while Rick found his brandy flask and took a swing.

Then, as they started back to Avalon, came the lecture which went on and on and lasted the whole drive. He understood half of it. He knew that it had little to do with him but was something going on in his poor father's fuzzy head. Mom was brought in, Grandma, Grandpa, Dan Mollman, all the Latchkids' parents, everyone, and it built up into a terrible fury that made the driving dangerous and Gene cower further into the back seat gloom.

It ended, eventually, with a terrible warning.

The name of Zuke was never to be mentioned again, and if he ever caught sight of Gene with her, he would confiscate the Mongoose bike. She was an evil-tongued hellcat, a troublemaker, a stigma on Avalon's good reputation.

His mother came home that evening and took over the role of scapegoat. There was an argument, another row, Rick over-drank, over-indulged and, as always happened, which he could not understand, they made it up once they were in their bedroom, leaving him alone again in the incomprehensible world.

A dismal week went by.

The cycling lost its novelty, he did not enjoy competing with the other boys, did not enjoy playing their team games. Though he preferred his own company he also became lonely and wanted a friend, the friend who understood him, with whom he had a bond, but who was now forbidden him.

Every evening at supper Rick Prestianni, sober or not, launched forth on his favourite topic by asking Gene if he had seen the pipsqueak shrew from next door, then elaborated on his theme of her evil deeds.

One night when he had rambled on longer than usual, Suzy Prestianni voiced the opinion that if he continued painting Zuke so black he would not only turn her into a martyr but a heroine in the boy's eyes, which was remarkably close to the truth. So much so, in fact, that the next day Gene decided to visit the Latchkey hideout.

Respecting their rules, he took up his old position in the garden behind Mayor's Folly, lay on his stomach for a long time till he was sure nobody was around, then he crawled to the secret entrance and eased himself through, experiencing a great feeling of belonging once he was inside standing in the empty, dusty, back rooms.

The place had not changed, even the spider's web in the corner of the kitchen doorway was still there. He went upstairs, climbed the ladder to the attic and found everything as it had been the last time he'd sneaked up.

He spent all the afternoon there looking through the magazines and playing with some of the games, especially a pocket computer which had a submarine darting across the small screen from left to right and back, avoiding the yellow explosions of bombs dropped by a red plane.

Bored with that he started opening the stacked cardboard boxes, most of which were empty, but in one he found a canvas bag and inside the canvas bag something bulky wrapped up in newspaper. Carefully he unwrapped it to find a parcel sealed with Scotch tape. Curious, he picked at the Scotch tape, opened up one end and pulled out a leather-bound book.

It was no ordinary book, not even printed. It was written in and he recognized Zuke's untidy scrawl. On the front page was the design of a scroll surrounded by flowers and leaves, and the legend, 'This Book Belongs to Zuleika Donoghue. Her Private Journal. Whosoever Trespasses Shall Perish.' It didn't frighten him, and he turned over the pages.

It started on Labor Day, went through the Easter vacations and right up to the week before. The last entry was undated, but followed the fifth of August.

Faced Liz Kleiner in Warshall's after she had followed me around and up and down 3 floors. She was very imbarased. She thought I was stealing. But I was not. No one trusts me. I miss J and B. Tomorrow I am being sent to the chicken farm

The entry before that mentioned him.

Gene is still on his stupid Mongoose.

Nothing else. The day before that . . .

Have moved this journal to Fort Knox where it will be safer. Ma tidied up and nearly found it yesterday. Dillon knew where it was and rescude it. He has been reading it I think.

Gene flicked the pages back, stopped at one with the heading *Operation SF*.

J, B, J and S are AOK at Fort Knox. All provisions there.

J, B, J and S officially missing. But no police activity. Coke and Monopoly keep them happy.

Further back still . . .

Little Gene dared break into Fort Knox today. I surprised him. But he was cool. I respekt him for it. He is good material for Latchkeys but has his parents. He would like to join but that cannot be aloud.

Several days later.

Put B's medallion on floor in SF's under fish tank. Told Gene. This is the BIG START of *Operation SF*.

Then . . .

Gene was right choice. Lush Rick made him go to the Sheriff.

He didn't want to see any more. He'd been used. Like a pawn. He looked at the back of the book.

Rules and Regulations for Latchkey Club Members.

1 No secrets between members, ever.
2 No punishments, ever.
3 Unity against adults at all times.
4 Any member can ask for help from any other member and they will give it unless it is impossible.
5 No member need explain why they have to refuse help. Their reason must be trusted.
6 Any member can ask for help under the No Question Operation clause.

NO QUESTION OPERATION. This allows for total secrecy till the member who has asked for it feels he can reveal the reason for the operation, safely.

Blue – Come to headquarters immediately.
Pink – Stay away.
Yellow – Make contact immediately. You are needed.
White – Instructions for you at headquarters.

Gene heard a noise.

He closed the book and quickly slipped it back in its wrapping and tried to stick down the Scotch tape, but he'd torn a strip off the paper and couldn't get it back the way it was, so he just packed it down in the canvas bag and replaced it at the bottom of the cardboard box.

Maybe she wouldn't notice.

What could Zuke do now but be friends anyway? He knew everything, could blackmail her if he wanted to. Take the book even. Show it to lush Dad or the Sheriff.

But he didn't want to do that.

He didn't want to become her enemy.

He left the attic, made his way downstairs, right down to the secret entrance. There was no one about. He'd just been nervous, had heard noises that were of no importance.

It wouldn't matter much anyway if he was discovered, providing it was by another Latchkey. But it would be terrible if he'd been followed by someone else, if he'd given away their hideout.

He pulled himself up and out under the verandah steps and waited for a long time before crawling away. Then he got up and made it through the laurel bushes to Dry Creek Lane and casually home to his parents and supper.

'I saw Sergeant Finch,' his father said. 'Told me that he's heard reports from the Rangers that Sam Finer is OK. He'll be back soon. Wants to see justice done, so that puppy bitch is going to be in trouble.'

He could smell the booze from where he was sitting.

'He's going to get her you know, Gene. He's going to get your friend.'

'She's no friend . . .' he protested, but felt himself flushing as his father eyed him.

Could he read his thoughts.

The lush?

The next morning Gene went out on his Mongoose heading for Balder Hill, but as he turned the corner of Cedar Avenue, he saw her, standing by a tree, as though she were waiting for him.

Zuke was back.

'Where've you been?' he asked, glancing over his shoulder to make sure he was out of sight of the house.

'Petaluma. The world's egg basket.'

'When did you get back?'

'Yesterday, both Dillon and me.'

'I'm not allowed to talk to you.'

'Tough.'

'Dad says he'll take away this bicycle if he sees me with you.'

'And the helmet?' she asked.

'Guess so.'

'You broke into Fort Knox, didn't you?'

'No . . .'

'Don't lie, Gene. You broke into a cardboard box, ripped open a parcel and read my journal. I've all sorts of ways to prove it.'

'No. I didn't, honestly.'

'There's a camera there that takes photos. Want me to show you? I've got proof. When the kids get back they'll rip you apart.'

Was there a camera up there? He'd have heard something, a click, seen it. He'd examined the place pretty thoroughly.

'OK so there's no camera,' she said, studying him as she always did with those piercing grey eyes. 'But there is Dillon. He followed you, climbed up the ladder and saw you. Know what I call him sometimes? Little Comanche, he's so silent and stealthy. Dill can creep up on you in an echo chamber and you wouldn't hear him.'

'I didn't mean to,' Gene said immediately. 'I was alone and had nothing to do . . .'

'You're a danger to me now. I'm not sure what to do with you.'

'Nothing . . . nothing. You trusted me so far, you must trust me some more.'

'Maybe,' she said, turning away, starting off in the direction he'd come from. Then she stopped. 'Your Dad's going to take that bike from you if he sees us together?'

'That's what he said.'

'Guess it's either the bike or me, then.' And she walked off.

It upset him.

For the rest of the day he didn't know what to do. When he eventually got home and put the Mongoose away, walked up to the porch, he felt someone breathe down his neck.

It was Zuke, right there on his own front doorstep.

'For Chrissake! If Dad sees you!'

She pushed the door open for him, but walked in first, straight into the living room where Rick Prestianni was dozing.

'Hi! Mr Prestianni! Gene and I have just been down to the lake. How was your day?'

He didn't pull out of the dopiness too quickly. The anger

didn't rise immediately, but he looked perplexed, puzzled, could not believe that this girl was actually sitting down on the sofa next to him talking away about what little she thought of the programme he was watching in his own home.

And all that Gene was aware of was the fear, the sheer fright freezing his back and making his knees buckle.

She was doing it deliberately to get her own back, though he knew enough about her to send her to jail.

She was standing up now, flicking a strand of hair away from her eyes. 'Got to go, Gene, feed little Dill. Nice day we had together, and thanks for the ice cream. Bye, Mr Prestianni.'

And she was gone.

He was rooted.

'She was lying, Dad . . .' he tried.

'Oh yes?'

Too late. All too late. She was everything his father had said she was.

'You know how much that bike of yours is worth? Two hundred dollars. Know what I'm going to do with it? I'm going to sell it. I'm going to sell it now, today, to Joe Tatillo who's offered me the full price for it because Warshall's have run out of stock and it's little Joe's birthday next week. And do you know what I'm going to do with the money . . .'

Gene knew. Gene knew exactly what he would do with the money. Even if his father believed him, even if he'd known all along that Zuke was standing on the porch waiting for him to pull off this trick, she had given him the excuse he had been waiting for ever since the gift had come into the house to exchange it for booze.

The bike was doomed. He could get down on his knees, cry his eyes out, beg for mercy, it was too late. The fact that his red-eyed father was holding a half-empty bottle of whisky and the fourteenth glass was about to be swallowed meant it was hopeless.

But then it occurred to him that maybe Zuke had not wanted revenge, but had acted for a quite different reason. What if she needed his friendship as much as he wanted hers? The bike had come between them and now he would be justified in defying his father. Now he would have nothing to lose by seeing her.

He stared at the grin of teeth, the glazed look that was trying to focus, the hand tightly clasping the small glass in case it slipped away.

He shrugged his shoulders in pity, turned on his heel and walked out.

He knew she would be watching from behind one of the boarded up windows, so he wasn't blatant about his approach, but patient and cautious. He had only one thing in mind and that was to join the Latchkeys, to have them as friends and abandon his own family. He would therefore have to convince her, somehow, that he was worthy of the group, regardless of having a parent at home looking after him. And to do that he would have to watch every move he made.

So he took his time. He hid in the long grass by the rusty old water tank and waited, observing, then moving slowly as he had before, crawling on his stomach till he reached the steps. He half expected the entrance to be blocked, that his way would be barred, but it wasn't. He slid the panel to one side, turned round and threaded himself into the hole feet first. Once inside he replaced the board and, feeling the wall in the dark, made his way to the opening which led into the house.

They were waiting for him in the kitchen area. Judd and Steve, the guards.

'What do you want?' Judd asked.

'I want to talk to Zuke.'

'OK. Wait here.' Steve waited with him. Steve might be younger and smaller, but he was stocky and possibly heavier. To attempt anything would be stupid and pointless.

He hated having to be tough. So he didn't move. He just stood there while Steve leaned against the wall and stared at him till Judd came back and told him to go up.

To his surprise Zuke was in the attic alone.

'He's sold my bicycle,' he told her.

'Tough.'

'To Joe Tatillo.'

'Lucky Joe Tatillo.'

'Look, Zuke, I know I have a dad who's supposed to look after me, but he doesn't. I'm in a worse position than any of you Latchkeys are.'

'Form your own club. The sons and daughters of underprivileged children of drunk parents. There must be quite a few in a shit-hole like this.'

'I can give you away, you know that.' He wasn't fond of his father but he hated it when anyone insulted him. He felt himself flushing with anger.

'The more you threaten the worse it'll get, Gene,' Zuke said with a smile. Then, by way of apology, 'Let me explain something to you, about us Latchkeys. Apart from helping each other we do have to contribute something towards the club. And the major contribution is our homes. We all go to each others' homes to eat and play. We wouldn't be able to go to your home because your dad's always there. End of story.'

'What if I got rid of him?'

'How would you do that?'

'Not sure. Help him get a job. Or get him to leave Mom?'

'Motivate a separation?' She was suddenly interested. 'That could be fun. How would you go about it?' she asked.

'No idea. That's why I came to see you.'

He was lying, but he realized he might be able to play Zuke at her own game, grab hold of her ideas and make her think they were his.

'I don't understand adults enough,' he said. 'But Mom and Dad are always quarrelling. They're not happy together.'

Zuke thought about it.

'What do they quarrel about, mainly? Sit down, make yourself comfortable, Gene, help yourself to a Coke. Let's talk this through.'

He had her interest. He helped himself to a can of Coke from the box, sat down on the big bean bag opposite her.

Judd came up.

'I'm in conference, Judd. What d'ya want?'

'Can we have a game. The sub . . .?'

'Sure.'

She waited till Judd had found what he wanted and disappeared down the ladder.

'OK, Gene. What do they quarrel about most?'

'His drinking I suppose. His not working. Her earning the money.'

'He just loafs around all day, does he?'

'All day.'

'But he feeds you, looks after you?'

'Sometimes.'

'Who cooks the evening meal?'

'Mom.'

'When she comes home after a day's work, she has to cook a dinner? What does she find, usually? What's he doing when she comes home?'

'Most times he's watching TV.'

'And you?'

'Upstairs in my room, waiting for her.'

'You've never thought of helping her?'

'No.'

Zuke sat silently for a long time, running the tips of her fingers along the lines of the carpet pattern.

'Why does he drink so much, do you think?'

He had never asked himself that question. It had never occurred to him that Rick drank for a reason.

'People don't just drink because they're thirsty,' she said. 'They usually drink to get away from something. To escape the inescapable.'

'I don't know,' he admitted.

'Do you remember when he started drinking?'

'When your dad left Avalon.'

'Yep.' She was saying it to herself as though he had just confirmed something she remembered.

'They were great friends,' he said.

'They were randy,' she corrected.

She got up and started pacing the squeaky floorboards. She wasn't wearing any shoes, or sandals, her grubby bare feet stuck out white from her blue jeans, her hands thrust deep in the pockets, red braces strapped tight over a smudged cream T-shirt.

'I'll tell you what I think, then you tell me if you think I'm right,' she said after a while. 'I reckon your dad and my dad were really great buddies, lifelong buddies from Vietnam. They went to the ball games together, wrestling matches together, picnics together, they did everything together. What they also did was fuck women.'

Gene looked up at her surprised.

He knew the word, heard it often enough, but it sounded really bad from her.

'That's what they did, Gene. All the time. They used to go to those nudie bars together where they have topless waitresses and naked go-go dancers. Then my dad left and your dad found himself alone. I heard them talk once about women and about their wives, your mom and mine. They were bored. Bored living with the same woman. That's why they went out. I think your dad drinks because he's bored and hasn't an idea how to entertain himself. My dad entertained him. Like he entertained everybody. He wasn't a loner, he could pick up friends easily, but your dad's different, he's a bit dumb sometimes too, if you don't mind me saying. I mean, in a partnership, there's always one who's brighter than the other. My dad was a lot brighter than Mom, but Suzy's brighter than Rick, she's the active one. Who do you get on with best?'

'Neither,' Gene said.

‘Come on. If you fell down the stairs and broke a leg who would come to help you?’

‘Mom. Dad would shout at me.’

‘If you need money who do you go to?’

‘I don’t.’

‘OK. Who do you lie to most, then?’

‘Well Dad. But that’s because he’s there.’

‘Do you give your dad birthday presents, your mom?’

‘Sure.’

‘Who do you enjoy buying one for . . .?’

He thought about it, remembered when he had gone to buy a bar of soap for his father and while wrapping it up had imagined it would be thrown back at him, which it had. For his mother he had bought a simple bowl of flowers, from Sam Finer’s as it happened. She had nearly cried.

‘Mom,’ he said. ‘Definitely. I usually know what she wants. Whereas with Dad I never do.’

‘Now we’re getting somewhere. Supposing you cooked the dinner tonight . . .’

‘I can’t cook.’

‘You can cook burgers. Anyone can cook burgers. Supposing your mom came back and found the table ready laid, the burgers cooked. How would she react?’

‘She’d think Dad was in one of his good moods.’

‘Right. How would he react to you doing that?’

‘If I didn’t burn anything? I dunno. He doesn’t like me doing things for her.’

‘Great! That’s where you start then. You start right there. You help your mother and annoy your father on every possible occasion. He’ll drink more and more till she’s had enough, and eventually they’ll split.’

‘But how long will that take?’

‘Two, maybe three months.’

‘Three *months*!’

‘It’ll keep you busy, Gene, I can assure you. And I’ll help out. Try it for a couple of weeks. If things start going well for you then maybe we'll agree to making you a provisional member of the Latchkeys.'

She crossed the room and got down on her knees in a corner to look through a pile of books. Finding the big one she was looking for, she flicked through the pages and read something with great concentration, running her finger along the small printed lines.

'You're half-way to losing him anyway,' she said. 'This is a medical dictionary. Listen to this: "Alcoholism leads to a great deal of misery, marital unhappiness and broken homes. Produces physical and mental disease, both directly and indirectly. In severe cases the alcoholic can die from cirrhosis of the liver though this is less common than pneumonia or some infection not usually fatal to healthy people. Drinking considerably lowers the expectation of life!" So buy him more booze, or steal some for him!'

'I guess now he's got money for my bike he'll do that himself. Trouble is he gets violent.'

'Get violent back.'

'You're kidding!'

'Study this. It may come in useful.'

She held the book up, grinning. There was a double page diagram of the human body, a grey skeleton with blue muscles and bright red circles over certain areas linked by green threads.

'Veins and arteries, Gene. Cut through that one when he's smashed and you don't have a father at all.' And she slammed the book shut. 'You'll be doing me a favour too.'

'How do you mean?'

'Revenge.'

'Revenge? What for?'

She had been smiling, it had been said as a joke, but now she was suddenly deadly serious, a seriousness and dejection he had never seen before. She looked down at the floor, talked in a quiet voice, not lifting her head.

'I've never told anyone this before, but I've always known who attacked me that night two years ago, who wore the mask and bundled me into the car. I knew the car, and I knew the smell of that man. It was your father.'

'My father attacked *you*?' He couldn't believe it.

'He drove me out to the Ridgemount Hills, parked the car off the track and, in the pouring rain, made me take my jeans down.' She put her hands up to her face at the thought of it, scrubbed her face with her palms because the memory of it was obviously so awful. 'He pushed me back against the bonnet, made me lie on the bonnet and, do you know what hurt most? The heat, the hot metal of that damned car on the back of my legs.'

'He was drunk?'

'Of course he was drunk.'

It explained his father's hate for Zuke. It explained his violence just after they'd dropped Sam Finer. It explained his determined defence of Sam Finer.

There was a noise from below.

Zuke sat up unsure who it might be, then Joleen came up the ladder.

'How long have you been back?' Zuke asked, delighted.

'Couple of hours.'

Joleen hesitated before saying any more, questioning Gene's presence.

'He's OK. He won't talk. If he does he knows I can make things really tough for him. How was Disneyland?'

'I didn't get to Disneyland. Mom sent me to a summer camp in Bakersfield instead. When they let Sam Finer go she decided to believe *his* story. Silly cow.'

'So did everyone else.'

'We kinda lost then?'

'Only a battle, not the war.'

Then Zuke stood up, smiled kindly, forgivingly, letting Gene know by a nod that the privileged interview was over.

He started down the ladder.

'Remember, Gene, side with your mom and antagonize your dad. It'll be hard work to begin with, but worth it.'

And she followed him down to see him off.

*

When Gene got home Rick Prestianni was waiting for him.

'Know how much I got for your bike?' The grin was more of a leer, his hair was standing on end because he'd passed his fingers through it and it was sticky and unwashed.

'No,' Gene said, quietly.

'Two hundred and twenty-five dollars! I'll give you some of it if you don't see your girl-friend again for a month.'

'OK, Dad,' he said calmly, 'I thought I'd cook supper for you and Mom tonight.'

Rick Prestianni looked up amazed.

Perhaps he hadn't heard right.

'Yeah? Well I don't know about that, Gene, your mother doesn't like you using the cooker in case you burn your pretty little fingers, but you can certainly clean up the mess you made in the kitchen this morning.'

The kitchen was in a terrible state. Gene stared at it. Was it always like this when his mother got home? Imagine if she came back and found it spotless.

He wasn't sure where to start, just stood there in front of the sink thinking of the comfort of his bedroom and his collection of cars, what he could construct with his Lego. Then he thought of the Mongoose. What he wanted to do more than anything else was ride on that bicycle. He turned the taps on and squeezed the detergent liquid over the crockery. He felt salt tears welling up in his eyes, stinging, and they clouded so quickly that he couldn't see. He was numb with anger and despair, just standing there, sobbing so suddenly.

The voice behind him made him jump.

'Tears at last, eh? You do care! It's your own fault, Gene. I told you not to see her. You went against my wishes, you deliberately went to find her and bought her an ice cream, so you have to be punished.'

His father put three dirty glasses and an ashtray in the sink and watched the cigarette butts and ash float to the top of the greasy water.

'There you are. If you're going to play Cinderella you

may as well have something to cry about. Don't break anything, your mother won't appreciate it, and don't expect a visit from any fairy Godmother. They don't exist.'

He closed his eyes tight and thought of Zuke and all she'd said. Two or three months . . .

The plates first, then the saucepans, the frying pan was black and filthy. He worked at it really hard with wire wool and scouring powder, it slipped out of his hands, drenched him and clattered to the floor.

He waited for the recriminations.

Nothing.

Not a sound.

The ogre, gone back to the television, was probably already asleep.

He did the glasses, the breakfast mugs, the forks and knives, the small sharp knife which his mother used for peeling potatoes, for slicing onions, for cutting the meat, even cleaning mud off everyone's boots in winter.

He started drying up. He hated it all. Hated the soapy wetness of the dishes through the cloth which somehow never quite wiped dry. Then the meat dish slipped and clattered to the floor. It broke. Two pieces.

'What the hell are you doing in there! Some people are trying to sleep!'

He picked up the pieces. Could they be stuck together? Could he stick them together? It was part of the set, the only meat dish. She'd never forgive him. It would mean another row, explanations of why he was washing up, why Rick had allowed him to, why he hadn't helped the boy . . .

Antagonize!

Easier said than done.

He was as frightened of his mother as he was of his father.

They both terrified him.

'Remain calm at all times,' Zuke had said on seeing him off. 'Imagine that you are absolutely by yourself and don't have to answer to anyone but yourself, because you're a loner. That is what a Latchkey is, a loner. He makes his own decisions, all the time, does not depend on anyone, and especially not on the whims of adults who continually screw up their own lives.'

He put everything away, plate by plate, glass by glass, finding the cupboards so untidy there was hardly any room. He dropped the meat dish pieces in the trash can.

He pulled open the table drawer and dropped the knives, forks and spoons in with a clatter. Unlike Zuke's neat kitchen there was no cutlery tray with separate compartments for carvers, or butter knives or teaspoons. Here you just dropped the lot in together. It wasn't even a matching set anyway.

He dried the sharp little knife and dropped that in the drawer too and stared at it. Zuke had indicated the jugular vein in the medical book.'Cut that one open and the man's dead.' Like the end of that film, with Jack Nicolson leaning over a sleeping Brando and waking him up. 'Know why you've woken up?' . . . 'No . . .' . . . Gurgle, gurgle . . . 'You've woken up 'cause I've just slit your throat.'

He closed the drawer quickly to shut out the fearful thoughts he knew would come in on him.

He turned round and looked at the empty sink.

It was satisfying, what he had achieved.

'Make the kitchen yours. Take over the house slowly but surely. Do one thing at the time. Tidy one cupboard or a drawer a day. They won't notice. It's good training. All of us have done it. Maybe you could ask your dad about sex, too. Find out if he's got another woman?'

Over the next few days Gene started spending more time at home, in the kitchen and in the garden with his rabbit. He was neither reprimanded nor congratulated for tidying up the place and the only time either parent came near to realizing what he was doing was when his mother couldn't find the coffee filter bags and he knew exactly where they were.

Rick remarked that he had noticed his son recently

playing housewife, but it didn't go further.

One Saturday, a dull hot afternoon heavy with clouds, a day when everyone else was down at the lake swimming, he stayed in his bedroom involved in building a garage with Lego.

It was a good construction, the best he'd ever tried, with five levels, pumps, car wash, a repair shop and parking area reached by a spiralling slope that went outside the main walls. It was this which was giving him difficulty because he didn't have enough bricks of the right kind.

As he knelt on the floor sorting out the necessary base pieces into different lengths and different colours, black, white, blue, he heard a vehicle drawing up outside.

He stood up, looked out of the window and saw a van. Tatillo's Wine Suppliers, and the van driver coming up the path holding a delivery note. The doorbell rang and he went to answer it knowing Rick would be asleep. But he was wrong. Rick was awake and already at the door.

He went back to his room, to the window. Eager Rick was out in the road checking what was in the back of the van, the driver pulling out a handcart and stacking it with one, two, three, four cardboard cases of J & B Whisky.

Rick led the way back to the house, but instead of going in, took the man round the side.

Was he going to try and hide and stuff from Mom?

Gene went to the bathroom and peeped out of the top window. They were just coming round, Rick leading the way to the shed, opening the door, looking in.

They exchanged words, laughed. The driver unloaded the cart and left. Rick went into the shed, stayed there for a little while trying to find room for the four cases.

Gene returned to his room, glanced out of the window to see the driver loading the cart again. Four more cases, and another four.

He raced back to the bathroom, peeped out again and just saw it, quivering, in the throes of its death agony, its neck snapped, the rabbit thrown on the rubbish heap with the hutch. Ulysses hurled out of the way to make room for more cases.

The driver looked a little surprised, but Rick made some funny remark and both laughed. Pencil from behind the ear, sign here please, Rick with shaking hand, signing, the driver giving a last look at the dead rabbit, off with his empty cart.

Gene watched, trembling, watched his father throw out the perished dinghy, throw out an old length of hose, an old petrol can then, with great love and care, move in the remaining cases.

He'd killed Ulysses. He'd killed Ulysses, sold the bicycle, bought the booze and killed Ulysses.

Rick came out, a manic smile on his face, holding a brand new bottle of amber liquid. He unscrewed the top, stuck it in his mouth and gulped greedily, wiping his mouth with the back of his hand.

It was then that he looked up and caught sight of Gene at the window.

'What're you staring at, Gene?' he shouted. 'Your rabbit? It's dead! You didn't feed it enough lettuce and it's dead! I told you animals had to be looked after. Come down right now and bury it before it stinks the place out. And get rid of that hutch!'

chapter eight

Zuke stood behind the boarded up window on the first floor of Fort Knox waiting for her club members to turn up. The first grand reunion since they had all been sent away.

She was nervous they might not come.

Judge William Craft had been clever ordering them all off

in different directions. He knew it could cause disunity among them, and perhaps it had. They'd been apart for two weeks in different environments, Bonnie, she knew, had had a good time with her grandparents somewhere in Oregon, Judd had trucked around with his father, Steve had enjoyed the sea near Santa Barbara with an aunt, only Joleen had had a bad time.

They had been alone, while she had had Dillon's company. There was no telling what effect that might have had.

She'd be pretty lost without the Latchkeys.

She wouldn't be anybody any more.

She'd still have Dillon to look after, and her mother's kitchen, but little else. So somehow she had to keep them together.

They'd nearly disbanded once, when the Sarson twins had left Avalon. That had been a blow. The nine-year-old boys had joined the club after Steve, but had only stayed three months. They'd helped in the Warshall raid and she'd thought of using them for raiding other stores as they were nearly identical, one providing the alibi for the other. But their parents had moved East. The emptiness after that, with only six members, had nearly destroyed them till she'd come up with the Sam Finer idea.

She'd have to dream up something new now. Something essential. Invent a situation that would threaten them all.

If they came.

She moved to the front of the house, looked through the gap in the shutters down Sherbrook Drive.

Not a soul. No one.

Then Judd, ambling, kicking a stone, whistling. She looked beyond him, searching for anyone following him. All knew that the moment they returned to Avalon they might be watched day and night.

But there was no one.

A creaking behind her made her turn round. Steve and Dillon were right behind her.

'Joleen's downstairs and Bonnie's on her way.'

She pretended not to care.

When they had all assembled, Zuke chaired the Latchkey meeting.

They sat in a circle on the carpet up in the attic and Zuke had a pad and pencil in front of her ready to take notes.

'Rumour has it,' she started, 'that the Juvenile Department is thinking of hiring someone to set up a special school for us Latchkeys for the rest of the vacation.' It was a lie, but it had its effect. 'Can anyone confirm?'

No one could, which wasn't surprising.

'Well I've heard,' she went on, 'that Judge Craft advised the Juvenile Department to advise the City Councillors that something would have to be done to keep us off the streets and that we'd have to report daily, either at the Junior High or the Methodist Church Hall.'

It scared them.

'I've further heard that Liz Kleiner, who hasn't anything better to do, has volunteered for the job. Has anyone got anything on Liz Kleiner?'

Everyone thought for a while, then Joleen said, 'She's a Catholic.'

'That doesn't make her a virgin.'

'But it might stop her working in the Methodist Hall.'

They fell silent.

'Does anyone think that this is a clever threat to get us to talk?' They were being dumb. She'd have to stir harder. Then Joleen reacted.

'Too subtle. They wouldn't think that way. I guess it's the City Councillors wanting to look as though they're doing something about what happened. I think if we came clean they'd drop the idea.'

'You serious?' Zuke asked.

'Yeah, I'm serious. I don't think anyone believes us and if we owned up that it had been a practical joke, it would all be forgotten and they'd drop the vacation school idea.'

Joleen was like that. She could lose face without it hurting.

'Would you take the rap?' Zuke asked her.

'Sure. I've paid already. Two weeks in summer camp, what more can Mom do? I'll say it was my idea if you like. I bribed Bonnie and the boys, and you can be kept right out of it.'

It was bringing them together, she could sense it. The loyalty to each other rising above everything else. Now she'd kill the idea and get them working against an outsider.

'I don't like admitting anything, Joleen. If we do that then we'll never be believed again and everyone will treat us like dirt.'

'I agree,' Judd voiced. A rare occurrence.

'If the City Councillors are looking for a way to clear their good name then maybe we should help them,' Zuke suggested. 'If we could somehow make our peace with Sam Finer, say sorry to *him* and make him believe that we were duped as much as he was, we'd be clearing his name and the Councillors.'

Dillon clapped.

But then Dillon understood her more quickly than the others. Intelligence just ran in the family.

'You mean someone else put us in the safe without Sam Finer knowing?' Bonnie asked.

'Something like that.'

'But who?'

She was ready. The answer had come to her as she was talking. Another perfect victim.

'Gene,' she said. 'Gene Prestianni.'

'How the hell would he get us to pretend we'd been in the safe for five days, and what for?' Joleen asked.

'For the bicycle, for the fame, because he's a creep,' Dillon piped up.

'But how would he do it, Dillon?' Joleen was really getting into it. 'Why would we help Gene?'

'Blackmail.' Zuke stated.

'What did we ever do wrong that he could blackmail us about?'

'Everything!' Bonnie laughed. 'My parents' place, Warshall's . . .'

'I mean what have we ever done wrong that didn't really matter, that Gene could blackmail us about without it being serious. 'Cause that's what we need here.'

'Smoking marijuana?' Zuke suggested. 'Gene caught us smoking.'

'But we never have,' Steve said.

'Speak for yourself, junior. Anyway that's not the point. We could tell Sam Finer that Gene caught us smoking pot, and threatened to tell our parents, or the police, if we didn't do as he asked.'

The idea wasn't bad and they all thought about it.

'Why would he have wanted us to finger Sam Finer?' Bonnie asked.

'Because Sam Finer encourages his dad to drink and his dad drinking causes him a good deal of trouble.'

'Gene's not that bright,' Joleen said. 'He'd never figure anything like that out. That's you, Zuke, that's pure you.'

'Sam Finer won't know that, nor the City Councillors. We make Gene out to be bright.'

'But he'll deny it,' Steve said.

'Four of us against a little boy? There are an awful lot of parents and kids who don't exactly like him right now, with his new yellow bicycle and new yellow helmet.'

'Wow!' Dillon said, hugging his knees.

'So how do you go about setting this thing up?' Joleen asked.

'First we have to antagonize Gene so he won't go around looking like he adores us all, then we have to find Sam Finer and tell him what happened.'

'Is Sam around?'

'Rumour has it that he's on his way back,' Steve confirmed.

Zuke dismissed the meeting and asked them all to await further instructions. Maybe they'd have to lose the Knox as a hideout to make the story ring true that Gene had found them up there smoking, but it was early days. They'd have to leave it to her. As to her part in accusing Sam Finer of rape she'd work something out on that too. Her problem.

The Latchkeys left, reunited, happier, with something to work for together, something to look forward to. Funny how she'd managed to get them together again. And the idea of making friends with Sam Finer appealed to her. Pity about Gene, but there always had to be a victim, he'd never be a Latchkey anyway, not enough guts, too fond of his parents. All that advice she'd given him had been a waste of time. He'd conform. Do as they said. She'd have to set him up now, get him to smoke some grass maybe so's he'd know what he was talking about, her mother still had some tucked under the mattress in a plastic bag. It would be good bringing up the marijuana bit, adults puffing away while forbidding their kids to do so. It might even upset quite a few of them. And it wouldn't be difficult getting Gene to hate her, hate them all. Just a matter of picking the right moment.

And anyway the whole reason for doing this was pure fiction, so maybe she wouldn't do anything at all, just tell the Latchkeys the danger was over, the idea of a vacation school had been dropped.

She'd play it by ear.

Gene's mother discovered Rick's cases of whisky in the shed half an hour after she came home from work.

She said nothing till supper time, then when Rick was a fraction more sober and she was a fraction more tired and irritated and both their moods were ripe for a confrontation, she started, using Gene.

'I haven't seen you on your bicycle lately,' she said.

His father glanced up from the paper.

'It's got a puncture,' Gene lied.

'Did you know that Joey Tatillo has got one exactly like yours, even the same helmet? His father gave him one for his birthday.'

The dart was not aimed at him of course. It sailed past him and hit its target dead centre.

Up went the eyebrows, down came the frown, the paper moved a few inches to the right to cover up.

It was going to be ugly.

'I heard Joey's father bought it secondhand from a customer,' she went on.

Gene kept his mouth shut. He wasn't expected to say anything.

The plate of chili-con-carne was smacked down in front of Rick. 'You're a shit, you know that, Rick? A real shit. It's the only decent toy the kid's ever had!'

The paper was hurled back and over his head, the plate picked up and thrown across the room at her, missing, crashing to the floor.

It was violent, loud, frightening.

'Mind your own business, Soo-zee! It has nothing to do with you!'

'Best go up and eat in your room, Gene,' his mother said gently, handing him his food. He knew the routine, knew when to take shelter.

The insults would build up, the outrage, the taunts, the scorn, then the big eruption with screams and tears and it would all end up in bed, their bed because that's where it always ended up and his mother would blame him in the morning, when she awoke with a headache and Rick had taken her up a sweetening cup of coffee.

He went to the bathroom and dropped the meal down the lavatory. He hated the stuff and couldn't eat anything now anyway. He pulled the chain.

He sat down on the edge of his bed, the light out, the door open, and waited to hear the argument develop. She would defend him, she would be angry on his behalf and that anger would rise and reach a crescendo, and then Rick would hit her, not able to stand any more.

But it took longer than usual.

This time it was different.

There was silence, so he tiptoed to the top of the stairs. The kitchen door was wide open and he could hear them munching, forks scraping plates, spoons scooping beans. They were probably staring at each other, sizing each other up like a couple of fighting cocks.

'How much did you get for the bicycle?' His mother, stern, her anger under control.

'Two hundred.'

'How much did you spend on the drink?'

'Half.'

'So?'

'So the rest of the money's in your drawer.'

'Is he upset?'

'He has to learn.'

'What?'

'To do what he's told.'

Silence.

'Why did you kill the rabbit?'

'Why do you think?'

'So you could hide twelve cases of booze from me?' There was a laugh in her voice. She thought it funny. 'You are an asshole sometimes, Rick.'

And he laughed.

They were friends. They were friends over a hideous deed against him. He felt the tears again. How did you fight an enemy like that?

'Can I have a glass of the damned stuff then?'

She was playing up to him, seeking his friendship. But why? Why? Why? Why?

'What did you do with the rabbit?' she asked.

'Buried it.'

'Thank Christ for that. I couldn't stand having it around. He had it in the house the other day and it left its pellets all up the stairs.'

It wasn't true. He'd cleared them all up. And why had she pretended she liked Ulysses? Why couldn't she have said? It was so confusing.

'Not now, Rick . . .'

They were smooching.

That was it, the barrier, the unbearable barrier that he would never be able to cross. Their loving, their touching, the sickening lust.

'*Rick*!!!'

His heart leapt. Anger? Had Rick gone too far? Even husbands had to stop somewhere. There seemed to be certain rules you just couldn't break, or only in the proper place, like the upstairs rooms.

The eating went on in silence, a long time, then he heard her ask quietly, 'Shall I tell him to come down?'

'No. Leave him up there. He's happy on his own.'

'It makes me feel guilty, us together down here and him all by himself.'

'Gene!' It was an irritated bawl.

He rolled over on his stomach then crawled back to his room. 'Yeah?'

'Want to come down? Mom's got fruit pie for you.'

'OK.'

Pretence time.

He knew this game as well. The loving family togetherness game when they would all sit and pretend to enjoy each other's company over the meal then go together and watch TV. Dad making efforts to be nice to Mom because he had done something wrong, and Mom being nice because she was too tired to handle another quarrel.

It's what happened.

Both together on the sofa holding hands with a glass of whisky each, himself alone in the armchair.

The programme was dull too, soap, jealousy, betrayal, suspected infidelity, the story of their lives without them realizing it.

Stupid.

And Dad dozed off and she reached out for his hand to squeeze before sending him off to bed with a loving kiss.

He fell asleep. The pretence contentment was enough, he

could fool himself with the best of them when he was tired, and he was tired. And when he woke up it was Sunday, which might either be a day of peace or a day of war, and this time it was a day of peace, all three going off in the car to Suzy Prestianni's boss, Jack McQuare's ranch, on the other side of Westcoat, McQuare's teenage kids ignoring him but allowing him to play in the pool all afternoon watched by Dad who was drinking himself into a stupor, laid back on a beach mattress while Mom took down shorthand inside the house from McQuare. The Avalon Fruit business was booming, contracts couldn't wait. Mom certainly worked overtime with Mr McQuare, but she never complained.

Then the battle positions were drawn up again across the kitchen table at supper time, her making, not his, her antagonizing, not him.

The opening salvo nearly went unnnoticed, but Gene picked up on it immediately.

'Young Billy called at the factory on Friday.'

'Oh yeah?'

'Did I tell you his father died two weeks back?'

'You told me he was ill.'

'Well he died.'

'Old Bill dead . . .'

There was a silence. Gene remembered old Bill, the chief packer at the canneries when his father worked there. He used to give him samples when no one was looking, miniature tins of cherries in syrup and strawberries in syrup.

'Young Bill must be twenty or so now, I suppose.'

'Twenty-two.'

'Is he?'

'He's come into quite a bit of money. Old Bill left a fair nest egg.'

'More than I will.' This followed by a short nervous laugh.

'He came specifically to see me, Rick. He wants to buy the boat. Offered five hundred dollars as it stands. Take it off your hands, no problems. You don't even have to go down there.'

It had happened before, such an offer, supposedly out of the blue. It wasn't true. Mom had a 'For Sale' notice up on the board in the canteen.

If Rick could sell the bicycle then he could sell the boat which he never used.

For years the *Water Fox* had been moored at the end of the old boardwalk on Lake Avalon. It cost little to have her berthed there and though offers had been made his father had always turned them down. It was like asking him to sell his whisky. He'd bought the small cabin cruiser when things had been good. Once, they had been a two-car family, a boat-owning family and only the husband worked. When the yacht was new they'd spent every weekend on her, roaring across the placid waters to Westcoat, or Devil's Creek, Hocum Bay, Spoof Cove, names Gene had made up. He had learned to swim because of the boat, had dived off her deck into the dark cold waters. He had loved it. Then Rick's job had failed, and nobody had wanted to buy the *Water Fox*, no one round the lake had any money or wanted to be ostentatious enough, and time had slipped by. To repaint it would cost, and no way would his father now get up enough energy to scrape and sandpaper and work at it.

'I've still got equipment and stuff on board,' he said defensively. 'I'd have to clear it out.'

'He'd like to know by tomorrow.'

'Why didn't you tell me earlier, so's I could think about it?'

'Because it doesn't need thinking about and you haven't been in any great mood to talk about anything.'

'What makes you think I'm in a better mood now?'

'I don't. I just don't have the time any more. We need the money, Rick. People will hear you bought in those cases of booze, they'll be round to help you drink it so don't give me any great stories about selling it. I want to clear up a few debts.'

It was time to make himself scarce again.

Gene started to get up but his father grabbed him hard by the arm and forced him back down on the chair.

'It's not my boat to sell,' he said.

'No, whose it it?'

'I gave it to Gene. That was part of the deal for selling the bicycle. I'd give him the boat, and we'd clean it up and go for picnics again as we used to. Wasn't it, Gene? The boat for the bicycle?'

The smiling, twinkling clever clever eyes were studying him, daring him to contradict.

Too late. This time, after the loss of the bicycle and the killing of the rabbit and Zuke's advice to settle for one parent or the other, he was going to act positively.

He got up quickly, away from Rick so that the heavy hand couldn't restrain, took his empty plate to his mother at the sink.

'I never made any deal, Dad. It's not my boat, and I don't want it anyway. But I'd like my bicycle back, or another if you sell it, if you get any money left over from the debts.'

The fist came down so heavily on the table that the cups jumped and toppled over.

'Don't talk to me like that you little motherfucker!'

Then it was the grand sweep. The extended arm reaching out across the table and clearing the decks straight on to the floor. The coffee pot, the cups, the plates, the jam, the peanut butter, salt and pepper, the glass fruit bowl, all went shattering to the floor.

Then it was her turn.

'I've had enough!' she screamed at high pitch. 'Enough, enough, enough! I'm leaving. I can't take any more. Unless you sell that boat I'm leaving and taking Gene with me!'

'Going home to mother?' Rick yelled, the twisted, victorious grin taking over from the anger. He knew she had nowhere to go, her mother was dead. Once, she had left, but that was some time ago, and she had come back. It was an empty threat, one that could not be carried out, the house was in his name, the car, the mortgage, everything, even the boat. 'The day you go, sweetheart, you'll never come back, so don't challenge me.'

He was making his way to the kitchen door, was out in the garden, on down the path to the booze stock. It was going to be an evil night.

'You'd best go upstairs, Gene. Thanks for telling me the truth, but maybe it doesn't help.'

She was genuinely scared for him. There was a fear and trembling in her voice. No one could tell what might happen when his father got out of hand, but he would be calmer after a few swigs, for a while anyway.

'Stay in your room till things quieten down. *Do* you mind if he sells the boat, we do need the money?'

'No, honest,' he said and, seeing the ogre coming back up the path, bottle in hand, he left the kitchen.

The same routine then, running up the stairs, leaving the bedroom door ajar, listening intently.

'I'll kill that son of a bitch one day.'

'I suppose I'm the bitch?'

'Right!'

'It's not his fault. He's forced to take sides . . . and never knows which way to jump.'

Silence, followed by the clatter of broken crockery and glass being swept up. The dust pan, the pieces being dropped in the trash can.

He heard his mother at the sink, cupboards opening and closing as she put things away. Then she went to the sitting room and switched on the television.

His Dad would stay put, sitting at the table drinking himself into oblivion. Mom would eventually go to bed.

The day was over.

The next morning Gene got up and looked out of the window. The sun was shining. He thought of his bicycle, managed to survive missing it with the thought of feeding Ulysses, then remembered that he had gone too.

So what would he do?

Tidy up the kitchen again once his mother had left? Put things back in the right places which she had moved. He couldn't understand how she managed to live like she did, never knowing exactly where things were, the coffee, the tea. The dairy products admittedly could usually be found in the ice box and the frozen foods in the freezer, but last week he had come across the shoe polish in the butter compartment and a deodorant spray in the oven. She was scatterbrained, that was all. Did too much thinking and day dreaming as she cooked.

When he got downstairs she was just leaving.

'Take care of yourself today, Gene, and tonight. I won't be home. Going to a seminar in Fresno with Mr McQuare. That's what that work was all about yesterday. So see you tomorrow.'

He listened to the front door closing, the sharp, smart clicking of her high heels down the front path. She would walk along Cedar Avenue to the corner and wait there for her friend Maisie to pick her up.

Same routine, every day.

He started the coffee machine going, three spoonfuls in the filter bag. He enjoyed doing that. He was a past master as making coffee for his Dad. Then the beast himself came down, hair standing on end, unshaven, tongue sticky, eyes bloodshot, looking terrible.

'Why did you tell your mother that you wouldn't miss the boat?' It wasn't asked aggressively, but whiningly, his little boy hurt act.

'Because I wouldn't. We never go out in it.'

'You want to go out in it?'

'Sure.'

'Well I don't.'

He served up the coffee, the toast, the butter, the jam, the honey. His father grunted. He went back to the sink.

'What are you doing?' Rick Prestianni asked.

'Washing up, tidying.'

'You really are a Mummy's boy aren't you? Hope you don't turn out to be a faggot.'

He was looking for a fight, spoiling for an argument. The best thing would be to get out of the house.

'More coffee?'

'Piss off, Gene.'

He managed to get past without trouble, went upstairs to his room and shut the door.

He would finish the garage, then maybe go for a walk, go down to the lake and have a look at the *Water Fox*. Grandma Olsen had once said that things never came in twos, but threes. Bad things usually. So the boat would be number three. The bicycle, the rabbit, the *Water Fox*.

He pulled the Lego box from under the bed and kneeled down to finish off the ramp. It looked really good, the best thing he had ever built. He went to the shelf, picked up all his cars, the lorries, the vans, set them in a line in front of the garage then, one by one, took them up the ramp, parking the vans on the top floor, the limousines on the second, the coupes on the first, then he took his favourite, the scratched red, green and gold Mustang, down the ramp to the pumps and filled her up.

The door opened.

'Wow! Did you build that?'

'Yes.' He didn't look up, didn't dare.

'*Very* good.'

He could smell the whisky now, felt the heavy breathing down his neck.

His father got down on his haunches to study the complex. His large hand settled on the Mustang, pushed it out of the garage forecourt and round.

'Can I play?'

'Sure.'

'Vroom . . . Vroom vroom!'

He took the Mustang up the ramp, then deliberately smacked it against the retaining wall, breaking it and crashing it down on the pumps below.

'Aw shit, Gene, this driver must have had a drink too many.'

He took one of the vans from the roof and shot it carelessly down the ramp, doing the same thing. Then he took another and drove that through the car-wash windows.

'Not too strong this building, is it?' He made a few rumbling noises and looked about him pretending fear. 'Did you hear that? I think it may be an earthquake!'

He threaded his hand into the main part of the construction, clenched his fist and pulled it out.

The bricks parted, the structure collapsed and, annoyed that some of the walls were still standing, he swung his other hand at it, sending pieces of Lego and toy cars flying across the room.

'Hurricane Force Nine too, Gene! Look at that!'

Gene said nothing.

It hurt. It was hard. But it was so childish and nasty that he nearly wanted to laugh. Anyway, deep inside him, he had expected it and was ready for it, knew that his father would not let last night's incident pass without some punishment.

'I'm sorry you don't want the boat, Gene,' Rick said, just to make the point of his action absolutely clear. 'It's not often you get the chance of becoming the owner of a fine yacht.'

'I wanted it, Dad, it's just that Mom also wants to sell it to get some cash.'

'So you were being generous?'

'Trying.'

'Trying!' And for some reason that made Rick laugh.

It made him laugh quite genuinely, quite unexpectedly, and through his laughter he said, 'Trying to be generous to your Mom . . . that's cute. That's really cute. It's also impossible, son. Impossible. Your mother forbids generosity. Forbids it. She likes to be the breadwinner, she wants to be in charge and numero uno.' And he slapped him on the shoulder, wiping his eyes of the tears, apologizing for what he had just done, but it had to be appreciated what a tough time he was having.

'How about you and me going down to the damn boat and

just seeing what she looks like, eh? Would you like to do that?'

An offer he could not refuse.

'I'll take some of this fuzz off my face, then we'll go. Tell you what, we'll spend the day on her, maybe take her out if she isn't too flooded. The pump might work. Think you can rustle up something to eat for lunch?'

It might never happen, but it might.

A day out. A day away from the house, a day with something to do. He liked the boat, he really liked to go out in her. Hadn't been on board her for a year. Things would go wrong because they always did, but it was worth hoping for a good day.

He got some cheese, ham, cucumber and lettuce together, shoved them in a brown paper bag with a number of bread rolls, added some apples and oranges, the sharp little knife, no time to boil eggs hard.

He sat at the table waiting. Perhaps he did have time to boil the eggs. He put the water on, waited some more watching the bubbles forming round the bottom of the saucepan, placed three eggs carefully in the water, checked the kitchen clock.

Three minutes.

By the time his father came down he could have boiled a hundred eggs, but he was sprightly and had lost that hang-over look. Jeans, striped T-shirt, sneakers, the boat gear, car keys in one hand.

'Just get myself a little stock for the journey . . .'

Out in the garden down to the shed, coming back with two bottles.

By the end of the day they would be empty, and he'd probably have to walk home.

They got into the car, front seat, all sunshine, the Lego garage forgotten, the bicycle in the past, the rabbit dead and buried. From the corner of his eye he saw Zuke and Dillon on their front porch looking bored. Well, if he was taking sides maybe it would be against his mother now. If he had a good day, just one good day with his dad on board the *Water Fox*, it would help him decide.

Rick Prestianni drove comfortably, slowly where he should, fast where it was safe, up to the highway, then left along the road to Lake Avalon and left again away from the Westcoat end where the rich lived, where the new marina was crowded with yachts, to the other end where the *Water Fox* was moored to the old boardwalk, well down in the water, green with slime, her blue and grey paint peeling.

'Still looks pretty good,' Rick said.

Maybe he was going blind.

He parked the car. No one was around. A few years back the boardwalk had been the centre of activity for the Avalon sailing community, enthusiasts had gathered at weekends in their hundreds to potter about in boats, pull out and launch their yachts, paint, scrape and varnish their cherished craft, but when the Westcoat marina was built everyone moved. There was nothing here for them now, no bars, no restaurant, no chandlers. It was deserted. Just the *Water Fox* and a fisherman's flatboat, a sunken dinghy and an upturned canoe on the bank with a huge hole in it.

They went on board. It swayed, the bilges slurped.

Rick was in the little cabin straight away looking for a glass, a container to pour himself a shot of whisky.

He found a beaker.

'Want some, kid?' He was joking of course.

'No thanks, Dad. Are we going to take her out?'

'Sure. As soon as I've had a look at the engine.'

But he sat down on the bunk, poured himself out a second shot then, fortified, came out and slid off the engine cover to have a look at the rusty mechanism.

'There's a lot of water down there,' he said, gauging the amount of oily space under the engine. 'Better try the pump first.'

The pump did not work because the rubber hose was rotten. Gene realized it would mean hours of baling out, on his knees, in uncomfortable positions, but he was ready to get on with it.

'I'll go find a new piece of hose, you just start,' Rick said, handing him the old scoop.

He watched his father potter about the boat, bottle in hand, pretending he was looking for the part.

Nothing would happen, nothing would come of it. He should have known better than hope. His father would eventually lie down on the bunk exhausted by the thought of helping and that would be the sum total of the day. He was wasting his time. It was madness, but he went on, baling out, scratching his knuckles on loose rivets, hating the yellow slime on the warped wood, getting his face splashed every time he failed to get the scoop over the side.

The frustration started to build up, the indignation, the fury. Thoughts of the garage, the bicycle, the rabbit, of Zuke and all her advice started taking over. Baling out was getting him nowhere, so he stood up, dropped the scoop and went into the cabin to see what was happening.

His father was lying full length on the bunk, his hands behind his head, the bottle and beaker balanced on his chest.

'Find the hose?' Gene asked.

'Not worth looking for. She'll never start.'

'We're not going out in her then?'

'You want to? If you find the hose and can bale her out I'll get her started.'

A length of new hosepipe was under the small sink unit in a tool bag. He might not be strong enough to fix it but he'd have a damn good try.

He took his shoes off, his jeans, sat down in his briefs on the bottom of the boat in front of the hand pump and studied the problem.

The ring and screw that held the perished hose was rusty, but with effort and determination using screwdriver and pliers, he got it off. Then he tried to push the new rubber hose on to the metal pipe, but he wasn't strong enough.

He'd noticed a bottle of detergent under the sink, so he got that, ignoring the encouraging noises his father made from the bunk, poured some on his fingers and down the tube and over the metal pipe and managed to slip it on. He fixed the retaining ring and tightened the screw.

'I got it on, Dad! I got the new hose on!'

A grunt.

He'd have to feed the pump now, pour water down it.

He did all that, enjoyed it, worked the pump handle till it started sucking the filthy water and the pumping got harder, but he at least got the satisfaction of hearing the bilge water splashing into the lake at the stern.

'It's working, Dad! It's working!'

More grunts.

He sat down and pumped knowing it would take an hour, maybe more.

It would be nice if his father came out to help, but that wouldn't be the order of the day, ever. He had been a fool to imagine it could be. But he wasn't unhappy. Monday on Lake Avalon, not a soul in sight, a dog barking in the distance, it was like being in a dead world, a lost world, and his mind allowed the boat to drift, down a river, the Amazon maybe, through jungle vegetation on either side, the waters swirling, alive with crocodiles, monkeys gibbering in the trees and he the key man navigating the steamship through fatal rapids.

Then, as he got cramp and changed position, changed hands, the boat rocked and there was a clatter from inside the cabin, the noise of a bottle falling. He left his post.

Rick was fast asleep, the bottle on the floor, whisky gurgling out. He thought of leaving it, letting it trickle away, but he'd get the blame, so he picked it up and stood it by the bunk and stared at his beloved father dead to the world this early in the day.

How could anyone be so useless?

Now he would have to wait till the man woke up to be driven home, or walk.

Oh to be a Latchkey without the burden of parents.

And he felt hungry and picked up the brown paper bag, dug his hand down in it for a roll and the ham and touched the knife.

As he got hold of the silk smooth wooden handle it reminded him of what Zuke had said when she'd held up the diagram of the human body, the skeleton with its blue muscles, green veins and red arteries. 'Cut that one and he's dead.'

Had she been hinting, or had it been a chance remark?

He stretched out and put a finger on his father's neck, felt the blood pulsate close to the Adam's apple.

Could it be that easy?

He put the point of the knife against the throat, kept it there for quite a while mesmerized by his own action. If his father chanced to move in his sleep, chanced to turn his head suddenly, then it would be fate.

If he had the impulse to press a bit more, push harder, it would change his whole life, put an end to all the misery, the fear, the injustice, pay back all the harm done him.

He took a closer look at the face, the skin was red and blotchy and dry and the eyebrows were frowning with stupidity and drink. A third of the bottle drunk already, on top of what he'd imbibed the day before it resulted in this. Stupor, coma, oblivion. He might as well be dead.

Without this man his mother might live quite happily.

He would live more happily.

It just needed courage.

And imagine what Zuke would say!

And he saw Zuke partly naked across the car bonnet.

And the impulse came.

He pushed.

He gripped the handle and pushed and the sharp blade went right in and blood spurted out so unexpectedly that he jumped back to avoid it and, in doing so, the blade slit the skin even more.

There was a terrible gasp, a sickening gurgle, more blood

oozed out, flowed out and Gene just stared, knife in hand, not knowing what to do.

He dropped the knife, kicked over the bottle and looked down at his blood-spattered body, his red speckled briefs.

He went up the two steps to the deck, glanced quickly to left and right and, seeing nobody, took down his briefs, wiped himself over quickly, threaded on his jeans, his T-shirt, his sneakers. He leaned over the side, washed the small briefs in the water, wrung them out. They were grey now with oil, but the blood spots hardly showed. He squeezed them into a ball small enough to hold in one hand then looked inside the cabin again and saw his father clutching his throat.

Would his fingerprints be on the knife?

He went back in, ignored the leg that was twitching, picked up the knife and held it by the blade. With his damp briefs he wiped the knife carefully, cleaned the blade, the handle, holding it through the cloth. Should he throw it in the water? Would that be sensible? His mother would miss it. Might guess what it had been used for. He dropped it in the paper bag with his briefs, picked that up and left glancing one last time at what he had done.

The face was now turned to the wall.

You couldn't tell.

He shut the door quickly, shot the bolt, climbed over the side and walked up the boardwalk to the cement path, past the car, up the grass slope and into the woods where he stopped and turned round to see if anyone had been watching him.

There was a woman with a dog walking along the bank some distance away. No one else. It was unlikely she would have noticed where he had come from, besides he didn't need an alibi, he had just left his father to sleep off another drunken morning.

In sight of the road leading to the Highway, he started running. Why was he running? Who was he running to? His mother? Is that who he was running to? And what would he tell her? That he had killed his father? Had slit the throat of his own father? She might understand. She might not.

Visions of the Sheriff, of Sergeant Finch, of the Court. The television people against him now.

What did they do to murderers in Avalon?

He ran, ran, he had to get home. He was nearly at the highway.

The dampness of his briefs started coming through the brown paper. The bag would tear, the apples and oranges would fall out, evidence that he had been running across this field.

He was frightened.

Terrified.

He knew that it would overwhelm him soon if he allowed it to. He hadn't just committed a crime, he had committed murder.

Murder . . .

He slowed down, walked with deliberately long steps, pleased that he could control his panic, pleased that he would have some time to think before facing his mother. The first questions would come from her. 'Where's your father?'

But not till tomorrow!

Not till *tomorrow*!

He'd forgotten she was away for the night at the conference with Mr McQuare!

He had twenty-four hours!

Even if she rang asking where he was he didn't have to know. 'I left him at the boat . . . midday . . .'

He had time on his side.

He walked at a steady pace, hugging the brown paper bag with both arms.

Grandma Olsen might see him. 'Where's your father?' . . . 'Stayed on the boat.' . . . 'Why didn't you stay with him?' . . . 'Why did you bring the picnic back, doesn't he want any lunch?'

The Sheriff would come to the house . . . 'Got bad news

for you, Gene . . . could you come along with us? Just a few questions. We found him with his throat cut, but he couldn't have done it himself. No knife or razor in the cabin.'

He should have left the knife right there on the floor, or even put it in his hand.

'The other thing that puzzles . . . the cabin door was bolted on the outside . . .'

He'd done it automatically. There was a hook on the inside, a bolt on the outside, the door didn't stay shut unless you bolted it.

He felt the chill numb his fingertips, his lower lip, his feet.

Should he turn back? Go back and maybe find him still alive?

What if he survived? What if he woke up and survived?

Monday afternoon. Trucks on the highway, hundreds of them. He waited, waited a long time, then crossed the first half, then the second immediately. Two fields, two roads to go and he would be in Cedar Avenue and home.

To what?

To wash.

He wanted to wash. Befor anything else, he wanted to wash, to make sure there was no blood on his face, on his hair.

He started running again, down the slope, hugging the bag, only a few minutes more.

Cedar Walk, Cedar Avenue . . .

He saw her from the corner, Zuke. Sitting on the verandah. Alone. She'd help. She'd have to help. He went straight up to her, panting.

She looked him up and down apparently not believing what had appeared before her.

'Jesus, Gene, did you see a ghost or something?'

chapter nine

She had seen him coming from a distance, but did not realize he was in a panic till he got to the end of the path. He was sheet white, his hair was wet, his face speckled with red paint. He stood there, out of breath, out of everything, unable to talk.

Something had happened. Something pretty terrible.

'You OK, Gene?' she asked.

'No . . .'

'Tell Aunty. What's the matter?'

'I . . . I . . .' His lower lip was trembling, his hands shaking, the brown paper bag he was holding was about to fall apart. She'd never seen anyone in such a state.

'Come in, you need a drink of water. Where's your dad?'

She led him through to the kitchen and sat him down at the table, filled a glass with water and handed it to him.

'Drink this, slowly. Don't talk until you're up to it.'

She reached for his hand. It was ice cold. She touched his forehead, wet with sweat, and that was cold too.

He sipped the water, holding the glass with both hands to stop it shaking, gave it back to her, stood up, took a few deep breaths and stared at her.

'I've just killed my father,' he said.

She believed it. Gene didn't lie. He wasn't inventive. And he'd said it in a very clear, very steady voice.

'How? Where?'

'On the boat. I cut his throat.'

'Jesus, Gene. Is that his blood on your face?'

He looked horror stricken, tried to wipe it off with the back of his hand. 'I have to wash.'

'What did you do with the body?'

'It's in the boat.'

'What did you do it with?'

'A knife . . . It's in there . . .'

'Christ, man, you ran all the way back from the lake carrying that?'

He nodded.

She handed him a damp dish cloth and watched him washing himself at the sink. He didn't just put soap on his face, he put detergent on his hair and scrubbed himself under the tap, his neck, his arms, his hands. Like Lady Macbeth.

'Have you told anybody?'

'No . . .'

She had to be very careful now not to do what an adult would do, that is think up all the bad things that could happen to him and point them out as a reproach. He needed help, but badly.

'Are you thinking of telling anybody?'

'I don't know what to do.'

'Want my advice?'

'Yes . . .' He was drying himself with the tea towel.

'Well for a start don't tell anyone until we can work something out.'

She looked inside the brown paper bag. Two apples, three eggs, two oranges, some bread rolls, cheese, a damp rag, and the knife that looked pretty clean.

'Did you plan it?'

'No.' He was emphatic.

'How did it happen?'

'He was asleep. I put the knife against his throat and it went in . . .'

'Did he take long to die?'

'I dunno. I didn't wait to see. Maybe he isn't dead.'

The guy was paranoid.

'Didn't you check?'

'I ran. I was too frightened.'

His lower lip started trembling again, then his whole body started to shake.

'Steady,' she said. 'Sit down.'

'Trouble is,' he said, 'the boat is locked. I did two silly

things, kept the knife and bolted the cabin door from the outside.'

'Who's likely to go there?'

'No one.'

'So we go along and unlock it, then let someone else find him.'

'But how would he have cut his own throat?'

'We take the knife back and leave it. When does your mother return?'

'She doesn't, not tonight. She's in Fresno, a conference or something.'

'With Jack McQuare?'

Gene nodded.

'Tell me everything, Gene, tell it me from the top.'

She listened.

It was an incredible story. The bicycle because of her, the killing of the rabbit because of the whisky stock, the Lego garage, the anger building up, the arguments between Suzy and Rick Prestianni, going out to the boat, the drinking, the death.

It was all understandable.

If he had been suffocated of course, he could have been tipped into the lake, but with a cut throat . . . Could people cut their own throats?

Dillon appeared in the doorway, leaned against the wall and studied them both.

'Can people cut their own throats, Dill?'

'Sure they can. You get a long knife and draw it slowly across. Painful maybe, but definite. Thinking of trying?'

'We can set it up as a suicide, Gene,' she said. 'Why don't you go back home and get yourself really cleaned up? Better still have a shower here because no one will think of looking for your family blood down our drains. And while you're doing that Dill and I will work things out.'

She smiled at him and he smiled back. It was an effort, but in the circumstances it was one of the bravest things she'd seen. 'Just one more thing, Gene,' she said, taking hold of his wrist and staring him in the eyes as he got up to leave the kitchen. 'Why did you do it?'

Gene shrugged his shoulders, looked down and away, then straight back at her. 'Maybe to become a Latchkey?'

'I guess you're surely one now.'

'So I get help?'

'You bet. And I'll tell you our password and motto, it's a phrase: "The adult is the enemy."' And she let him go.

As he went up the stairs she pulled the wet rag out of the paper bag, shook it and held up the briefs for Dillon to see.

'Know what these are? A murderer's pants! Grim aren't they?'

Dillon wasn't too impressed.

'Know what you're going to do?' she went on.

Dillon shook his head.

'You're going to stay here and make absolutely sure he doesn't leave the house. Entertain him and keep him happy because that, up there in the shower, is one big unhappy boy who could get into a whole lot of trouble.'

'Where are you going?'

'The less you know the better, but I'll be back pretty damn soon. Meanwhile get him to wash these, dry them over the oven and put them back on, or in his drawer at home, and tell him I've taken the knife.'

'What about the great marijuana plot?' Dillon asked.

'The great marijuana plot is ditched. We're into murder now, Dill, which could be a lot more exciting.'

First washing it, then wiping it carefully so as to erase any fingerprints, she wrapped the knife in newspaper and left by the side door.

Her heart was beating fast. Very fast. If adrenalin could be felt to flow, she was feeling it. The prospect of seeing a dead man, a murdered corpse, excited her more than any sensation she had ever experienced.

She walked quickly down Cedar Avenue, right into Cedar Walk to the fields, across the fields, kicking at the long grass, over one fence, over two, the smell of the fruit orchards in the valley, the afternoon sun being reflected off the slanted corrugated roofs of the Canneries in the far distance.

She reached the highway, crossed it at the pedestrian bridge, went round the golf course and eventually down the steep slope to the south side of the lake.

The Prestianni Lincoln was parked there dangerously in evidence. Gene hadn't mentioned it. Time, therefore, was more precious than she had reckoned, for the damned car was telling the world where its owner was.

She started along the boardwalk and went past the *Water Fox*, not stopping till she got to the end, then went up the slope and into the woods where she got down on her haunches among the hidden safety of the bushes.

There was little activity around, an old fisherman on the lake in a flat-bottomed boat sorting out his tackle, a number of sailing dinghies at the other end of the lake, small white triangles that she need not worry about.

She watched the *Water Fox* intently for several minutes trying to discern any movement on board, but it was as still and as peaceful as the lake itself.

So the man was dead.

What could happen?

If he was left there till reported missing, the police would go aboard, find the cabin locked, the body inside with its throat cut and foul play would immediately be suspected.

If she crept on board and unbolted the door, threw the knife in and they found him like that, then it would certainly be less suspicious. But how did a man really cut his own throat?

He didn't.

If he wanted to take his life with a razor he would slit his veins down the length of his wrists so as to make sure there would be no hope of healing, or he would take drugs, or shoot himself, or hang himself, or drown himself.

He would not cut his own throat.

The body, therefore, would have to disappear.

The boat could be se on fire, but that would only draw attention instantly. It could be sunk, it was very low in the water. Two or three of them might be able to take it out into the middle of the lake and sink it; the object of that would, of course, be to make it look as though an adult had murdered him and tried to cover up. Someone who knew he was on board, someone who had seen Gene leave, someone who wanted him dead.

She had managed to throw suspicion on an innocent party before, old Sam Finer, there was no reason why she shouldn't do it again. It was only a matter of manipulating adult imagination. A missing Rick Prestianni in a missing boat might take the heat off the interest in the Latchkeys and cause a different sensation, turn everyone's head in another direction.

She left her hiding place and walked down to the mooring, hands in pockets, carefree to the onlooker, but watching out for anyone who might see her.

If someone was watching then she would be throwing away any hope of the Latchkeys helping Gene. What she was doing was dangerous. If anyone came now she might well be suspected of having killed the man herself, after all she was even carrying the murder weapon.

She climbed aboard quickly and ducked down. She sat on the bottom of the boat for quite a while then peeped over the side. No one about. Not a soul. The fisherman had moved off farther away.

She reached out and pulled back the bolt. The door squeaked on its hinges and slowly swung open.

The smell that came out was sickly, rather like stale fish, but sweet. She went down the two steps and saw the distinctive shape in front of her on the floor, the figure lying head down in something black and sticky.

It was blood.

Rick Prestianni in a pool of his own blood.

Dead.

She backed out, left the door ajar, sat down in the fresh

air aware now of the boat's movements, of the water slurping in the bilges.

She dared look up and around.

Still no one about.

Quickly she unwrapped the knife and, still carefully holding it with the newspaper, threw it into the cabin. Whoever had killed him had found the knife there, used it, dropped it and left in a hurry. But who? Who would behave like that? Who would want to kill Rick Prestianni?

If Suzy Prestianni wasn't coming back till tomorrow, then they had a whole night in front of them to incriminate someone.

Funny how she wanted to protect Gene now. She'd wanted to see him to rile him, make him hate her, hate the Latchkeys for the great marijuana plot, but now she'd get the others to help him.

He'd won her over because he'd killed.

It was that simple.

She admired his guts.

And what better to get all the club members together again under her control than involve them in a murder they didn't know had been committed . . .?

But she'd have to tell Dill to keep his mouth shut.

She got home much later than intended and found Gene watching TV with Dillon, pale, distraught, nervous, jumping up as she came in.

'You been here all the time?'

'Yes.'

'Good. Now Gene,' she said throwing herself back in the armchair, pretty tired. 'We've got to think through the whole of your day. You went out with your dad . . .'

He was trying to say something.

'Yes?'

'Is he dead?'

'Oh yes, he's dead. I boarded the *Water Fox*, unbolted the cabin door and there he was lying on the floor, quite dead. You're half-orphan now, Gene. Congratulations.'

She thought it quite funny, but he was close to tears. Were they of grief, joy or remorse? She realized that he'd had time to think, too long a time probably, and that maybe she could have been less blunt. But the deed was done and he would have to live with it. It was essential that his mind should be kept occupied, too.

'So Gene, we've got to think through your day. You went out with your dad, you baled out the boat, he drank his bottle of whisky and fell asleep. So you walked back here to play with Dillon and me. What would you normally do next?'

'Wait for him to come home.'

'OK. So you wait. You have waited. He doesn't come home, what would you do?'

'Nothing.'

'You wouldn't ring up your mom?'

'I don't know where she is. Fresno somewhere . . .'

'Is she likely to ring you?'

'She might ring Dad.'

'Then we must be ready for that. When would she ring?'

Gene shrugged his shoulders.

'How late might she ring?' she asked.

'Ten?'

'So if she does, what will you say to her?'

'Dad hasn't come back. I'll tell her I came here, and that he still hasn't come back.'

'Will that worry her?'

He gave it some thought. 'No. She'll probably tell me to go to bed.'

'OK. So we go over to your house and wait till ten for her to call. When my mom comes home we'll say you're a bit worried, but not more than that. You didn't do it, Gene, you see. All you did was walk home alone leaving him on the boat dead drunk.'

They went over to Gene's house and settled in the living

room to watch television. Suzy Prestianni did not ring, but Angela Donoghue did.

They heard the phone through the windows they'd left open and Zuke rushed over hoping it would be the sad news that her mother wouldn't be home till late.

'Hi, honey . . . Mr Greenhook's got a whole lot of real important friends here tonight and wants me to stay on . . .'

'Don't worry, Mom.'

'Everything OK?'

'Everything's fine.'

They had till two, maybe three. She sat down by the phone and rang the other Latchkeys immediately.

Joleen was alone as always and free to rendezvous at the lake, in the woods overlooking the boardwalk. Eleven o'clock.

Selina Reidy answered her call to Judd but got him to the phone. He'd come as soon as his mother was asleep, which would be early enough.

Steve answered when she rang him, Dan Mollman was on duty till dawn, he was as free as he was excited.

Bonnie was the only problem, she used the code word 'skateboard' to signify that she was being overheard and watched, but added 'one cheeseburger' which meant only one parent was with her so things could work out.

All that was needed now was to organize Gene and Dillon, and get themselves over to the lake without being seen.

It was a hot, dark night. Zuke lay full length on her bed going over every detail of her plan. They would need nothing but the fisherman's flat-bottomed boat which Gene had assured her was always tied up at the boardwalk close to the *Water Fox*. Joleen and the four boys would be enough if Bonnie couldn't make it, the more hands the better obviously, but they'd manage without her. Maybe she would leave Gene behind as lookout, though Dillon was the most reliable for that and Gene would be necessary on the cruiser if something was needed.

Black faces? Special clothes?

No clothes. They would pretend they were having a midnight bathe. Two torches, one for signalling danger, the other simply to see by. And silence. That was the essential. Silence and making absolutely certain they were not seen. This was Operation Death. Rick Prestianni's death and their own death if they were caught.

She switched the light on, checked her watch. Ten forty-two. If she went ahead of them now she could go over the whole plan on the spot and iron out any unexpected problems.

They could all swim so there was no danger of anyone drowning, the coming back would be no sweat, only the paddling out of the cruiser and keeping everyone quiet. Sound travelled dangerously over the water, she knew that.

She went downstairs to the kitchen, ate a banana, a couple of cookies, drank a glass of milk and crossed over to the Prestianni house.

She gave Gene and Dillon her strict instructions. Gene was to follow her in thirty minutes, hide in the woods overlooking the boardwalk until he could see her by the boat, he should then proceed to the far end of the boardwalk, the north end, where everyone was to meet. Dillon was to follow ten minutes after him and meet at the same place. The best way to get there was down Cedar Walk, across the fields and over the pedestrian bridge. If they saw anyone they must try to remember what they looked like, so notes could be compared afterwards.

She set off at a good pace, but slowed down immediately on seeing someone coming the other way. It was a young man, jogging, plugged into a Walkman, humming. She started running herself as soon as she turned the corner.

It was an ideal night, a thin crescent moon giving no light, but comfortingly up there. No wind, no breeze, enough traffic around to make a general background noise, and hot.

She saw no one else as she crossed the fields, but there

was a figure on the pedestrian bridge over the highway. She held back till they were down the other side, then started running again. She skirted the wood and reached the slope leading down to the boardwalk from the north. The *Water Fox* was still there, the Prestianni car, but also the fisherman's flat-bottomed boat.

First thing was to find the paddles.

She waited in the shadows, not able to see much because of the dark, then made her way down to the boardwalk realizing that the noise of the water lapping up against the struts would cover any undue sounds they might make later.

The flat-bottomed boat was tied with a rope, not locked with a chain which she had feared, and she found a boat-hook as well as two paddles neatly stowed away in the locker under its long flat deck.

She sat down and looked up at the slope, the tops of the black trees. It was a good vantage point, she would be able to spot any silhouettes against the skyline to the south and see everything that was going on around her. Her eyes were getting accustomed to the dark.

Then she heard a plopping sound beside her.

Something small dropping into the water from a height, or a fish, jumping?

It unsettled her. She looked across the water at the cruiser. Rick Prestianni's ghost? The body was in there, lying in its pool of sickly blood.

And there was another plop.

She froze, tried to work out what it could be then stood up when a pebble hit the side of the boat. She saw the figure stand up slowly right there in front of her next to the post round which the flatboat's painter was tied.

Joleen.

'Come aboard . . .' she whispered. 'How long have you been here?'

Joleen joined her, sat down next to her and gave her a big hug. 'I came down as soon as you rang.'

'Anyone see you?'

'No. And no one's been down here. They're all up the Westcoat end. What's the emergency?'

'It's a no-question operation. We have to take that cruiser out into the middle of the lake and sink it.'

'That's Gene's father's boat.'

'Yep.'

She could sense Joleen was burning with curiosity, but all her Latchkeys were well trained. A no-question operation was a no-question operation. They would be told all about it in due course.

'How's it been?' Zuke asked.

'Lonely. The Nelson twins have been forbidden to play with me and I haven't seen Marilyn since I came back. Everyone thinks I'm evil.'

'You are.'

'There's someone up there in the woods, see, to the left of the tallest tree.'

Zuke saw something white moving. Small, running.

'Judd or Steve, I expect.'

'Both. There's another. They must have come together.'

'They would.'

The two figures disappeared for a while then reappeared.

'There's someone up there, far left,' Joleen pointed out.

It was Gene. It was strange how you could recognize a person from the briefest movement. He was being very careful because she didn't see him again though she knew where he was going.

'Dill will be along in a minute, so we may as well make a move. Take the boathook and leave it on the boardwalk in front of the cruiser as you pass. I'll bring the paddles.'

She got off the boat, followed Joleen, left the paddles by the *Water Fox* and studied its position for a moment. The old cruiser looked as though it was stuck in the mud. Maybe they'd have difficulty getting her away.

She moved on.

When she got to the end of the boardwalk she was

surprised to find everyone there, Bonnie, Gene, Judd, Steve, Dillon all sitting in a line on the grass with Joleen.

'OK,' she whispered, 'Gene Prestianni's joining us. We're going to take his dad's boat out into the middle of the lake to sink it.'

Two of them gasped with excitement.

'Dill will stay on shore here as lookout. If he signals a circle with his torch it means someone's coming. If anyone does come our story is that we're having a midnight swim. Let me do the talking. Gene, Bonnie, Judd and I will take the cruiser, we've got a hook and two paddles. Joleen and Steve will take the flatboat and follow us, but you'll have to use your hands. We're not in a hurry and we've only one thing to be careful of and that is noise. The cruiser team will go first, Gene leading, Gene will cast off with Judd. I'll paddle on the right side, starboard, Bonnie will paddle on the left side, port. Judd will take over from me, Gene from Bonnie. Once we're away, Joleen and Steve will follow. Any questions?'

'Where are we heading for?' It was Gene.

'The middle of the lake, aim for the green neon Westcoat Diner sign, it's brighter than the others. Anything else?'

'There's a paddle in the cabin, under the port bunk, shall I get that?'

'No,' Zuke said, pleased that he'd given her the opportunity of giving them a warning. 'No one must go in the cabin, the timbers are rotten. Besides two paddles will be enough.' She waited. No one asked anything more. 'OK. Let's go to our positions, Gene leading, Bonnie, Judd, Joleen, Steve then me.'

She kicked off her sneakers, left them with Dillon, the others did the same and disappeared one by one into the night.

'If you hear a car coming this way, Dill, and its headlights might catch us, whistle. Sorry you can't join us and have more fun but you're the best at lookout. Besides I'll make it up to you.'

'How?'

Zuke planted a firm wet kiss on his forehead.' How about a bicycle like Gene's?'

'When?'

'I promise it for your sixteenth birthday.'

Bonnie hadn't picked up her paddle, so Zuke took it on board with her and handed it to her. Of them all, Bonnie was the least practical. Good with a needle, useful for any delicate work, but had to be watched on occasions like this. She was feminine, whereas Joleen could be relied on to do anything without guidance.

She bolted the cabin door when no one was looking then sat down on her side, Bonnie on hers, while the two boys untied the ropes and started pushing the cruiser.

It didn't move.

'It's stuck!' Judd whispered loudly.

'We'll go up front . . . rock her a little,' Zuke whispered back, and took Bonnie's hand to lead her up on to the deck above the cabin to the very edge of the bows.

They started rocking, as Gene and Judd pushed.

The *Water Fox* shifted.

Slowly at first, then quite suddenly, launched out into the deep black waters, her stern sinking right down so that the surface was only five inches below the top of her sides.

They would have to keep her very steady if she wasn't to ship water too soon.

Zuke waited till Gene and Judd had clambered on board before going aft, then did so very cautiously. As she took her position on the starboard side the cruiser listed, the water coming to within an inch of the edge, but when Bonnie had settled down she steadied, and both started paddling.

There were bubbles and gurgles and sounds of water swirling inside the cabin as the *Water Fox* dipped forward as though taking a nose dive. Zuke followed Bonnie's stroke to keep the cruiser straight on course, it was hard to begin with but once they'd got a momentum going they moved at quite a speed, too fast for Joleen and Steve to keep up in the flatboat.

Zuke counted the strokes. Fifty would be enough, then she'd call a change.

They changed, Gene taking over from Bonnie, Judd taking over from her.

The boys were better at it, she had to admit. They got into a rhythm very quickly and somehow seemed stronger. Judd had done a lot of canoeing, she knew.

She looked behind but couldn't see the flatboat. Joleen would be all right, and Steve was reliable, a born commando.

It was cooler out on the lake, peaceful, she could enjoy the adventure now, and there was no torch flashing from the shore. She and Bonnie took over after the boys' fifty strokes, got into a rhythm without losing speed, then the boys took over again and when she next studied the shoreline Zuke realized they had done extremely well. They were level with the end of a line of trees on the south bank, the breeze was up and there were ripples on the water. This would be as good a spot as any, equal distance from the three nearest banks, and a mile from Westcoat at least. She hissed and the boys stopped paddling.

'This'll do. We'll wait for the others,' she whispered.

They waited.

There would be no difficulty in sinking her, just the four of them standing on one side would tip her, though an air lock in the cabin might cause a problem. The portholes would have to be opened.

She wasn't going to ask Gene to go in there, that might be asking for trouble, so she did it herself. She unbolted the door and stepped down.

The smell was worse than before.

She felt something soft and sticky with her bare foot and recoiled. There was no way she could reach the bunks and the portholes without stepping on that body, and she might leave a footprint on its shirt, in its blood, who knew? She grabbed hold of the top of the cabin door and swung herself in the void, getting a foothold on one of the bunks. It needed some agility, but she had that and was soon kneeling on the damp mattress trying to unfasten the porthole.

It was rusted up.

There were three on each side, all were solid, so there was only one way of doing it and that was by breaking the glass.

Suddenly the boat lurched and started listing heavily. If it sank she'd be trapped.

She didn't take any chances. Terrified of drowning in the cabin with that body floating around her neck, she stepped on its flaccid stomach and hurled herself forward out of the door.

Water was pouring over the sides and the cruiser was rocking, listing to port, turning.

'Abandon ship!' Gene hissed.

She didn't hesitate. When she heard the others diving off she clambered up on to the cabin roof and, holding her nose, jumped feet first into the warm, ink-black water.

She was alone.

Her orientation lost, she was frightened for a moment that the others might panic, but then she saw Gene to her right and Judd to her left.

'Where's Bonnie?'

'Over here!'

She'd looked at the *Water Fox*. The stern was way down under the water but the bows were up, the weight of the engine countered by the air in the cabin. They'd have to break those portholes.

Someone hissed behind her. It was Joleen in the flat-boat. All swam to her and hung on to the sides, survivors of a torpedoed liner, rescued by a sister ship.

'We have to break those portholes,' she whispered.

'I'll go.' It was Steve, and before she could stop him he was swimming to the wreck, and clambering on board.

They watched. His movements were not too clear in the dark, but there was enough light to see him kneeling on the cabin roof and over the side with the end of the paddle trying to smash the glass.

The first smack resounded, the second. Then the third was followed by the tinkling of broken glass.

He moved to the next one. Broke it first time. To the next one, which was tougher. He crossed to the other side. The cracking was duller, quicker, Steve putting all his energy behind every attempt.

Then suddenly there was a stifled scream followed by a splash. Steve disappeared and the cruiser, amidst a gush of air and swirling water turned right over on her side and sank below the surface.

It was quick. A matter of seconds. What had been there one moment disappeared the next. A whole little world, bunks, mattresses, washbasin, doors, brass fittings, engine, ropes, everything, everything went down, down into the deep black waters of the lake.

And she couldn't see Steve.

'Steve?'

No answer.

'Christ! Can anyone see him?'

Silence as everyone peered into the darkness.

Then a whistle, and the splashing of water. He was OK.

They waited, and spotted him, swimming towards them, pushing one of the paddles in front of him.

'There's a whole lot of junk floating up,' he said.

'Let's all get aboard the flatboat, then we'll have a clear up operation.'

They clambered on board one at a time, pulling themselves up and over at the stern on the little flat deck, then they paddled over to where the *Water Fox* had been, to haul in the flotsam.

Gene was sitting next to her and she glanced at him.

It was in his eyes, the same thought.

What if he came up?

What if one of the others grabbed hold of a wet hand, a limp arm?

But then he turned away and she realized he might be crying.

She had been pretty insensitive to everything he might have been feeling. After all, down there was his father. She patted him on the back, then squeezed his arm. 'We've got to find our paddles and the boathook, and scatter everything else that might have our fingerprints on it, so don't relax just yet, Gene, keep those big brown eyes of yours skinned for anything that's floating.'

chapter ten

Gene was on his own again, but not alone.

He belonged.

At last he belonged.

He was part of something, part of a group, he would be able to help them as much as they had helped him, and anything he did from now on which was exciting would be shared, with her and with the others.

The surprise was how nice they had been, how easily they had accepted him without question, and with apparent pleasure. They were really a great bunch of kids.

He padded about the house with nothing on, eating his peanut butter and pickle sandwich.

Four in the morning.

In just the one day he had got ten years older. That's how it felt. Suddenly he was his own boss, his own man. Every time he thought of doing something, anything, he first hesitated because his Dad would forbid it. Then he felt the tremendous relief of his new found freedom.

There was a tough time ahead, but it would be nothing

compared to what he had been through. And he was no longer alone! That was what was important. Fear could be shared, as well as joy.

He finished his sandwich staring out of the front room window at the deserted avenue, then decided to see how he felt facing himself with reality.

'It's going to take some getting used to,' Zuke had said. 'The best thing is to get him out of your system by forcing yourself to think of him. That's what I did when Dad left. For days I tried not to think about him at all, then one day I went the other way and touched everything that had belonged to him, made myself look at his photographs, I even put on some of his clothes.'

He went upstairs to his parents' bedroom. The bed was unmade. He got into it, lay down full length on his father's side, butted his head back against his father's pillow, and sniffed. Deliberately he inhaled the smell of the sheets, the smell of the bed.

It was there, the lingering odour of alcohol and scent, a mixture of them both.

Would his mother miss him?

Would he?

He got up, went to the bathroom and switched on the light, opened the cupboard above the washbasin and took out the electric razor, unclipped the head.

The powdery shavings of his late father's beard fell like a small cloud of dust on to the white porcelain. He never cleaned his razor, Ma did that for him once a month when she remembered.

Would she miss him?

He clicked the head back on to the razor, flicked the switch.

That brought him to life.

The noise. That particular sound. He held the vibrating razor up to his face and closed his eyes.

Already he had difficulty in remembering what he had looked like. The vision that haunted his mind was not his father, but the boat, that moment when it had suddenly turned over and sunk.

So quick.

He switched off and opened his eyes, put the razor back in the cupboard and left the bathroom. He should try to get some sleep but it wouldn't be easy. It had been some day!

They had nearly sunk the flatboat on the way back in their enthusiasm, he, Steve, Judd and Joleen, two paddles, two lengths of wood from the *Water Fox*. Red Indian shooting the rapids time, he couldn't remember what had got into him, a need maybe to get away. Only Zuke's sudden fury had stopped them, but they'd got a terrific speed up.

They'd had to bale out the flatboat with their hands.

He'd walked home alone, wearing only his jeans, swinging his T-shirt about his head, carrying his shoes. He had savoured his freedom realizing he'd be able to do almost anything he wanted from now on.

He got into bed, pulled the top sheet over himself and lay back. Imagine waking up in the morning and not being afraid, not having to sneak a look into the bedroom to see if he was asleep or awake or drunk or sober. It's the best thing he had done in his life.

Those tears on the lake had not been for Rick Prestianni. They had been for the *Water Fox* and all the good times he should have had aboard her but which had always been denied. They had been tears of exhaustion, of relief, and now he felt sleep coming in on him and let go, allowed himself to be overwhelmed, thankful that it was over. Tomorrow he would have to act the part of the innocent, the part of the concerned son, he would have to be in control. In his mind he went over the sequence of events which he would report had happened, a sequence he and Zuke had discussed right up to an hour ago sitting on the stairs of her house waiting for Angela Donoghue to come home. When they'd heard the car coming round the corner he'd left the house by the kitchen door, and Zuke had shot up to bed.

Shortly after midday he had left his father on board the

Water Fox in a drunken stupor, had come home, watched television, fed himself, waited, worried, had not known where to ring his mother, had gone to bed deciding his Pa would eventually come home. In the morning, when he woke up, he would go down to the lake to see if his father was still on board the cruiser, and the moment he discovered that the boat was missing but the car still there he would behave absolutely naturally, ask anyone around if they had seen his father then, maybe, show panic. What he would secretly have to observe was whether there were any signs of the *Water Fox* on the lake's surface.

With these thoughts circling his mind, he fell asleep, and when he awoke it was eight o'clock and the sun was shining.

He got up, went into his parents' room, found the bed unmade but not slept in, went downstairs expecting to find his father asleep on the sofa, as he was on some occasions, but there was no one there. He went into the kitchen, drank an orange juice, went back upstairs to dress, did not brush his teeth but went straight out of the house and walked off, into the morning sun, the way he had come back the night before, the way he knew, across the fields, across the bridge over the highway, and when he eventually reached the slope overlooking the boardwalk he half-expected to see a crowd of people lining the banks. But there was no one. Not a soul. Not even the *Water Fox*, nor any sign of her. Only the Lincoln parked where it had been parked before.

His father must have taken the cruiser over to Westcoat, and he realized he was slipping quite easily into the part.

The fisherman appeared, walking slowly out of the woods with his two rods and net and fishing tackle bag. Gene ran down the slope towards him.

'Excuse me,' he said anxiously. 'Do you know my father? Rick Prestianni, owns the *Water Fox*?'

'Yep. Not there this morning . . . wasn't in too good a shape to take out either . . .'

'Have you seen him?'

'Nope. Only just got here myself. I haven't seen no one.'

He walked along the north shore staring into the distance. There was no sign of any cruiser. He looked along the edge of the bank, but there was nothing.

Rick must have taken her across to Westcoat, it was the only explanation. He'd sailed her across the lake to Westcoat, met up with a drinking partner and probably slept on board. Should he walk the distance, or go home?

He decided to go home.

When he reached Cedar Avenue he saw Dan Mollman cleaning his windows.

'You haven't seen my father around, have you?' he shouted.

'No, Gene, I haven't. Has he gone missing?' There was a smile in the voice, the reminder that Rick Prestianni was always thought of as a bit of a joke in the community. 'When did you last see him?'

Gene walked up the path and told Dan Mollman his story.

'I expect he took the boat out to the other side of the lake and stayed the night there. Met some friends, had a few drinks . . . Have you been alone all night? Want some breakfast?'

So he had breakfast in the Mollman house, straight into the lion's mouth. Steve, as always, indifferent to what was going on around him, concentrated on the TV programme he was watching.

'If you're worried about your dad I can ring up the Westcoat Yacht Club, see if anyone's seen him around the Marina.'

'I guess he's OK,' Gene said.

No one would worry. Rick had his reputation.

'Will you two boys be all right? I've got to get along to the office. Lunch is in the ice box.'

'Why don't you drop us down by the lake on your way, Dad?' Steve suggested. 'We could wait for Mr Prestianni to come back.'

'If you want.'

So they drove over to the lake and Dan Mollman got out to check the Lincoln, then left them to their own devices getting Steve to promise he would go home for lunch, share the meal with Gene.

They sat on the edge of the boardwalk, their legs dangling over the water.

They threw pebbles, watched the fisherman cast his line, thought of going for a swim.

A few yards away a bottle bobbed up and down against the boardwalk post. It was a whisky bottle and Steve noticed it. 'Do you think your dad was on board the boat when we sank it?' he asked.

'That's sick,' Gene said. 'He'd have woken up anyhow,'

'Not if he was drunk.'

Gene shrugged his shoulders. 'We'll never know, will we?'

'No unless they bring her up.'

They remained silent for a while longer, then Steve piped up again. 'Your dad didn't come home last night, we know he couldn't have gone over to Westcoat, so where is he?'

'It was a no-question operation,' Gene said.

And Steve apologized, then suggested they should do something else because he was getting very bored.

They went home for lunch, hard-boiled eggs, finely chopped carrots and lettuce salad, cheese, ice cream. Gene then followed Steve to the old house and for the first time entered Fort Knox as a welcome guest.

Steve had found a message from Zuke summoning all members to headquarters, a simple piece of blue tissue stuck in a hole of the garage wall. Blue paper, he explained, was a summons to headquarters. They used different colours as codes and had found that people never removed tissues. They'd have to look for a message hole around his house somewhere, the shed at the back would probably provide a suitable crack.

It explained Zuke's entry at the back of the journal, the stock of tissues Gene had seen up in the attic. It was true, tissues were so commonplace that no one would think of removing a piece from anywhere in case someone had used it to blow their nose.

Upstairs they found Zuke sitting at a small portable typewriter tapping away with great concentration with one finger. Joleen, Bonnie and Judd were sitting on the floor watching her.

Zuke zipped the piece of paper out of the machine and read it through to herself, then she looked up and smiled. 'Hi, Gene!'

The others laughed. The oldest joke ever, 'hygiene', he must have heard it a thousand times, but somehow the laughs were nervous.

'I've told everyone your dad's dead,' Zuke said. 'Steve, you've just heard. Gene lost his dad, but no one else knows.'

'Was he on the boat when we sank it?'

'Yes, he was on the boat when we sank it.'

'Did we drown him?'

'No, he was already dead. Gene killed him by accident yesterday, but the police might call it murder, so we're covering for him. He's a Latchkey now.'

Gene wanted to hug her, hug them all, but Zuke didn't give him the chance.

'Did he have a typewriter at home, your old man?'

'Yes,' Gene replied.

'Do you know where it is?'

'Sure.'

'Good, then we'll go and type this out on it for you to give to your mom.'

'What is it?' Gene asked.

'A delaying tactic. It's a note from your father which will stop her looking for him immediately. I'll read it out.' She cleared her throat. 'Quote: I have had enough of the underdog life. I am going away to think of divorce. I will contact you when I have made up my mind. I have taken the boat to Westcoat Marina to sell. Signed Rick. Unquote. Does that sound like something he might have written to your mom?'

Gene shrugged his shoulders. 'Maybe?'

He didn't like it. He didn't like the idea of any note, typewritten or anything else. It's not the sort of thing his father would have done.

'You don't look happy, Gene.'

'Why would he abandon the car? If he was going away he'd take the car, not the old boat.'

'Good thinking. Why would he abandon the car, kids?'

'To leave it to Suzy, a kind of goodbye present?' Bonnie suggested.

Zuke looked at Gene for confirmation.

He shook his head. 'If he typed the letter at home he'd leave it at home. It all sounds a bit too planned for Dad. If he decided to leave, he'd just leave.'

'A note would delay things though,' Zuke pointed out. 'A delay would be good.'

'Why don't I just hint it to Mom?'

'How?'

'Say something like . . . Dad mentioned going over to Westcoat to sell the boat and not coming back for a while.'

'Could you handle that?'

'Sure. Why not? He was always making threats.'

'OK,' Zuke said, screwing up the paper. 'When will you say all this?'

'Best over the phone. I think I should ring her soon. I'd be kind of worried by now, not having heard from him.'

'So let's go ring her.'

He left first and waited for her in his own house, in his own front room, staring out of the window again at the familiar scene in Cedar Avenue, at the house opposite that always looked empty though people lived there, some of the time, at night anyway, when they got back from work.

Zuke took her time, then he saw her coming down the street holding a brown paper bag. She'd been shopping; if anyone was watching, her call at the house would seem like a chance one.

She came in, sat down cross-legged on the floor and brought out two cans of Coca Cola from the bag and a double carton of strawberry ice cream.

'Want some? Got any spoons?'

He got some spoons, a plate, put the phone on the floor between them and sat down. Before eating he would ring his mother. It would be the big test, it wasn't an instrument he used often.

He picked up the receiver and dialled the Fruit Canneries number.

'I'm Gene Prestianni,' he said to the operator. 'Do you know where I can contact my mother? It's urgent.'

'Hallo, Gene, hold on. I think I may have a number for her.'

He waited quite a time, then she came back to him.

'Have you a pen and paper? It's a Fresno number and it's a hotel. The Arbuthnot.'

He took it all down, and she even gave him the Fresno code.

'Is everything all right?' she asked.

I think so,' he said, managing to sound as though things weren't.

He next dialled the hotel.

'I'd like to speak to Mrs Suzy Prestianni please.'

'Is she a guest there, madam?'

He hated that. His high voice always had them calling him madam.

'Yes, I think so.'

'Hold the line please.'

A minute, maybe two, watching Zuke eating her ice cream.

'Hallo, madam, Mrs Prestianni is not in her room at present, would you like to leave a message for her?'

'Yes. Could you ask her to ring me as soon as possible.'

'Certainly, madam.'

And he nearly hung up, but the receptionist asked who might be calling.

'Gene, her son.'

'Does she have your number, sir?'

'I'm at home.'

'Very good, sir.'

He replaced the receiver and looked at Zuke again. 'She's not there.'

'So we wait. Want a Coke?'

He opened the can and took a sip.

'A lot of what's going to happen next is going to depend on your Mom, you know that?'

He nodded.

'Her reaction, her behaviour. If she panics it'll be more difficult for us. Do you think she'll panic?'

He shrugged his shoulders. They fell silent. Ate.

'Did I tell you that Mom got the sack because of my part in the Sam Finer trial?' Zuke said.

'No. Isn't she working then?'

'Oh she got reinstated, but she was fired. She never believed my story about the abduction. She went along with it because she thought she'd get something out of it, like you got the bicycle, but things didn't turn out that way. Avalon was split. Pro Sam Finers and Anti Sam Finers. When someone at the Greenhook said something about me being behind the whole thing and called me a lying little bitch, she came to my defence, or so she said. She came back one morning with her bags, sat down in the kitchen and accused me! "Because of you, Zuke, my sweetie pie, because of you," she said. "I heard the manager insult you saying that you were a bitch and only wanted attention, so I told him it was nothing of the sort and said a few things more which weren't too polite. All in front of customers. So here I am." Can you imagine? Holidays and Mom at home. It would have been unbearable, a real punishment. My whole freedom suddenly cut, her kitchen her domain reclaimed. But old man Greenhook himself rang and asked her back. Mothers are strange creatures. They behave most of the time as though they hated you, hated having had you, but the moment someone says something against you they really react. So lay it on that your dad was a bit mean yesterday morning. A bit violent, OK?'

It was beginning to be enjoyable.

It was beginning to be fun, life.

And Zuke was opening up.

'You know who tipped the balance against me over Sam Finer? Liz Kleiner.'

'She's trouble,' he said.

'I'm going to get my own back one day. She's really two-faced. "We're friends," she said to me. "Trust me". Thank God I never did. Everything I told her went straight back to the DA. "I know everybody thinks I fantasized about my abduction because my daddy left me," I told her. "But I didn't mind Daddy leaving home," I lied. "I was pleased," I said. "You see, he used to paint me. He used to stand me up naked in the bath and paint me different colours. My arms red, my legs blue, my bum green. I didn't like that," I told her. And it went straight back to the DA.'

He wasn't sure whether it was true.

'He didn't really paint you, did he?' he asked.

"Course not, dummy. It was just a story for old Kleiner to lap up. Great stuff for parent psychologists. Crazy! The DA got really concerned, asked me what colour Dad had last used. So I told him I'd made it all up to throw Kleiner, and that threw him. I think maybe that's why he gave up.'

The phone rang and Gene reached out for it.

'Hallo?'

'Gene, did you ring me?'

'Yes, Mom.'

'Oh God, what's happened? Is Rick there?'

'No . . .'

'Where is he?'

'I don't know . . . . well that is . . .'

'You OK honey? He hasn't hurt you or anything?'

The concern was there, the guilt at leaving him alone with the ogre.

'I'm OK. It's just he didn't come home last night.'

'He didn't? Do you know where he went?'

And he told her the story, as rehearsed.

'Was he drunk?'

'Kind of . . .'

There was a big sigh at the other end.

'Have you been back to the boat?'

'Yes. It isn't there.'

'What do you mean it isn't there?'

'The boat's gone. The car's still there, but the boat's gone.'

'You think he went out in the boat then?'

'He must have. He said something about . . . about . . .'

'About what, Gene? What did he say to you?'

She was gentle, persuasive, concerned.

'He was mad at me for doing something to the pump, you know how he gets, and said something about going to Westcoat to sell the damn boat, but not coming back. Ever. He said . . . he'd had enough of me . . . and you.'

There was a long silence at the other end, a silence from her but not behind her. She was in a room with someone else, and he held the receiver up to Zuke's ear for her to listen.

She came on again.

'OK, Gene. Obviously your Dad's on one of his moods I'm quite some distance from Avalon and I'm not sure what to do. How did you manage last night?'

'I'm OK by myself, Mom. I can look after myself.'

'What of Zuke next door? Can you get some help from her or her mother?'

'Sure, if you'll allow me to.'

'Well I guess that if your father's decided to take off I've no objections.' There was a pause, then she asked, 'Gene, did he by chance load the boat up with his booze?'

'I dunno.'

'Would you like to go have a look see, count the number of boxes left in the shed. It is important.'

'Sure, will you hang on?'

'No. Take your time, count them carefully and ring me back. Better still I'll ring you. I'll ring you in ten minutes.'

'OK, Mom . . .'

And the line went dead.

Zuke had heard most of it and was frowning.

'We hadn't thought of that. If your father intended going for a cruise somewhere he'd have taken his booze, that's for sure. How many cases are there?'

He went to see.

Walking down the garden path reminded him of the rabbit, and the rabbit reminded him of the bicycle. He'd never see either again. He'd never see quite a lot of things, smashed plates, broken bottles hurled against walls, would never hear rows again.

He counted the cases of whisky. Out of the twelve that had come in there were ten left. He went back to tell Zuke.

'He'd take at least three on a trip, wouldn't he? If he hid them in the boot of the car, he'd take three. How the hell do we get rid of three cases of whisky?'

'Pour them down the pan.'

'Sure. The contents is easy, but what about the bottles? Thirty-six whisky bottles? No easy matter. They'd really be traceable. The cardboard boxes can be burned, but the bottles?'

'Break them up on the dump, in the Folly garden,' he suggested. 'Bury them?'

'We have to think this one out carefully. There are seven of us . . . seven fives are thirty-five, plus one . . . Could we each take care of five bottles without being noticed?'

'Round the back of Joe's bar there's a dump. Hundreds of bottles!'

'Right! We can get rid of some there, the others we drop in other people's bins.'

The phone rang.

'Seven cases left, Gene,' Zuke said. 'Seven.'

He picked up the receiver. 'Mom?'

'Yes, Gene. Did you go and have a look?'

'Seven cases left.'

She sighed. Was it a sigh of relief because it meant he was on a planned trip and nothing serious had happened, or was it relief that he had just gone?

'Do you think you could stay with Zuke tonight, Gene? You see I'm at this conference and there's an important meeting tonight . . .'

'I'm sure I can. They're always asking me over.'

'Tell you what, Gene, ask Angela Donoghue to ring me collect at the hotel when she gets home, OK?'

'OK.'

'And look after yourself sweetie, Mommy loves you.'

'Mom?' Gene said, just before she could hang up. 'Where do you think Dad's gone?'

'I guess he's just taken a break. He'll probably turn up tomorrow. Tonight even?'

'What if he does and finds me at Zuke's?'

'I'll deal with that, Gene. Ask Angela to ring me, and don't worry, it's just Dad being Dad when he's had a few too many I expect. OK?'

'OK, Mom.'

And the line went dead.

Zuke was staring at him, smiling at him.

'Did you get the feeling she was with someone?'

'Maybe.'

'Why is she in Fresno?'

'A conference. Something to do with the Canneries.'

'Got the number of the hotel?'

He handed her the name and number. 'What are you going to do?'

She didn't answer.

He watched her dial.

'Hallo. Is that the Arbuthnot Hotel?'

He listened, unable to hear the answers.

'I'm trying to contact someone attending the Fruit Canneries Conference,' she said, then held the receiver up.

'I'm sorry, miss. What conference?'

'The Fruit Canneries Conference.'

'No, miss. We have no conference here. We have no conference hall. This is a country club hotel. May I suggest you try the Roeding Hotel.'

'Thanks,' she said, and hung up.

Gene made a face, not understanding.

'Your Mom never went to a conference, Gene, she's shacking up with some guy, which is why she's in no hurry to get back to you. That's how much she cares for her lovey-dovey son.'

And Gene felt a little emptiness in his stomach, a sense of insecurity again, and he was very pleased when Zuke patted him on the back and smiled.

'Cheer up, kid. You're staying with us and we've got to get hold of the others. There are thirty-six bottles of booze to get rid of – and we have to do it by morning!'

And with remarkable speed and efficiency she organized him and Dillon to get the other Latchkeys to come round to the house. When it was dark they moved the three cases of whisky from Gene's shed to Zuke's kitchen, poured the contents of the bottles down the sink, then each took a similar number to the four corners of Avalon where their emptiness would not be noticed.

Gene now entered a phase of happiness he had never experienced before. He became, for several days, the complete centre of his mother's attention. She was sweet and kind and considerate and made a great effort to look after him. She sorted out his clothes and bought him new ones, she helped him tidy up his room and throw out a lot of junk that he no longer wanted, she took him to the Canneries one day so that he would not be alone at the house and allowed him to sit down behind her desk and play with the computer she worked, even taking him into the boss's office where Mr McQuare proudly gave him a publicity brochure about the fruit orchards around Avalon.

Back home Suzy sat with him and watched the programmes he wanted to watch and answered all his questions without questioning them herself. Over meals she talked casually about his father, allaying any fears he might have that she was unhappy about his departure, convincing herself that Rick had found another woman, presumably rich, who was looking after all his needs and that as she had not found the *Water Fox* at the Westcoat marina he had actually sold it and it was in some boatyard for repairs.

As Gene listened to her he realized that he was believing every word she was saying, that is, believing every word that she was believing, for all her information was based on the assumption that Rick had left her, left them with no intention of returning.

She invited Angela Donoghue over for drinks and both discussed divorce at length, and the difficulties they had as Latchkey mothers, balancing duty towards employers and duty towards their homes, their constant fear of the children having accidents, the nagging guilt of not sharing their lives.

Angela Donoghue suggested that Gene should come over and stay, sleep in Dillon's room if he wished, there were two bunk beds. Having three children in the house looking after each other would make little difference, even help, and if Suzy contributed for Gene's upkeep she would then be free of the worry of him being alone during the day and any of the nights she had to work late.

So Zuke and Dillon helped him move his stuff across, a few vital toys, his clothes, his toothbrush, and just before she left for work on the first day of their separation, his mother hung the latchkey of the front door round his neck, making him promise never to take it off, and certainly never to lose it. He fingered the green cord with which the key was tied, he fingered the key, and made a great effort to remind himself what it had cost, but somehow the guilt never matured. Rick Prestianni had disappeared beneath the surface of Lake Avalon with his throat cut and it had nothing to do with him.

Suzy, in fact, dropped into the Donoghue house most evenings that first week, then she started staying away nights, not telling him where but just satisfying his curiosity with the story that Avalon Fruit Canneries were opening up their own supermarket chains soon and she had a great deal of public relations work to do.

From somewhere Zuke acquired a video machine, telling her mother it was borrowed from a friend, and from somewhere else she got a succession of tapes. Afternoons, therefore, were spent in the Donoghue living room viewing with the other Latchkeys, Joleen, Bonnie, Judd, Steve and Dillon. Most of the films were pretty boring, adult movies of naked men and women licking each other between the legs and grunting a lot. There was never any action and it didn't interest him too much, but now and again Zuke got a fantastic tape, violent to a degree that really scared him, detailed murders and decapitations with so much blood that Dillon jokingly put a bucket under the TV set before running 'The Jackhammer Massacre' for the third time.

He was aware that Zuke often watched his reaction to these movies with interest. Whenever someone cut someone else up, she always glanced sideways at him to see if he would flinch or shut his eyes. But there was no relation between what he saw on the screen and what he had done. Movies always led you up to the bloodshed, the carnage, the butchery, they geared you in advance, made you look forward to the horror.

It wasn't like that in real life.

There wasn't any music for a start.

He hadn't heard thundering drums or screeching violins when he had picked up the knife.

Real murder was not exciting at all.

Just messy.

chapter eleven

Zuke convened a meeting at Fort Knox to swear Gene in as a full Latchkey member.

Normally this ceremony followed immediately on a task set by members and was followed by a swearing in, but the act of killing his own father in order to become a Latchkey was deemed sufficient proof of future loyalty and valour, so it was now a simple matter of ritual.

Zuke had read, in a book entitled *The Forbidden Garden*, a certain passage she had sensed was the key to the unity that some adult couples possessed. It was obviously something to do with sex, but it also had to do with knowing people and dropping all inhibitions. Inhibitions made you shy and shyness led to all sorts of communication problems. The passage, which she knew by heart, read:

> I used to wonder what my friends and
> acquaintances looked like naked till
> I went to a nudist colony and learned
> that it didn't matter.

So she had insisted that the Latchkey ritual should be performed with all the members stark naked.

It was to embarrass, to force the newcomer to be known, and to know that he was known, it was to get rid of all inhibitions between themselves. The younger ones didn't care, but it was hard on the older ones who were naturally shy, and she herself did not find her own ruling that comfortable, but afterwards, apart from the unadmitted thrill, the excitement that always pervaded the body, all agreed that it was good.

To overcome the embarrassment of undressing, she had devised a moment in the ritual when they all stood in a circle holding hands then, on a nod from her, took off their clothes together. It was forbidden to close your eyes and it was forbidden to look away. You had to look at each other and get to know the fellow members visually. Then everyone kneeled down to drink a loving cup of natural Avalon fruit juice, which symbolized their purity.

To her surprise, Dillon was late.

Gene, Joleen, Bonnie, Steve and Judd all more or less came together but Dillon, who should have come early to help her prepare the room, clear the carpet where they would form the ritual circle, was late.

She had left him at the house with Gene that morning, had gone shopping for the fruit juice, then come straight to the secret attic. She had written up her journal, taken notes from it for the meeting, and the members had arrived.

After a half hour of waiting she decided to go ahead without him. Something or someone might have delayed him, she was quite sure Dillon had not forgotten or would ever think of opting out.

They all formed the circle, Gene opposite Zuke, held hands, and when she nodded they all took off their clothes.

To her surprise Bonnie had developed quite a lot since the last ritual, much more than herself, and so had Steve who, for a boy of his age was surprisingly well equipped. Gene was in a state of semi-excitement, blushing to the roots of his hair, but he soon got over it and when they started chanting, very quietly, and then knelt to drink the loving cup, he managed to look across the circle at her and smile.

At the end of the ceremony he was presented with the Latchkey cord, made by Joleen from a leather thong, on which Zuke threaded his latchkey, before hanging it round his neck.

They got dressed, sat down again in the circle, and Zuke was about to start on her notes but admitted that she was worried about her brother. It was so unlike him that she suggested she should go and check up at the house to see if anything unusual had happened.

At the house she found no sign of him. His bed was unmade, there was an open book on the pillow, his clothes had gone, it was as though he had left in his usual dreamy mood. She asked Grandma Olsen if she had seen him; she had not, and Zuke returned, concerned, to Fort Knox.

The meeting, she decided, would have to be postponed. It could not take place without all members being present, and now she thought it urgent that Dillon should be found.

She designated areas to each member for a search and told them to meet back at her house at six, or make contact by phone the moment he showed up. If there was no news of him by then she would first contact her mother, then the hospital, then the police.

Back home, alone, she had a bad time.

Her imagination went quite wild, so wild that she found herself having to rush to the lavatory to be sick, cramped with stomach pains, her guts reduced to jelly. In wild flashes she saw Dillon under a bus, under a car, swimming in the lake and drowning, perhaps misunderstanding the venue of the meeting and going to the woods where they sometimes went, falling down a disused well, her own worst fear, a subsidence, to be knocked unconscious and waking up among snakes and spiders and worms, unable to get out, unable to see.

Had he got trapped somewhere? Gone for one of his adventures and found another derelict house where a wall had collapsed on him?

She held her hands out and saw the tips of her fingers shaking. She was cold with fear, the sheer fear of losing the only person she really loved.

She went to his room and felt the tears welling up in her eyes as she looked at the posters he had stuck up on his walls. No Batman or Superman or Darth Vader or some pop idol for Dillon, he had a map of the world, a portrait of Albert Einstein and a history chart of his own making listing the names of those prominent in the Civil War.

If she lost him as well as her father, life would become unbearable.

At six all the Latchkeys assembled with nothing to

report. No one had seen Dillon, no one had heard from him, so Zuke picked up the phone and rang her mother at the Greenhook Chalet Motel.

The conversation was a strange one.

Her mother did not seem very surprised that Zuke was ringing her, though she very seldom did, but where she did react, indeed over-react, was on hearing that Dillon had been missing since the morning.

'You don't think he could have been abducted, do you?' she asked. And it sounded so false, so rehearsed even, that Zuke instinctively got the feeling that maybe, maybe, the whole thing had been set up.

'I think we should call the police,' Zuke said. 'Or at least the hospital.'

'Well wait till I get home, honey, let me think about it a little. I'll come right away.'

Think about it a little or talk about it a little to whoever else was involved?

Was she being too imaginative? Was she crediting the adults with more cunning than they had? But wouldn't it be a wonderful way to crack the Latchkeys, kidnap one of them and see the reaction of the others? It would mean that someone somewhere was suspicious of all the events that had taken place in Avalon, that someone was actually working things out.

Zuke said nothing of her suspicions to anyone, but waited patiently for her mother to turn up. When she did, she was so surprised to find all Zuke's friends in the house that she forgot, for the first few vital minutes, to be more concerned about her son's disappearance than why such a reunion was taking place. Then, when she remembered Dillon, she went over the top.

Zuke knew her mother when she was acting, and she was acting now. The sooner she got the kids out and away and arranged to see them by themselves later, the better. She was convinced it was a trick, and she would have to go along with it till she found out who had dreamed it up. It certainly could not be her mother. She wouldn't have known where to begin, let alone understand the subtlety of giving anyone a bit of their own medicine to unsettle them so that they would drop their guard.

It was going to be stimulating.

There would be signs, all sorts of signs to show whether Dillon's disappearance was genuine or not. If it were, her mother would have to be at the centre of the plot, but having taken on this responsibility, possibly at the instigation of the police, she was now going to find that she had bitten off more than she could chew. Her actions would be as clear as crystal, she'd read her like an open book.

Angela Donoghue's performance went from bad to worse, and she made the major error of mentioning abduction again, in such an obvious way, that it pained Zuke to think she must have inherited some characteristics from her.

'I know that Sam Finer isn't around anymore,' said her mother, as though she had given it a great deal of thought. 'But do you think . . . if he has come back . . . that to get his revenge he might have kidnapped Dillon?'

What was she playing at? Had a group of adults decided on a plan of campaign to get her to admit that the whole SF Operation had been her doing?

'Revenge for what?' Zuke asked.

'Accusing him . . .'

'He was guilty, Mom.'

'But it was never proved.'

It might be the defence lawyer still trying to clear his client's name? Then came a ploy which had been well thought out.

'I'd rather go see the Sheriff, Zuke, speak to them myself. I don't like talking on the phone, it's too impersonal. So I'm going along to the station. Do you mind stopping here while I'm out, in case the phone rings with news of Dill?'

That was how she got out of calling the police, of getting

involved with the authorities. But dear Mom had forgotten Gene.

As she went out, dressed up a little too colourfully for the mission, young Prestianni came in, kicking his heels and looking a lot sadder about the missing child than its mother.

'I want the police station watched,' she said to him when they were alone. 'I want to know if Mom's really going there. She's taken the car so it should be parked in the area. If not, hang around. I think Dill's disappearance may be a set up to draw us out.'

She sat down on the porch steps and waited.

Her mother came back soon, mistiming how long a chat with the police would take. Where had she gone? For a drive? Got bored by herself? Made a call to Mr and Mrs Mystery?

Half an hour later Gene returned, still kicking his heels and looking forlorn. A better actor.

Zuke was in the kitchen, watching her mother peeling onions, a vegetable she seldom used but today chose in order to make her eyes red and watery.

She couldn't talk to Gene, couldn't communicate immediately, but eventually they found themselves alone, upstairs in Dillon's room.

'She never went to the police station, I saw the car parked outside the Armaflex offices, saw her come out of there too.'

Dan Mollman worked from there, and Dan Mollman would have the brains to dream up something.

That night she found she could not sleep. Visions of something horrible happening to Dillon haunted her, the adults' abduction plan failing, going terribly wrong and him getting hurt. What would he do without his books? Did they know what he liked to eat? She was being stupid, the details hardly mattered, but they had never been separated before, ever.

Then an unexpected give-away disturbed the middle of the night. Her mother snoring. Two o'clock, the house silent, the streets outside silent, but in the room next door, her mother snorting in dreamland.

Zuke got up.

She went into the room, made quite a lot of noise, put on the main light and watched the slumber of the untroubled, the contented. Though her mother might be indifferent to her children most of the time, she wouldn't be that unconcerned if Dillon had truly vanished. The light woke her up.

'What's happening?'

'I couldn't sleep,' Zuke said.

'Why not? . . .' Then she remembered. 'You want to come in the bed with me?'

It wasn't her favourite place, her mother slept across the bed, legs everywhere, but things might be said in the intimate darkness that could cast light on what was happening.

It was strange to be hugged, suddenly, by a mother who hadn't hugged her since Dill was born.

'What do you think could have happened to him?' she asked.

'I don't know, honey. The thing is to try and get some sleep so we can be fresh in the morning and have enough energy to cope when we hear if it's serious.'

Wasn't it serious now? Not knowing?

When the other Latchkeys had disappeared every household had been up all night, countless nights, the whole town had known. The abduction of another boy now, and nobody seemed to care. Not even Dan Mollman had come round to sympathize. Wasn't that strange? They did not understand that the give-aways were not what you did, but what you did not do.

They were fools.

And her mother, instead of tossing and turning, or chain smoking, or getting herself a drink, just turned over and went to sleep again.

Some abduction!

*

Joleen called the next morning while they were preparing breakfast. She wanted to know if there had been any news. At least that was the up front excuse.

Zuke was cautious, took her time before easing her out of the kitchen and up the stairs to her room.

'What?'

'He rang.'

'Dillon?'

'Yes.'

'Where is he?'

'Talpona.'

'Where the hell's that?' She had never heard of it.

'What did he say?'

'Nothing much, he didn't have time. Just . . . "It's Dill, tell Zuke I'm OK. I'm in Talpona . . ." And he hung up.'

She went to Dillon's room, looked along the line of books on his shelf, found the National Geographic mapbook of California. Talpona wasn't in the index. Either it was too small to be in such an edition, or it wasn't in California.

It was blue tissue time. A meeting at the Knox as soon as possible.

And they were all there in half an hour.

'We've heard from Dillon,' Zuke told them, aware that she was over excited, really keyed up. 'He rang Joleen this morning from a place called Talpona.'

'That's where my uncle lives!' Steve piped up.

'Your *uncle*?'

'Yep. Dad's brother. He has a farm out there.'

'Where is it, for God's sake?'

'Near Reno, Nevada.'

It fitted. Confirmation that the enemy was Dan Mollman.

'Think your dad could be behind Dill's abduction, Steve?'

Steve gave it some thought.

'Could be,' he said after a while. 'But why?'

'Dill's the youngest of us, your dad might think he could get him to talk in isolation?'

'He's been reading screwy kind of books lately,' Steve admitted.

'What kind of books?'

'Books on children. Psycho stuff . . . He usually reads about cops and detectives.'

Dan was a strange man, a bigot, with narrow-minded views on how children should behave and be brought up.

Zuke disbanded the group and asked them all to be on the lookout for developments. If she could she was going to blow Dan Mollman's little plot, she was going to expose it to get Dillon back as soon as possible.

The evening gave her an opening for a good move. Dan Mollman had not calculated on her mother's poor acting. She was just unable to keep up the supposed worry. For one thing there was obviously something going on at the motel that night, as she dressed up and left Zuke and Gene alone at the house again with the request to stay by the phone in case news came through of Dillon. It was so ridiculous that she decided to act.

Leaving Gene by the phone, she borrowed Bonnie's bicycle and made her way across town to the Greenhook Chalet Motel where a party was in full swing, a band, adults dancing, drinking, generally behaving like assholes.

She found her mother serving drinks behind the bar surrounded by friends and hotel clients.

She waited till one of them had finished telling a joke before stepping forward so that she could be seen.

'Zuke! What are you doing here?' Guilt, anger at being found enjoying herself. It registered in the eyes, in the twist of the lips.

'I've found Dillon.'

'*What*?' Complete amazement. It made no sense.

'He rang up. He's with Steve Mollman's uncle, said he'd been there all the time, and that you knew.'

Confusion. No joy at hearing her lost little boy had been found. Just confusion.

'Excuse me,' she said to everyone, flustered. 'This is my

daughter. A slight domestic problem, wouldn't you know?'

The women were slightly interested, the men slightly peeved, making way for her as though she were a leper. Children were not in their scene.

'Can you tell me that again, Zuke?' her mother asked, moving to a dark, quiet corner.

'Dillon rang, says he's at Steve Mollman's uncle's place in Talpona, and that you know he's there.'

'How could I know?' She was clearly in an impossible situation, had no idea how to play for time, was incapable of improvising. 'Well, I know he was invited there,' she tried. 'But I didn't know he'd actually gone.' Then inspired, 'He must have left with Steve.'

'Mom! You're talking about Dillon, your own son for Chrissake! Steve's been here all the time. If you knew Dill had gone there why didn't you *tell* me?'

'It's a very long story, Zuke and I can't tell you now. I promise to explain everything in the morning. This is a business party and I have to entertain the guests.'

She could make it worse, become really difficult, or help her mother out.

'OK,' she said. 'It's kind of a relief though, isn't it?'

'Of course it is, honey. Of course it is.'

'I'll go home then,' Zuke said.

And she headed for the main lobby entrance aware that her mother wasn't going back to the bar but to the offices. She hadn't asked how she had got to the hotel, she hadn't suggested accompanying her back, she had no motherly interests in her at all. Angela Donoghue was all unaware selfishness, never really thinking about anyone but herself or her immediate surroundings or what she wanted to do.

Zuke left, walked across the pink neon lit car park to her bicycle down the short driveway. She cycled off, then stopped and turned into the bushes. Dropping the bike on the grass she stole back through the undergrowth.

She knew the layout of the motel more or less. The offices were round the side, on a night like this all the windows would be open. She skirted the pool where several people were swimming, made her way behind a line of suites to the yard where the kitchens spilt out their bottles and garbage. She saw her mother now, quite clearly, standing in her office, phone to her ear, ringing Dan Mollman, no doubt.

She crept up to the window, ducked under it and listened, but by the time she got there the conversation was over. She moved back into the shadows to observe.

Her mother didn't leave the office. Instead she lit a nervous cigarette and paced the floor, up and down, back and forth. What was going on in her head? What was she so worried about?

Lying to her own sweet little daughter or letting Dan Mollman down, screwing the whole thing up by not knowing what to say? That's what it would be. 'You must have given it away!' That's what would really worry her, the thought that Mollman might think her unreliable. It would all reflect on her. Everything always had to reflect on her. Her, her, her.

Zuke got back to the bicycle and started pedalling home. It was a warm night, she felt pleasantly carefree.

As she got to the end of Cedar Walk and turned the corner into the Avenue, the lights of a car parked ahead came on, dazzling her.

When she drew level with it a shadowy figure stepped out and signalled her to stop.

It was Dan Mollman himself.

'No lights, Zuleika, on a major road. That's dangerous.'

'Hi, Mr Mollman,' she said. 'Not my bike.'

'Your mother just rang, said you'd heard from Dillon.' His tone was severe, intimidating.

'That's right.'

'He rang you?'

'That's right, from Talpona where your brother lives.'

'Who told you that, Steve?'

'No, Dillon told me.'

Dan Mollman was clearly upset.

'Did he tell you anything else?'

'Nope. He just said I think I've been abducted, but don't know why.'

'I think you're making this up, Zuke. I don't think Dillon rang you up at all.'

'How come I know he's in Talpona then?'

'I'm not sure that you do.'

Zuke shrugged her shoulders.

'I'll walk you home, Zuke, I think we need to talk.'

She got off the bicycle and wheeled it on to the pavement where he joined her.

'Did Dillon ring you?' he asked, more gently, but with some insistence.

'No.'

'So how do you know he's there?'

'Would you believe I'm psychic?'

Her humour irritated him. 'I am aware that you kids have some very clever way of communicating, but I don't think you're psychic.'

Zuke said nothing. She wasn't sure why he couldn't believe Dillon had rung. Was the phone hidden away, or cut off or something?

'Did Steve tell you he was there?'

'I don't think Steve knows.'

He was worried that his own son had spied on him.

'Why won't you believe that Dill rang me, Mr Mollman?'

'Because he has no access to any telephone.'

'So he is there.'

'Yes, he is there.'

'Why?'

Dan Mollman took a deep breath, let it out through a long sigh.

'A lot of strange things have been happening in this town this summer and I've come to the conclusion that in one way or another they're connected with you.'

'How come?'

'You're the leader of a gang, Zuleika, everyone knows that.'

'What gang?'

'The Latchkids.'

'I don't know what you mean, Mr Mollman.'

'Children talk you know. Bonnie, Joleen, Kathie, they're not as loyal to you as you think.'

They made such errors, adults. They were always making errors. Kathie? What had she to do with it? Kathie Stone? Her mother hung a latchkey round her neck, but that didn't make her a member. They lumped everyone together. Poor Kathie Stone wasn't bright enough to be part of the group, but she said nothing.

'You'd like your brother home, Zuleika?'

'Of course I'd like him home.'

'You like your kid brother?'

'Certainly more than my mother does.'

He picked on that, stopped and turned to face her.

'Is that what it's all about? Revenge against your mother?'

She was in the hands of an amateur child psychologist. She'd be able to tell him anything.

'What revenge?'

'Sam Finer, Zuke. Why did you accuse him? What did he ever do to you?'

'I don't know what you mean.'

'You can have your brother back tomorrow if you tell me why you accused Sam Finer of abducting Steve.'

At least he was coming out in the open. He had taken Dillon from her, with her mother's knowledge, in order to bargain. He had taken Dill away from *her*, no one else.

'Sorry, I don't know what you're talking about, Mr Mollman.'

'I think you were responsible for putting those kids in Sam Finer's safe, Zuke. I also think you are responsible for Rick Prestianni's disappearance.'

She let her jaw drop open. The amazement in her expression was genuine and it helped cover her sudden concern.

Had she made a major mistake, somewhere?

'I had a long session with Sam Finer after his release, Zuleika, and he remembered you, you know. He remembered employing you, and giving you the key to his back gate. He also remembered you giving him the key back, but the wrong one, the copy you had made secretly because you kept the original by mistake.'

'I don't remember anything about that, Mr Mollman. I don't remember anything about any key. I don't know what you're talking about.'

She wheeled the bicycle up the garden path and leaned it against the wall.

'You're the only one who could have known anything about the inside of the Old Bank, Zuleika. And his birthmark. You could have spotted that one day when he was in the bathroom. He says he's never been particular about closing doors.'

She just stared at him, wide-eyed, waiting for more.

'As to Gene's father, I'm the only one in town who thinks this, but I don't believe he sailed his boat across the lake. I believe you kids did, and sank it, and you were so scared of him that you've locked him up somewhere too.'

'How d'you figure all that out, Mr Mollman?'

Dillon couldn't have talked. Even if he had been tortured he wouldn't have talked. The man was just thinking things out correctly, that was all. Or nearly.

Dan Mollman took a deep breath to expand his chest and make himself taller, make her feel smaller. What he was about to tell her was clearly going to impress.'

'The lake water smells, did you know that, Zuleika? It has a stagnant smell. People in my profession are trained to recognize smells, and I recognized the lake smell in Steve's damp clothing one morning. The morning after Rick Prestianni's boat happened to disappear.'

'And you think we sank it and are keeping Gene's father locked up somewhere?'

'That's what I reckon, Zuleika.'

It was pretty good. It was imaginative. Wrong, but imaginative.

'I don't know anything about the boat or Mr Prestianni, Mr Mollman,' Zuke said, going up the front porch step. 'But maybe the Spiders do.'

'What spiders?'

She'd put some distance between them and was now standing above him.

'The Spider Club,' she said. 'Kathie Stone . . . I'm not a member. It's a secret society though.'

He was staring at her, frowning, trying to gauge her honesty, her integrity.

'They meet at the Web,' she added.

'What web?'

'That's what they call it, but I don't know where it is. They have these meetings, these rituals.'

'Who?'

He was really hooked. He was about to crack the hard nut at last.

'Who you said. Kathie Stone and others.'

'Is Steve a member?'

'I reckon.'

He looked down. Perhaps he'd got it wrong. Perhaps it had nothing to do with her. His doubts were written all over his face.

'OK, Zuleika. Go to bed now, but make sure the doors are locked first.'

She went in, closed the door, ran to the sitting room window and watched him walk back to his car.

The Spiders and their Web!

She'd work on it. They all would.

Dillon was delivered to the front doorstep the following afternoon looking none the worse for wear.

Angela Donoghue was at work, having departed earlier in the morning than usual in order to avoid Zuke and Gene. On the kitchen table she had left a note, 'Dillon will be back today, Love Mom.'

When he arrived, driven in from Talpona by Dan Mollman's brother, Zuke and Gene sat him down in the kitchen, handed him a strawberry milkshake and grilled him. How, when, why, where, who . . . all at once, unable to control their eagerness to know everything.

'Cool it you guys, I'll tell it to you from the top if you just listen!'

And they had to wait while he sucked the pink milk slowly up the straw, taking his time and making a great deal of noise just to annoy them.

'OK. It was like this. I was on my way to the Knox, down the Avenue, when Dan Mollman drew level with me in his silver satin limousine. It was a beautiful day, the sun was shining . . .'

'Cut the weather report, Dill, let's just have the facts,' Zuke requested.

'OK. So he leaned out of the window and told me that Mom had something for me at the motel, a kind of surprise. The way he said it, it sounded as though it were a present or even . . .' and he hesitated. 'Or even . . .'

'Even what?' Zuke asked, puzzled.

'I dunno, Zuke. The way he said Mom had a surprise, I guess I thought Dad might have come back. I asked where you were and he said you might be there too. That's why I went. I wouldn't have gone otherwise.'

He fell silent, as was his habit, thinking over what he had just said, working out whether he had got it right. She always had to urge him to go on.

'Go on, Dill.'

'Well, when I got to the motel, Mom was there waiting for me on the doorstep and she said I was going to stay for a few days on a farm, Steve's uncle's farm. I asked why and she said there was a surprise there waiting for me, not to ask questions but just to go with Dan. I asked if you would be going and she just said "maybe".'

'How was she when you asked that? Worried, nervous?' He fell silent again, thinking, considering the question, recalling the moment.

'I got the idea she wanted to get rid of me. Wanted the

moment to be over. Like she is with meals, you know? Let's get this over.'

'What happened after that?'

'Dan Mollman took me for this long drive. Really long drive. I didn't think we were going to go that far. Jesus I thought it would never end. Then we got to this farm which was real nice. A ranch.'

'And what was the surprise?'

'A pony.'

'For you? A present?'

'Not exactly. They just said it was mine while I was there.'

'How did you feel about that?'

'Shitty. It was then I started to think I'd been got down there for a reason, but a girl took care of me, a niece of Dan's I think and she showed me around. It was big. They had twelve horses, a lot of cattle, pigs, snakes even in a special cage, but they didn't have any books, you know that? I couldn't find a book anywhere.'

It didn't surprise Zuke. The adults hadn't thought it out, hadn't considered the needs of the boy at all. Abduct a kid of eight whose main interest in the whole wide world is reading, and his mother didn't think of providing him with a book. If they had settled him in a corner with just two new books they wouldn't have had any trouble from him for hours.

'The girl, what was she like?'

'Sixteen. Pretty dumb. I asked her if she had something to read and she gave me a romance magazine about this doctor who hates this nurse but she makes him fall in love with her because he's got curly red hair. They didn't even have a Reader's Digest!'

'Did they lock you up? Stop you doing anything?'

'No, they never made me feel I was a prisoner. I was free to do what I wanted.'

'But Mollman left?'

'He stayed the rest of the day, went back in the evening.'

'What did he say to you, what reason did he give for you being there?'

'No reason. Well, just a break before school started because neither of us had been anywhere this summer. That's when I twigged it must be a trick. He said Mom had decided to surprise you with a trip to Disneyland.'

'What?' She couldn't believe it. 'Why would I want to go to Disneyland? And without you? You might want to go to Disneyland, but why me?'

Dillon shrugged his shoulders. 'Guess they couldn't dream up anything better. Mom was going to take you to Disneyland as a surprise, it was an expensive trip and only one of us could go, and as I was interested in horses they thought that I'd like it better on the farm.'

'Where do they get goofy ideas like that?'

It really depressed her. Just what went on in her mother's head? Dillon interested in horses! He hadn't shown interest in animals, ever.

'Why horses, Dill? You've never even been near a horse.'

'*Black Beauty* I guess, Zukie. Remember *Black Beauty*? That edition Dad gave me? I used to carry it around with me all day long, even took it to school with me and slept with it under my pillow.'

'But that was over two years ago.'

'Mom isn't too observant.'

'The telephone was the other joke,' Dillon went on. 'They hid it, or tried to. I mean, as soon as I got to the house I asked if I could ring you up to tell you where I was, and they said they weren't on the phone. I mean . . . for something like five miles we'd driven along this dirt track along which the only thing to do was count the telegraph poles!'

'Where was the phone?'

'In a cupboard under the stairs. They just didn't think I'd look. All I had to do was trace the wires from the outside into the hall.'

'Why did you ring Joleen?'

'By then I didn't think it was safe to ring you. Joleen was first on the list.'

'What list?'

'The list in my head. Joleen's *3478*, Judd's *4692*, Bonnie's *6327*. Telephone numbers in the right order.'

She had never thought about it that way. In her head she remembered the names first in alphabetical order, then the numbers.

'I rang Judd as well, but it was engaged. And I didn't risk anymore.'

He fell silent again and she handed him an apple.

'How did they treat you?'

'Like a three-year-old, speaking to me rather loudly, slowly, explaining everything. And you know what? At the first meal this girl set out a spoon for me to eat with. Just a small spoon. I mean, I don't think they knew anything about kids at all, I'm sure they didn't even know whether I had teeth, except Dan who gave me a new toothbrush. He knew what I was about, well he would with Steve to look after . . . but once he'd gone . . . Jesus!'

'Did any of them ask any questions about us, about what you did in Avalon?'

'Not really. They were all too busy feeding the animals and feeding themselves. They do a lot of eating on those ranches.'

'What about Dan, didn't he question you during the drive?' Gene asked, biting into an apple himself.

'Sure. He tried. He didn't get too far.'

And Zuke understood even if Gene didn't.

Dill the silent, Dillon the dreamer, the reader. If he didn't want to talk he could keep his mouth shut for hours and return any questions asked right back from where they'd come.

'Didn't you ask why Steve wasn't joining you?' Gene insisted.

'No. I just knew he wouldn't.'

'So what did you think was happening?' Gene asked.

'I thought maybe they'd found your father and were going to arrest you and Zuke and didn't want me around.'

'Were you worried?' Zuke asked.

'About you, Zukie? I'd never worry about you.'

chapter twelve

'Could you do me a favour?' Zuke asked. 'Could you go over to Steve's and see what's happening. Something is wrong. Judd saw a pink tissue on a bush outside his house. He's probably unable to come out, and I don't want to go there myself.'

Gene had nothing to do, was only too pleased to be of service. A few weeks back he had been famous, his face on local TV, in the local papers, he had found new friends with his bicycle, had a rabbit, then it had all gone wrong, and since living with the Donoghues he'd hardly gone out at all, except to the Knox.

So he went happily along the Avenue to the other side of Cedar Walk and the Mollman chalet, a one-storey building painted cream, with a low pink slate roof.

He wasn't sure he particularly liked Steve, but he was curious about the house. He was always curious about other people's houses, they were always so full of surprises, like the electric chairlift on the stairs in Grandma Olsen's, fitted for Grandpa Olsen before he died because he couldn't walk. And Joleen's mother's bedroom with all those mirrors you could swivel round. Joleen had sat him on the bed and by turning two or three of the mirrors he'd been able to see both sides of his face and the back of his head at the same time without moving. Mad!

He knocked on the glossy brown front door, there was no answer, no sounds from within, so he walked round the side to the back garden which had a big tree in the middle of a neat lawn and banks of flowers all around. At the end Steve and his father were sitting on a white bench, a game of checkers between them, Mollman in his Security Officer's uniform, grey shirt, grey trousers, silver badge on the breast pocket.

He moved slowly towards them, unnoticed, studying the relationship.

Was Dan Mollman playing the game to please Steve, or was Steve being dutiful? He'd never played a board game with his own father, only kicked a ball around, and then had had to let him make the scoring rules.

Dan Mollman looked up, did not show particular surprise, but seemed pleased, very pleased.

'Hallo, Gene. Come and join us.'

Gene sat down on the grass in front of them.

'Would you like an ice-cream soda? I'm about to make one for Steve. Strawberry, orange or lemon?'

'Orange,' he said. 'Thank you.'

Dan Mollman turned his attention to the game, taking one of Steve's men.

'Now you've got to take me here,' he pointed out.

Steve took the white piece, only to see two more of his being confiscated and his father gaining a King.

'You have a go after this, Gene,' Mollman said, waiting for Steve to make the unavoidable final move. Then he slapped his piece across the board taking the last of the black men and the game was over.

Mollman got up slowly, suggesting Gene should take his place and ambled across the lawn to the house.

It was funny, Gene thought, but his whole life seemed to be spent in back gardens, on front lawns or in kitchens, the suburban life. Where the hell did kids play in New York, 'Frisco or LA? It must be even deadlier. Country kids had ranches, mountains and deserts to play in.

The moment Mollman was indoors Steve looked up from putting out the men.

'Something wrong?' Gene asked.

'I think he can lip read,' Steve hissed. 'And he may have binoculars behind those blinds.'

'You in trouble?'

'We all are.'

'Why?'

'They've found some wreckage floating on the lake.'

'And the body?'

'Not so far. But I'm being grilled daily, nightly. No let up, man. I've had to give some things away.'

'Tell.'

'The Knox. I made a lot of things up but I had to name the hideout. You've got to warn everybody.'

'He knows where it is?'

'Yeah . . .'

Gene sat down and slid a piece on the board, then when Steve made his move he noticed the watch.

'New watch?'

'Yep. Dad gave it to me yesterday. The latest quartz from Japan. This bit's a geiger counter in case the Russians drop the bomb, but I haven't been able to test it yet.'

The idea sounded screwy.

'Can I see it ?' Gene asked.

Steve took it off and handed it over. It was very thick for a quartz watch, with a stainless steel waterproof shield at the back, but instead of a micro computer keyboard under the digitals there was just a rectangle of meshwork.

Then he realized what it might really be.

Didn't Dan Mollman work at Armaflex, the security people?

'I think it's loaded,' he said in a whisper, handing it back. 'It's a bug.'

Steve looked at it, then stared at it horrified as though a tarantula had landed on his wrist. 'Shit! That would explain . . .'

'Sshh!' Gene whispered. 'We'll examine it later, he's coming.'

They both watched his father come back with a tray of

three drinks, two orange with white foam bubbling round the straws and over the top, the third a straight lemon probably laced with vodka.

They played the game, Mollman sitting on the grass watching, tutting when Steve made a dumb move, sipping his drink. He seemed pleased with himself.

Gene won easily and looked up. 'Want a game, Mr Mollman?'

'No time, I'm on duty, afternoon shift.'

He helped Steve set up the board again and they started another game.

Again he won.

'I have to go, Steve,' Mollman said, finishing his drink and standing up.' I'll be back about seven, eight. Stay and play on if you want, Gene, you're good, maybe you could teach him a few moves.' He gave his son a manly pat on the back, put his peaked cap on and walked off with big official strides. He was a cop, to all intents and purposes.

They both listened for the car to start up and drive off, then Steve covered his wristwatch with his hand.

'It must be recording. He can't be listening now!'

'Let's go in and see what we can do.'

They went into the house to the sitting room and Steve took the watch off. Gene asked for it, placed it under a cushion, then led the way out to the garden again.

'We mustn't talk in front of it. Do you know how to open it?' Gene asked.

'No.'

'I think I do, I'll need a sharp knife.'

'He did ask me not to. He said it had been given him by a client, for me, and it was very delicate and expensive. Whatever else I wasn't to open it up.'

'It must be a bug. Who'd want to go around with a geiger counter? And how does it warn you about radiation anyway?'

'Makes a noise, you know, kind of a rattle.'

'Bullshit, Steve. Your dad's spying on you. If you need to

say anything while we're looking at it, just signal and we'll come out here again. OK?'

They went back into the front room and he knelt down in front of the sofa and the offending watch. Steve found a knife, not unlike another he'd used for a less delicate operation, and he got down to it.

He'd seen army bomb-disposal squads dismantling explosives in movies and using the point of the blade to prise the back off made him feel just like one of those English stiff upper lip officers risking life and limb. Then he realized the cover unscrewed quite easily and inside there was a tiny round device very much like the battery, but wired to the mesh.

He pointed to it and signalled Steve to join him outside. He placed the open watch under the cushion and both went out to the garden.

'I think that small thing's the microphone, so somewhere there must be a speaker or a recording machine.'

'How big would it be?' Steve asked.

'No idea. Size of a typewriter, maybe more, maybe less. It could be tiny.'

'What do we do with the bug?'

'Isolate it.'

'How?'

'Drop it in water or better still put the whole watch in the freezer.'

'How do you know?'

'Gene Hackman, my namesake, he does all those kind of things in movies.'

They placed the watch in the freezer and went back out into the garden.

'OK. Now let's hope we can talk freely. Where would your dad hide a recording device?'

'In his room. His office. But I'm not allowed in there.'

'Why not?'

'He has secret files, all to do with his work.'

'Don't you *ever* go in there?' Gene asked, surprised at how obedient Steve was.

All the time. I know the files inside out. Had myself a spare key made.' His grin was evil.

He led the way to his own room, a small sky-blue cubicle with a bed and a few shelves of tidy toys. From inside the head of a plastic E.T. he brought out a ball of tissue paper and unwrapped a key.

They went along the short corridor past Dan Mollman's bedroom, a double bed, a cupboard, little else, to the door at the end. Steve opened it, found a switch and Gene looked into a large box-room, no windows, a bright overhead spotlight beaming down on a desk laid out neatly with rows of pencils, pens, scissors, rulers, a calculator, typewriter, and all around shelves of files.

'What are those?'

'Secret records on the people employed at the places he works at, in case there's a robbery.'

'Anything on my mother?'

'Nope. The Canneries don't use Armaflex Security. Most are to do with banks and the Solar Energy place down in Chittuck Valley.'

Steve got down on his knees to slide back the door of a steel cabinet, but it was locked.

'He's got recording equipment and stuff in there, I know.'

'How can we open it?'

'The key . . .' and Steve climbed up on the black leather chair and reached for one of the files, took it down, opened it; there were several keys in it.

'Very secretive, my dad. Says he's going to set up as a Private Eye when he's got the money together, but he isn't very bright. He can't spell for one thing.'

'Doesn't he suspect you come in here?'

'Nope. I'm only interested in baseball on TV and geography at school. He thinks I want to be a spaceman when I grow up. That's because I asked for a model toy of the Shuttle last Christmas.'

'What do you want to be?'

'Do you know what *you* want to be?'

'Free.' Gene said.

'Right!' And Steve inserted the key in the lock. 'He's got guns in here usually, A Smith & Wesson and a Charter Arms AR.7.'

'What's that?'

'A survival shotgun. Comes to pieces.' Steve opened the steel cabinet and slid back the door exposing a recording machine with tapes going round very slowly, a red indicator light on.

'Shit! It's recording.'

'Us?'

'Better be,' Steve said, switching if off and rewinding, 'because if he's bugging someone else I'm now really in trouble.'

He stopped the tape and pressed the playback button.

The end of their garden conversation came out very clearly.

'Want a game Mr Mollman . . . I have to go Steve . . . I'll be back at seven . . . It must be recording . . . He can't be listening now . . . Let's go and see what we can do . . . We mustn't talk in front of it . . . Do you know how to open it . . .'

Then a muddle of sounds and nothing.

Steve stopped the tape again, rewound and erased.

'He won't get that bit anyway.'

Gene watched Steve set the machine on again, close and lock the cabinet, replace the key in the file.

'It's a mistake to be neat and tidy, you know?' Steve said. 'Sure you can spot immediately if someone's been at your things, but the intruder can remember where things are supposed to be so much more easily. So what do we do now?'

'Go see Zuke,' Gene suggested. 'She makes the best decisions.'

And Steve switched off the light.

Gene was over the moon.

And so were the other Latchkeys.

It was just the kind of fun they all enjoyed and it was his idea.

After testing Steve's bug-watch and discovering it had a range of about a thousand meters, certainly powerful enough to send a signal from the Knox to Steve's house, he explained the Mollman spying set up to Zuke on a walk to Balder Hill Woods with Judd and Dillon. He suggested using the device to their advantage, talking into it so as to misinform Dan Mollman, a whispered conversation maybe about where his father might be, Florida or New Orleans or somewhere, or even hinting that he *was* dead and buried in the woods.

For a moment Zuke thought they'd get a lot of laughs if they said the body was buried in Mollman's garden, she could visualize him digging up his own lawn in a frenzy, but then decided that that would only be telling the world that they knew Rick was dead. Better to invent a fictitious situation, and Gene came up with the idea of a Black Mass burial ritual, supposedly taking place in the Mayor's Folly garden-dump.

Now they were all in the attic of the Knox, Zuke, Joleen, Bonnie, Judd, Steve and Dillon, sitting in a circle round a pile of books on which Steve had placed his watch. They had run through and written up a fantasy sequence in which Zuke would play the High Priestess, imitating Kathie Stone's Southern drawl, and the others would participate. Gene was in charge of special effects. Steve more or less directing the production.

When they were all ready, he signalled Zuke to start.

'We of the Spider Fraternity,' she chanted.

'We of the Spider Fraternity,' the others repeated.

'Call upon the Spirit.'

'Call upon the Spirit.'

'Of Marvin Taylor.'

'Of Marvin Taylor.'

'Deceased by our hands and buried in the Ring according to our vows.'

The others repeated it all in the form of an incantation.
'We call on his blood.'
'We call on his blood,' they repeated.
'To rise out of the earth.'
'And out of the ring.'
'And give us the force we beg for.'
Zuke paused, looked at the others, frowning at Joleen who was about to burst into a fit of giggles.
'Spirit of the Spider,' she went on, 'we honour thy grave and call upon Rosie Fieldstein, deceased by our hands and lying beside him, and Tommy Lubicks, deceased by our hands and lying beside her and Fido the dog, deceased by our hands lying at their feet, to come out of the ring and cover us with the force.'
All repeated this, chanting, Gene hitting the sides of three glasses with a pencil to simulate High Mass bells.
'In sacrifice and in payment for the force-gift, we will water your graves with the potion according to the book of Jod, blood from each of us mingled with water from the stagnant pool,' Zuke went on, 'tonight, at midnight, under the crescent moon, in the garden.'
'In the Garden,' they all repeated.
'The Garden of Despair.'
'The Garden of Despair,' they repeated.
Then they all mumbled away a mantra, sighed and hissed and Gene reached for an empty biscuit tin and thumped it gently while others started clapping their hands and thumping the floor till Steve waved at them all to stop.
Zuke then signalled Steve to muffle the watch between two cushions and take it downstairs out of harm's way, after which she instructed each Latchkey to take as many items as he could and hide them, as this might be the last time they would be meeting in the Knox.

The next day Gene waited with Zuke and Dillon for developments. In the morning he helped clear out the Knox completely, dumping the empty coke tins and cardboard boxes in among the rest of the garbage round the house, rolling up the carpet and hiding that inside an empty oil drum.

The attic was now empty, deserted, obviously used by some kids at some time, but no longer an active headquarters.

Steve came by as Zuke was preparing lunch, a Spanish omelette she was trying from one of her mother's recipe books but which wasn't holding together too well.

'He's heard it,' Steve said, holding up his wrist to show them he wasn't wearing the watch.

'How do you know?'

'He asked me about the Garden of Despair.'

'Where it was?'

'In a roundabout way. He was very careful. I was with my rabbits and he came down the garden holding this magazine and a pencil as though he were doing the crossword puzzle. "Does the Garden of Despair mean anything to you, Steve? Something from a poem you may have learnt at school?" '

'Subtle!' Zuke said appreciatively.

'No, I said, not from any poem. Then he played really heavy . . . "But it does mean something to you? Something to do with Black Magic perhaps . . . Spider Fraternities?" And I froze, I looked really frightened. "I don't belong anymore, Dad," I said. "It's Kathie Stone and her crowd." And I told him everything we agreed I should tell him, and he went away very happy.'

'Did he check his files, do you think?'

'Oh yes, he checked his files, because I went in there and checked after him. All three were on his desk. The Marvin Taylor, the Rosie Fieldstein and Tommy Lubicks, all stamped MISSING. I read through them again, they're just personnel who left without saying goodbye and collecting their last week's pay packet. There were seven others. He must have checked them all.'

As Zuke served up some floppy pieces of burnt egg yolk

on a plate with three raw tomatoes, Judd came in, dripping with sweat and panting.

'Guess what!' The excitement was making his eyes water.

'What?' they all screamed at him.

'They're digging up Fort Knox.'

'Who are?'

'The police. Quite a few people around looking.'

They ran all the way.

To Gene's amazement there seemed to be an army of cops digging up the garden dump and even a bulldozer standing by.

Zuke couldn't believe it either. She hoisted herself up on to a wall and sat down to watch.

Gene joined her, the others sauntered off to get a better view from the old verandah.

'What's happening, Joey?' Zuke shouted to young Joey Tatillo who had come on Gene's old bike.

'They're looking for something buried in the garden.'

'I can see that, dummy. But what?'

'Old coins.'

'Old coins? You're kidding.'

'That's what Dad said. They've heard from the museum, the arkalogical department.'

'Archaelogical,' Zuke corrected.

Dan Mollman was there, the Sheriff, Sergeant Finch and a few town dignitaries who didn't have anything better to do.

'If they find out that this is a trick too . . .' Zuke said, but stopped smiling on realizing Mollman was looking at her.

The search went on for several hours. First they carefully took off a layer of earth with spades and pick-axes, then they brought in the bulldozer which moved mounds to various corners where they were carefully examined by experts.

No bodies, no bones, no skulls, no clothes. Nothing except a great big boulder which jarred the driver and forced the manual team to dig round it with spades and pick-axes.

Probably because he felt guilty at having started the whole wild goose dig, Dan Mollman took up a pick himself, and when Steve went to him asking why they were using an excavator for fine work, he got a short answer that suggested he should get lost.

Then Mollman glanced at his son's naked wrist.

'Where's your watch?' he shouted.

'At home.'

'I told you to wear it all the time.'

'Think there might be radiation here, Dad?'

Gene had never seen Steve being cheeky. 'Insubordination' Liz Kleiner would have called it. The relationship between son and father was horrendous. Steve didn't care a damn about his father.

'Is this your doing, Steve? Was that all made up about the Garden of Despair?'

'The tape you mean, Dad? That you bugged off me?'

Controlled rage. Fury in the eyes. A tightening of the fingers aching to get round the boy's throat. 'Yes, Steve, what I bugged off you.'

'Best ask Zuke,' Steve said, waving his hand in her direction.

Exasperated, Mollman stuck his pick in the earth, wiped his hands on his shirt and came over with his big official stride to face Zuke as she sat on the wall.

'So, what was it?' he asked.

'What was what?'

'The mumbo jumbo you all knew I was recording on Steve's watch.'

'Ah . . .!' Zuke said. 'Probably the celebration of the Feast of Fido.'

'The Feast of Fido?' he repeated patiently.

'Well,' she said, getting down, 'I don't suppose you could know 'cause it's made up. Some of us, lonely kids, Latchkids I think you call us, ganged together a while back after Joleen, Bonnie, Judd and Steve got mixed up with Sam Finer, and we sort of formed a secret society. It's not real.

It's just a game. The Feast of Fido is a pretend feast based on a legend we made up. Three people started digging for gold in this garden way back in the days of the goldrush, and they found a gold dog called Fido. When they tried to get it out of the ground it pulled them in because it had magical properties and this is the Garden of Despair. It's a sort of Western mixed up with Fairies.'

Gene was quite amazed. He had never heard the story before and knew she was making it up on the spur of the moment.

'We circle the bodies, which are pretend, of course, and they come out of the earth and give us strength to continue living without the help of our parents. In exchange for the gift of the force we give our blood, which isn't our blood but water, to Fido, the gold dog.'

Mollman was looking at her, studying her, joined now by the Sheriff who was very nearly amused.

'You weren't digging for real bodies, I hope, Mr Mollman, because you heard of our game?' Zuke asked innocently.

'No. I wasn't doing that. I was digging up for bodies because you named them. Marvin Taylor, Rosie Fieldstein and Tommy Lubicks.'

'They had to have names, Mr Mollman.'

'But why those names?'

'I don't know. I think Steve suggested them.'

'From my files, Steve?' Mollman said, turning on his son.

'Guess so.'

'How did you get into the room?'

'I didn't, Dad. If they're names from your files I must have seen them lying around in the kitchen or your bedroom. You do work in the kitchen sometimes when eating, and in bed . . .'

'Put it down to coincidence,' the Sheriff said, patting Dan on the back. 'But I'll need a report from you to justify the expenses, and maybe you could enclose a copy of the tape.'

And he moved off.

Then all the Latchkids shrugged their shoulders in sympathy and, as one man, walked away from him too, leaving him standing in the middle of the garden staring in despair at the mounds of churned up earth.

'At least, Dad,' Steve shouted over his shoulder, 'it's cleaned the place up.'

The next morning the telephone rang as Gene was brushing his teeth.

He went down, picked up the receiver.

'I've heard they're going to drag the lake,' Judd said.

'What for?'

'Your boat.'

'Where did you hear that?'

'My dad. He was over at the Westcoat Marina boatyard yesterday delivering timber, or something, and he told Mom he'd heard people talking. Some wreckage of the *Water Fox* showed up a while back and the police want the lake dragged.'

'Are you real sure about this?'

'No. But Dad was telling Mom.'

'Any idea of when they'll do this?'

'No. None at all.'

'OK, Judd. I'll tell Zuke. Thanks.'

He went up to her bedroom. She was lying there under the top sheet in her pale pink cotton pyjamas, wide awake, one eyebrow cocked questioningly.

'Judd. He's heard they're going to drag the lake for the *Water Fox*.'

She sat up.

'How come today? Any connection with Mollman, do you think?'

'It may not be today. He just heard that that is what they were going to do. Could be coincidence.'

'Could be.'

He watched Zuke get out of bed, take her top off, drop her pants. She stood naked in front of him, then walked about the room looking for her clothes. He knew she was doing it on purpose, to make him blush, to make him feel awkward, so he stood his ground and stared.

'Like what you see?' she asked, pulling on her jeans, not bothering about knickers.

'You'll be OK in a couple of years,' he managed, in a pretty steady voice.

'Fuck off, Gene.'

They smiled at each other. It made him feel really good, really warm inside. He liked her a lot.

'First thing is to find out whether this is all just a rumour or the truth. Best to make contact with the others and get them out in the field. Let's meet as soon as possible in the garden and, by the way, I've decided we should call ourselves the Fido Club now and look for new head-quarters.'

When Angela Donoghue left, he rang Judd and Bonnie, then Joleen, but sent Dillon down the road to get Steve, and when they had all gathered, looking like a pretty normal batch of kids getting together to play some game or other, Zuke explained the new situation and what she thought they should do.

Bonnie was instructed to drop in on Marina Sharp's hairdressing salon and listen to the gossip, Joleen was asked to cross-examine her mother, while the others mixed with adults in shops and supermarkets and anywhere else they might pick up some news.

Sure enough three of them came back with the rumour that was doing the rounds. Rick Prestianni's boat had been found sunk in the middle of the lake with his body on board.

Gene felt himself icing up when Zuke told him, but she was as calm as ever. After three weeks there was no reason to think that the police would suspect any of them, but just to make sure the rumour was true she sent Dillon down to the lake to have a look see.

When he returned it was clear he had rehearsed the

description of what he had seen over in his mind. Of late he had been reading a book on journalism and fancied himself as an ace reporter, which, Zuke pointed out, could prove useful.

'The boardwalk's packed with onlookers and the action is out in the center of the placid lake, like a pageant. There are two white yachts and four dinghies in a circle and in the middle you can just see the upturned bows of the *Water Fox*. That's about it.'

'What are people saying?'

'They're saying that several drowned on board and that one bloated body has been found so far which they've taken to the morgue.'

Gene decided he didn't want any lunch, which prompted Zuke to take hold of his hand and lead him upstairs to her bedroom. She told him to lie down on the bed, then knelt down on the soft mattress beside him, crossed her arms and studied him for quite a while before saying anything.

'You scared?' she eventually asked.

'Yes.'

'Because you think the whole world's going to be looking at you?'

'I guess.'

'Well, you're guessing wrong. I'm going to ask you a few questions about a matter we haven't discussed, your mother, and through your own answers you'll get a very different picture of what people will start thinking than the one you've got stuck in your head.'

'OK,' Gene said. He liked being alone with Zuke, he liked being questioned by her, being her focus of attention. She'd once admitted, when they were watching a torture film of Gestapo men beating the shit out of some innocent Pole, that she would like to be an interrogator in the next war. She was good at ferreting out the unexpected.

'How long has your mother been working at the Avalon Fruit Canneries?' she started.

'Dunno . . . two, three years?'

'Longer than that. She was there when both our dads were there. It must be at least four.'

'True.'

'Do you remember anything about her first going there? What you were doing?'

'I was at school. Going into second grade. I remember now, we started the same day, more or less, 'cause she said "We're both new boys today," . . . It was the day I moved up to second grade.'

'Which is what . . . four years back?'

'Yes.'

'And what did she do at the Canneries?'

'She wasn't a secretary. She was a receptionist. On the telephones.'

'When did she start working for the boss? When did she become McQuare's personal secretary?'

He thought about it, remembered her coming home and saying she'd got promoted and there'd been a terrible row, the first of many on the subject. 'It was after Dad got the push. He told Mom it wasn't because she had brains but in way of compensation for him losing his job.'

'That was a short time after my dad went to San Diego.'

'Must be.'

'What hours did your mom work, to begin with?'

'Nine to five . . . then six, later she had to work more because we had no money.'

'Did she stay away nights often?'

'No. Weekends sometimes. Like she went to Fresno with Mr McQuare.'

'Right, Gene. Are you getting a picture?'

This was where Zuke was sometimes tricky. She understood things he didn't, the way adults behaved. When she looked for trouble she usually found it. He shook his head.

'Your dad goes missing, your mom invites you to the office and Mr Big is nice to you. A few days later she and my mom agree you should come stay with us so's she can be more free. What for?'

'Work . . .?' he suggested, shrugging his shoulders.

'When your mom goes off to Fresno with her boss, what do you think they do after work?'

One of the adult movies he'd watched had been about an executive and his secretary going to a hotel together and undressing in one of the bedrooms.

'They're shacking up together, you mean?'

'Of course that's what I mean.'

He didn't see the importance.

'So, dummy, if your dad's body has been found and foul play is suspected, what do you think the police will look for first?'

'A motive.'

'Zap! Have you got a motive? Would a twelve-year-old kid kill his own father to be rid of him? Unlikely. But . . .'

'You think they might suspect Mom?'

'Why not? Her or Mr Big.'

'But they were in Fresno!'

'You sure?'

'Of course I'm sure. I rang her. You were there when I spoke to her.'

'You rang her late the following evening. Where were they on *the* night?'

'Mom wouldn't kill Dad.'

'Shit, Gene, *you* did! And if you think she's more innocent than you, what about Mr Big? I looked at the map. Fresno's less than a hundred miles from here, he could have come over and gone back in a couple of hours in the middle of the night. Who would know? And look what we did in a couple of hours.'

'So what are we going to do?'

'Very little. You're twelve, that means the police will treat you like you were six, you're naturally wide-eyed which makes you look even less guilty, just let me paint a new picture in your mind of the events that took place. You went with your dad to the boat as was, you started baling it out as you did, he got drunk as he did, went to sleep, all that, you got bored and decided to walk home. But why?'

Gene shrugged his shoulders then realized she wanted

him to think up a reason. 'Watch television. Saturday afternoon. Batman?'

'Right. As you walked away from the lake did you notice any other car but your own?'

'No.'

'Think again.'

'A white Mercedes?'

'Better. But why a white Mercedes?'

'McQuare's car.'

'How do you know?'

'I saw it in the car park at the Canneries and asked Mom whose it was.'

'Then forget everything I've just said. Wipe it from your mind. We must find something less obvious.'

'To finger him?'

'To finger *them*.'

Gene sat up. He wasn't sure he wanted to involve his mother. Zuke was asking him to accuse her. He didn't want to do that.

'Why the frown, Gene? Worried about getting your own mother into trouble?'

He nodded.

'You can always confess at the eleventh hour, but it's your skin I'm trying to save.'

He started biting his thumbnail, something he had only recently started doing.

And Zuke slapped his hand away.

Gene's mother called from her office in the afternoon asking him to go to the house and wait for the Sheriff who wanted to see them both. She didn't think she would be late, but thought it best not to keep the officer of the law waiting outside. 'Offer him a drink, one of your father's whiskies, or beer, there's some in the ice box.'

He hadn't gone back to his own home for two days, so he was rather surprised to find it changed when he went in. It was tidy. That was the difference. Spotlessly clean, everything in its place and, indeed, the ice box was stocked with cans of beer and white wine, which was strange because he had never seen his mother drink much of either.

Then upstairs, in the bathroom, he found a cigarette stub in the ashtray on the john, and his mother didn't smoke.

So, OK, she'd had someone staying.

The Sheriff arrived and he let him in, ready to answer any questions, relaxed after a further session with Zuke who had drilled it into him that he had left his father drunk on a bunk and had never seen the boat again.

The Sheriff accepted a whisky, pouring a generous measure out for himself, and was quite happy to stand by the window of the front room and look out.

'Who lives opposite you?' he asked.

'The Weiss's, old couple. They had a Great Dane but he died last year.'

'He wasn't called Fido, was he?' It was said with a broad grin.

'No.' Gene grinned too.

'Who are your neighbours?'

'The Donoghues on the left, Old Grandma Olsen on the right.'

'Old Grandma Olsen eh? She's still around.' The Sheriff seemed to remember her from way back. 'Nice avenue,' he added and seemed perfectly content to be looking at the scene and to be sipping his drink.

Suzy Prestianni drew up outside in the Lincoln. She parked the car behind the Sheriff's and got out. Both watched her coming up the path, patting her hair, taking out her compact and glancing at herself unaware that she was being observed. Gene glanced at the Sheriff who was amused. The woman was vain. Her appearance to an unknown man mattered. She wanted to look good.

Come to think of it, she had settled down to her life without Dad pretty damned quick, she'd even collected the car from the lakeside within hours of returning from Fresno, had driven it around ever since like it had always belonged to her, was her possession retrieved.

She came in, all smiles. 'Hallo, Sheriff. Sorry I'm late. Hope Gene looked after you.'

'He looked after me fine.'

'I'll just freshen up, then I'll be with you.'

She nodded to Gene to follow her. They went into the kitchen.

'He asked you anything, tell you anything?'

'No.'

She was as nervous as hell and obviously knew what had happened, but for some reason was pretending she didn't. Zuke had said that maybe the Sheriff was coming to break the news, officially. Someone had to do it officially, and though they might have spoken on the phone, perhaps she had asked him to come along and help her out. After all, breaking the news to a twelve-year-old that his father and constant companion was dead couldn't be too easy for anyone.

'What's he here for?' Gene asked.

'I don't know, darling. He rang me at the office and said he'd like to see me, and maybe you. Can you look after yourself? I think I ought to speak to him alone.'

Zuke had got it right.

Zuke always did.

On the other hand maybe his mother didn't know. Maybe she had no idea at all what had happened.

And that left a little hollow in his stomach as he realized that he didn't want to follow Zuke's line of campaign and have his mother accused.

She went into the living room and closed the door. He tiptoed after her to listen, but only murmurs came through. So he made himself an orange milkshake with real juice because they had no flavour syrup, only the milk curdled and it didn't taste too good.

When she came out she wasn't crying, but her eyes were a bit pink round the edge and she was even more nervous. 'The Sheriff would like to speak to you,' she said.

He'd been found out. He was certain. He had left a clue,

or had been seen, the police had already arrested Zuke and the others. It was over, he should never have tried to cover up. He felt his face flush, his feet grow cold, the very tips of his fingers turn to ice. He walked in.

'Well, Gene, this is none too easy for me. Your mother asked me to break the news to you . . . We found your father this morning, he had a kind of accident in the boat, in the *Water Fox* . . .' It came out all in a rush. 'He must have taken the boat out into the middle of the lake and it sank . . . he was on board, probably couldn't get out.'

'Is he dead?' Gene asked. He turned, his mother was behind him.

'Yes, dear.' And she pulled him to her and gave him a hug which was so unlike her that he felt embarrassed.

Neither of them cared, damn it. Neither of them would regret him. Since he'd gone they'd both had the best time of their lives.

Adults were terrible hypocrites.

'Now you were the last one to see him, Gene, and it's important for us to have all the facts, so could you answer a few questions?' The Sheriff sat down after helping himself to another measure from the whisky bottle.

Gene sat down, the Sheriff glanced at his mother, the question bounced unasked between them, would the child speak more freely without her in the room?

'I'll go make some coffee,' she said, and closed the door behind her.

Alone, the Sheriff tried a sad smile.

'So, Gene, can you remember the day when you last saw your father?'

And Gene told him the events of that day as he remembered them, the afternoon walk home, coming into an empty house, waiting till the following morning before ringing up his mother.'

'Where did you ring her?'

'At her office. They gave me the number of the hotel where she was staying. I knew she was at a conference or something in Fresno.'

The Sheriff noted that down in a notebook he took out from his shirt pocket. 'Do you remember the name of the hotel?'

'Began with A . . . Arbuthnot I think.'

'And you stayed here all night alone?'

'Yes.'

'What did you do, all by yourself?'

Gene shrugged his shoulders. 'Made myself a peanut butter and pickle sandwich and watched TV I guess.'

'You saw no one. No one called here, or rang?'

'No . . ..'

'And you didn't go back to the boat?'

'Not till the next morning. I didn't get worried about Dad till then because . . . sometimes he didn't come home nights.'

'Was your father drunk when you left him, Gene? I know it's a hard question, but I also know he had a drink problem. The truth will help.'

'He was asleep, but he had been drinking.'

The Sheriff got up, crossed the room and opened the door.

Gene's mother was just about to come in with the coffee tray, she was right there outside the door.

'What conference was it you were attending, Mrs Prestianni, the weekend Rick disappeared?' he asked, as she put the tray down on the low table.

'The Californian Fruit Council's annual seminar. We have discussions on the crops, new species, cloning of rare fruit trees, mutations, that sort of thing.'

'And this was at the Arbuthnot Hotel in Fresno?'

She lied and the Sheriff knew it. The Sheriff knew the Arbuthnot wasn't big enough for a conference. She had incriminated herself.

'Oh no. I stayed at the Arbuthnot. The conference was down the road at the Roeding.'

Gene reported the setback to Zuke the next day, but she didn't seem in any way upset.

'The whole of Avalon knows about your mother and Jack McQuare, Gene,' Zuke said. 'They've been sleeping together for years, I got it confirmed by Joleen. We'll just have to finger them another way. Give me the key of your house and leave the rest to me.'

He took the latchkey from around his neck and handed it to her, then, on her suggestion, went for a ride on Joleen's bicycle over to Boulder Hill to see if his old friends were still playing there, but they weren't. Either the cycling craze was over, or they had moved to new ground.

There didn't seem to be anything to do, so he cycled back to his house and when he got there was surprised to see the Lincoln parked outside. His mother had come home from work.

He went straight in.

'I've been given the afternoon off, Gene, we could spend it together if you want. We're invited to swim at the McQuare ranch if you'd like.'

Her eyes were reddish and she was pale, shaken by something.

What had Zuke done now?

'You OK, Mom?'

'I had to go to the mortuary, Gene, to identify your father. It wasn't very pleasant, that's all. I'll get over it.'

They drove over to the ranch where he had the pool to himself, the lilos, swam around all day while his mother lay on a beach mattress sunbathing and gossiping quietly with a friend from the office who had joined them. No other McQuares were around as he had feared, not even Jack's wife.

When they got back home late that evening his mother rang Angela Donoghue to tell her Gene would be staying with her that night, she needed the company in the house after what she had been through. 'Five weeks in the water, Angela, he was quite unrecognizable and . . . well I'll tell you another time.'

Nothing else happened over the weekend, he stayed with his mother who tidied up the already tidy house and asked him to help clear up the shed. Unknown to him Joe Tatillo had come one day to take back all the whisky and she intended getting him a new Mongoose bicycle and if he wanted he could get himself a rabbit.

Then, on the Monday, the day before he was due to go back to school he woke up early, about six, to find a policeman in his bedroom telling him not to worry but to stay right where he was.

He made the excuse that he wanted to go to the bathroom and was allowed to do this, and found his mother dressing in a hurry with a woman cop standing by her door.

'What's happening, Mom?'

She seemed to be in a state of shock, hardly able to speak.

'I'm going down to the station, Gene, to help the police with their enquiries.'

'Is it about Dad?'

'Yes . . .'

Downstairs were two plain clothes officers opening cupboards and drawers, looking under the carpets, under the furniture.

Whispers, low talk, then it was suggested he should get dressed and go next door to Zuke's.

He went to the Donoghues', unsettled, and joined Zuke and Dillon and their mother who were looking out of their front window at the activity in the avenue. Two police cars were parked, uniformed drivers waiting, then he saw his mother being led down the path to one of the cars and behind her one of the detectives carrying a flat black leather case, wrapped in clear plastic, as though it were a bomb.

'What's that he's got, Gene?' Zuke asked.

He knew what it was.

'One of Mom and Dad's wedding presents from way back. A set of silver handled carving knives. Dad only used it to carve the turkey at Christmas and Thanksgiving.'

'Do you think one of them's missing?' Zuke asked.

Or was she telling him?

Angela Donoghue turned away from the window, closing her eyes, and patted Dillon on the head in way of suggesting they should all move to the kitchen. And when she had gone Zuke switched on the television and sat down in front of it to wait for one of the local morning news bulletins.

When it came on, Gene got a shock.

His mother's picture was flashed on side by side with Jack McQuare's, and an excited female voice told the world that Suzy Prestianni and Jack McQuare had that morning been arrested for the bloodthirsty murder of Rick Prestianni, one-time employee of Jack McQuare, President of Avalon Fruit Canneries who, for seven years, had been secretly co-habiting with his personal secretary Suzy Prestianni and had just recently been separated from his wife. It was believed that on hearing that Jack had got a divorce agreement from his wife Suzy had tried to get a divorce agreement from her husband and on being refused had taken a knife to his throat. The murder weapon had not yet been found, but a family silver handled carving knife was missing from a set and the police were treating it as homicide.

'Shit, Gene,' Zuke said, switching off the television. 'If your dad had given your mom a divorce and she'd married McQuare you might have lived in luxury over at the ranch!'

'Did you take that knife?' Gene asked.

'The no-question operation, Gene. You're going to be an orphan.'

'I'm not sure I want that,' he said. 'I don't think I want Mom to be wrongly accused.'

'Kind of late in the day to change the evidence, Gene.'

'I could confess.'

'And get us into trouble as well? You've sworn loyalty to the Latchkeys, Gene. You can't do that. Besides you wouldn't want the electric chair.'

'I wouldn't get the electric chair. I'm a minor, and I'd say why I did it and get sympathy.'

'Why did you do it?'

'Anger.'

'Because he killed your rabbit and sold your bike?'

'And because he . . . attacked you.'

'Is that why you did it?' She thought it pretty funny.

'Maybe . . .'

'Because I told you he tried to rape me, you killed your father?' Her voice was tight surprise at the revelation.

'Yes.' The vision of his father, drunk and violent, attacking Zuke was still with him.

'Oh come on, Gene, you know me better than that.'

He didn't understand.

'It was fabrication,' she explained. 'It wasn't true.'

He actually felt his heart double beat, a thud within a thud that made him catch his breath.

'He didn't try to rape you?'

'Of course not.'

'Why did you lie to me then?'

'To see whether you cared. I reckoned that it might make you do something pretty stupid. I wanted you to, naturally.'

'Why?'

'Power. I like to know I can manipulate people. Like I know I can manipulate you.'

'You can't manipulate me!' He felt himself flush with anger, with hurt pride.

'No . . .?'

'No!'

Quite unexpectedly she got up, crossed the room to stand right in front of him, and gripped his chin between her forefinger and thumb, forcing him to look at her.

'You're mine to do with as I wish, Gene, when I wish. You're shit scared. You're going to live in terror all your life because of what you did and the only person who's going to be able to help you is *me*. Remember that!'

And he realized she was right.

He realized she was the only person in the whole wide world he'd ever be able to run to for comfort.

Fiction

☐	**The Chains of Fate**	Pamela Belle	£2.95p
☐	**Options**	Freda Bright	£1.50p
☐	**The Thirty-nine Steps**	John Buchan	£1.50p
☐	**Secret of Blackoaks**	Ashley Carter	£1.50p
☐	**Lovers and Gamblers**	Jackie Collins	£2.50p
☐	**My Cousin Rachel**	Daphne du Maurier	£2.50p
☐	**Flashman and the Redskins**	George Macdonald Fraser	£1.95p
☐	**The Moneychangers**	Arthur Hailey	£2.95p
☐	**Secrets**	Unity Hall	£2.50p
☐	**The Eagle Has Landed**	Jack Higgins	£1.95p
☐	**Sins of the Fathers**	Susan Howatch	£3.50p
☐	**Smiley's People**	John le Carré	£2.50p
☐	**To Kill a Mockingbird**	Harper Lee	£1.95p
☐	**Ghosts**	Ed McBain	£1.75p
☐	**The Silent People**	Walter Macken	£2.50p
☐	**Gone with the Wind**	Margaret Mitchell	£3.95p
☐	**Wilt**	Tom Sharpe	£1.95p
☐	**Rage of Angels**	Sidney Sheldon	£2.50p
☐	**The Unborn**	David Shobin	£1.50p
☐	**A Town Like Alice**	Nevile Shute	£2.50p
☐	**Gorky Park**	Martin Cruz Smith	£2.50p
☐	**A Falcon Flies**	Wilbur Smith	£2.50p
☐	**The Grapes of Wrath**	John Steinbeck	£2.50p
☐	**The Deep Well at Noon**	Jessica Stirling	£2.95p
☐	**The Ironmaster**	Jean Stubbs	£1.75p
☐	**The Music Makers**	E. V. Thompson	£2.50p

Non-fiction

☐	**The First Christian**	Karen Armstrong	£2.50p
☐	**Pregnancy**	Gordon Bourne	£3.95p
☐	**The Law is an Ass**	Gyles Brandreth	£1.75p
☐	**The 35mm Photographer's Handbook**	Julian Calder and John Garrett	£6.50p
☐	**London at its Best**	Hunter Davies	£2.90p
☐	**Back from the Brink**	Michael Edwardes	£2.95p